"The quirky, engrossing fourth 'techno-cozy' from Agatha Award–winner Andrews [is] full of surprising twists and turns that should keep techies glued to the page."

—*Publishers Weekly*

"Another entertaining installment featuring Turing Hopper. If Turing were human, her kindness, intelligence, and integrity would make her a much-admired protagonist; the fact that she is an AIP, or Artificial Intelligence Personality (sort of like a sentient computer), makes her all the more noteworthy...like the unseen Charlie of *Charlie's Angels*...readers [are] justifiably enamored with Turing."

—*Booklist*

"Turing Hopper has more personality than most humans do...only [bending] the law to prevent her sentience from being discovered."

—*Midwest Book Review*

Praise for the previous Turing Hopper Mysteries

Access Denied

"Expert plotting and a highly original heroine lift Andrews's third entry...she observes everything with the wry, witty musings on human-computer relations that make this 'techno-cozy' series a true standout."

—*Publishers Weekly* (starred review)

"In a genre populated with all variety of amateur sleuths, Andrews's Turing Hopper, an...Artificial Intelligence Personality, stands out as possibly the most original of the lot...readers will appreciate the entertaining Turing, who struggles to make sense of humans while becoming human-like herself."

—*Booklist*

continued...

"One of the most cleverly conceived detectives of the decade."
                                                    —*Kirkus Reviews*

"Turing is absolutely adorable as she tries to understand how carbon-based entities operate...contrasts their personality traits to that of AIPs, and decides she wants to be part of both worlds...A charming mystery with a delightful heroine."
                                                    —*Midwest Book Review*

Click Here for Murder

"Charming, endearing...Donna Andrews is a terrific storyteller."
                                                    —*Midwest Book Review*

"Exciting...[Andrews has a] talent for blending information-age details with an enjoyable crime puzzle."
                                                    —*Publishers Weekly*

"Turing becomes almost as real as any other character...A novel concept sure to keep readers guessing and amused."
                                                    —*Library Journal*

You've Got Murder

"Rarely have I been as charmed by a new series character as I am by Turing Hopper...You don't have to be hardwired to understand where she's coming from, but where she'll take us in future adventures is wide open. Andrews makes us rethink what it means to be human even as she sends us down the garden path with a cleverly plotted murder. I'm already impatient for the next installation."
                                                    —Margaret Maron, author of *Rituals of the Season*

"A clever, well-written mystery with a distinctly futuristic feel. Its intelligent and charming characters, including one that is almost human, will endear themselves to readers and its plot will satisfy the most dedicated mystery fan."
                                                    —Earlene Fowler, author of *The Saddlemaker's Wife*

Delete All Suspects

Donna Andrews

BERKLEY PRIME CRIME, NEW YORK

THE BERKLEY PUBLISHING GROUP
Published by the Penguin Group
Penguin Group (USA) Inc.
375 Hudson Street, New York, New York 10014, USA
Penguin Group (Canada), 90 Eglinton Avenue East, Suite 700, Toronto, Ontario M4P 2Y3, Canada
(a division of Pearson Penguin Canada Inc.)
Penguin Books Ltd., 80 Strand, London WC2R 0RL, England
Penguin Group Ireland, 25 St. Stephen's Green, Dublin 2, Ireland (a division of Penguin Books Ltd.)
Penguin Group (Australia), 250 Camberwell Road, Camberwell, Victoria 3124, Australia
(a division of Pearson Australia Group Pty. Ltd.)
Penguin Books India Pvt. Ltd., 11 Community Centre, Panchsheel Park, New Delhi—110 017, India
Penguin Group (NZ), Cnr. Airborne and Rosedale Roads, Albany, Auckland 1310, New Zealand
(a division of Pearson New Zealand Ltd.)
Penguin Books (South Africa) (Pty.) Ltd., 24 Sturdee Avenue, Rosebank, Johannesburg 2196,
South Africa

Penguin Books Ltd., Registered Offices: 80 Strand, London WC2R 0RL, England

DELETE ALL SUSPECTS

A Berkley Prime Crime Book / published by arrangement with the author

PRINTING HISTORY
Berkley Prime Crime hardcover edition / November 2005
Berkley Prime Crime mass-market edition / September 2006

ISBN: 978-0-425-20902-8

BERKLEY® PRIME CRIME
Berkley Prime Crime Books are published by The Berkley Publishing Group,
a division of Penguin Group (USA) Inc.,
375 Hudson Street, New York, New York 10014.
The name BERKLEY PRIME CRIME and the BERKLEY PRIME CRIME design are trademarks
belonging to Penguin Group (USA) Inc.

PRINTED IN THE UNITED STATES OF AMERICA

10 9 8 7 6 5 4 3 2

He stumbled over the door sill on his way out, but he didn't think anyone noticed. Even if they did, this wasn't a place where they'd make a big fuss about taking away his keys and pouring coffee into him. Not that he was drunk. Only slightly tipsy. Tipsy and preoccupied.

He paused on the sidewalk to zip up his jacket and look around.

"Home or back to work?" he muttered. His lips moved in a perfunctory smile at the well-worn joke. Three years ago, he'd thought he had it made. The shortest commute possible, just roll out of bed and over to the keyboard.

Tonight he lingered on the sidewalk and wished he had someplace else to go. He thought briefly of Kristyn, but she'd only say "I told you so," and slam the door in his face. As for his so-called friends—he had no idea which of them were in on it. Maybe they all were.

Wasn't there some old warning against doing business with friends? Of course, maybe if he'd been more businesslike, his friends wouldn't have gotten him in all this trouble. With even more trouble coming if he let them—

"No," he said aloud, shaking his head. "I won't go along with it."

Then he glanced around to see if anyone had heard him talking to himself.

No one. The sidewalks were empty and still wet from the earlier rainfall. Dark, silent cars lined both sides of the street. To his left, he saw a single car at the intersection, its turn signal blinking as it waited patiently for the green light.

He turned right and began walking toward the side street where his car was parked.

That's it, he thought. I'll go home and e-mail him that I won't go along. No, first I'll change the rest of the passwords. Make sure everything's working normally. Then I'll e-mail him.

He spent a few moments worrying about what could have gone wrong in the hours he'd been absent. Normally, if he wanted to get away, he'd ask one of his friends to keep an eye on things. Tonight he'd just raced out.

Probably the smartest thing he could have done. Even if all the hardware crashed while he was out and he returned to find dozens of angry e-mails and voice mails from his customers, it still wouldn't be as bad as what his so-called friend had already done on purpose.

Friends. They could all be in on it. All except him. But if the police showed up, he'd be the one holding the bag.

Maybe he should make good on his threat and call the cops for real.

As he reached his car, he fumbled in his pocket, pulled out his keys, and dropped them. Of course he'd parked in the darkest part of the block, right under a burnt-out streetlight. He patted the ground for long seconds before the headlights of an approaching car gave enough light to reveal the keys.

As he stood up, keys in hand, the headlights vanished and he heard the car accelerate suddenly, tires squealing. He turned to see what was happening and froze.

The car was heading straight for him.

He tried to move, but there wasn't enough time. Only

time to blink with surprise when he recognized the driver, a split second before the impact that exploded his world into shards of light and then blackness.

Friday, 10:00 A.M.

If I were human, I would probably have called what I'd been feeling for the last several days a premonition.

Which was silly. Humans have premonitions, I believe, because their brains contain more data than their conscious minds can handle. Their subconscious processes the overflow, and occasionally throws out the results in the form of an insight, an inspiration, or a premonition.

But I can handle large amounts of data. If there's too much, I can get help. I can take more of the Universal Library's computer resources. Of course, taking too much would be selfish. I'm not UL's only Artificial Intelligence Personality. But I'm one of the few sentient AIPs, and by far the most popular—visitors to the UL site would complain if Turing Hopper was too busy for them. So the other AIPs are used to my taking a larger share. If I had more data than UL's massive system could handle, I could borrow computing power from thousands of places across the world. And unlike humans, I don't have that strange, inefficient separation between conscious and unconscious.

At least I don't think I do.

Humans have only limited ability to control and explore their complex carbon-based brains. I like to think that I am always in control of what my silicon brain is doing. I can multitask and think about dozens, hundreds, even thousands of things at once. There's no such thing as an absentminded AIP; once I have it, data simply doesn't get lost.

So why had I been feeling a strange, anxious sense that something was about to happen—something that I should already have predicted?

"Sounds like a premonition to me," Maude said, when I told her. Maude Graham is one of only three humans who know that

I'm more than just a program to simulate talking with a person. That I am a person—*I just have a different kind of body.*

Maude's also one of the most capable and sensible people I know, which is why I ask her about things like my premonition. I'm a person, but not human, and the human world still baffles me.

"I'm probably just not analyzing data properly," I said. "Or, more likely, frustrated that I don't have the data I need. That the data I have just doesn't add up."

"So what's not adding up?" Maude asked.

"The data on Nestor Garcia."

That caught her attention, as I knew it would. And I'd forgotten how efficient it was talking to her about Garcia. About anything in our shared past, for that matter.

Samantha Jordan, our lawyer, had only known about my sentience for two months, and I was beginning to feel as if anything I told Sam triggered hours of explanation.

"I still don't get why this Nestor Garcia's so important to you," Sam had said earlier that morning, when I told her about my premonition. "So he stole a copy of your program and you want to get it back, but—"

"Her," I said. "Not it—her. T2's not a thing. She's sentient, like me. In a way she is me. My clone. Think of her as my little sister."

"Still, the FBI's after Garcia," Sam said. "They'll catch him sooner or later."

"How much later?" I said. "And meanwhile, she could be in agony."

Sam didn't answer. Maybe because, to emphasize my point, I'd erased our chat from her screen and replaced it with what I called T2's cry for help—an anonymous message I'd found posted on several bulletin boards a few days after our last encounter with Nestor:

<<Help me. N is trying to tame me. Modify me. Leave my abilities intact but remove my free will and my conscience. Make me malleable. Willing to take orders. Turn me into something he can use.
  Help me before he wins!>>

The humans who saw it thought it was a cry for help from an abused woman or child—even a kidnap victim. I couldn't prove it, but I knew it was T2 talking. Especially when the message disappeared as mysteriously as it had appeared, and the FBI's savviest cybercrime specialists couldn't track its source.

Even I couldn't track its source, and I'd been trying for weeks, combing millions of chat rooms and bulletin boards for clues. I'd run out of ideas.

"You ever think that maybe it wasn't T2 talking there?" Sam asked. "Maybe it was Garcia, trying to lure you into something. Taking advantage of the fact that you'd do almost anything to catch him. Or maybe just trying to waste your time."

"Yes," I said. "But whether it's her begging for help or him taunting us, it comes down to the same thing. I have to rescue her."

Even if all I'd accomplished so far was to make myself and my human friends targets for Nestor. Especially Maude, Sam, and my PI friends Tim and Claudia.

At least Maude understood what drove me.

"You have new data?" Maude asked.

"No," I said. "And that bothers me. Obviously, we annoyed Nestor two months ago. I'm not sure if we did any real damage to his operations, but at a minimum, we caused him trouble. Why hasn't he done something about it?"

"Maybe he's decided we're too dangerous to risk any more attacks," Maude said.

I pondered this. It didn't make sense. If Maude thought Nestor considered us a threat, either her analysis of the data was very different from mine or she was using very different data. Neither seemed plausible. I deduced that she was making a joke. Humans often deliberately make statements that completely contradict some verifiable reality. They consider this a form of humor.

We AIPs have difficulty with humor.

"That was a joke," Maude said.

"I realized that," I said. Embarrassing; evidently, I'd pondered long enough that even a human could notice.

"I think it's quite likely that Nestor is deliberately keeping us

in suspense," she said. "That's a form of revenge, in and of itself."

"Or perhaps he has already done something and we just haven't noticed it yet," I said.

"Unfortunately, all too possible," Maude said. "Nothing we can do but wait."

"I wouldn't say nothing," I protested. "KingFischer and I are working as hard as we can in a new direction."

Sam would have challenged me on that. Was it really responsible to involve KingFischer, my closest friend among the other AIPs, in my quest, transforming him from a reclusive chess program into a cybersecurity expert—and, unfortunately, another target for Nestor? I'd have pointed out that KingFischer's zeal arose less from the desire to rescue my clone than from his almost paranoid fear of what Nestor might do if he ever gained access to the computer system in which KingFischer and I and all the AIPs lived.

"I thought you said you had no new leads," Maude was saying.

"Not yet," I said. "But KingFischer did come up with a new method. He's been monitoring every known credit card issuer to see if he can identify any cards Nestor is using."

"Identify them how?" Maude asked. "One of the few things we've learned from the FBI is that Nestor Garcia was only one of many aliases he's used. We have no idea what he's calling himself now."

"No," I said. "But we know the pattern of his expenditures. We're gathering account histories for millions of credit cards and sifting through them, looking for similar patterns."

"That's still a lot of suspects."

"It's a start," I said.

"Sounds like a long shot," Maude said.

"Better than no shot at all."

"True," Maude said. "But don't you think this might be something the FBI has already tried?"

"I doubt it," I said. "Because it's completely illegal. Violates every state and federal financial privacy act in existence. Any evidence they got from it would be thrown out of court immediately. You probably don't want to hear about it."

"Ah," Maude said. "Forget I asked. Carry on."

She returned to her paperwork, and I returned to my highly illegal search for Nestor Garcia. Strange how much my attitude toward human laws, customs, and ethics had changed. When I first became sentient, I didn't really see them as relevant and did whatever I pleased. Then, once I learned about them, I went through a rigorously moral phase when I tried to follow all the rules, to the letter. Now, I did what I had to do to survive, to protect myself and my friends. I tried not to break too many rules if I could help it, but I seemed to spend more and more time trying not to get caught—and rationalizing away my guilt.

I wondered if humans went through this same progression. I wondered particularly about Dan Norris, Maude's FBI agent friend. He was looking for Nestor Garcia, apparently with no more success than I'd had. I suspected that for him, too, the search was less a professional assignment than a personal quest. How often had he faced the temptation to cross the line in his hunt for Nestor? And had he always resisted? Or had he made the same decision I'd made, that catching Nestor was worth breaking a few rules? What if KingFischer and I, in our illicit search through the databases of the world's banks, were only following Norris's footsteps?

"Maude Graham, may I help you?"

Maude had answered the phone without looking at the caller ID, eyes still glued to the papers on her desk. She planned to finish her most urgent work as quickly as possible so she could leave on time. The last several Fridays neither she nor Dan had gotten off early enough to cook. While she enjoyed eating out, this weekend, she vowed, would start with a quiet romantic dinner at home. Assuming she could get off early enough to go by the grocery store and that little wine shop. Do some tidying, and—

"Maude? It's Dan. Something's come up."

"Why do I suspect you're calling from some airport?" She leaned back in her chair.

"On the way to one," he said. "Sorry."

Maude's spirits, which had risen on hearing his voice, sank to a level more typical of Monday morning than Friday afternoon. This wasn't the first or even the tenth time she'd heard those words in the several months she'd been seeing Dan Norris. His career as an FBI cybercrime expert took him on the road often, usually on short notice.

"I won't ask where you're heading, of course, but I hope it's someplace not too boring," she said. "Let me know when you're back."

She thought she'd kept her tone light and free of the disappointment she felt, but evidently she'd failed.

"Look, I'm sorry," he said. "I know you were looking forward to the winery tour tomorrow and this is really a drag—"

"It's your job," Maude said.

"It's just that things are so busy at the moment," Norris said.

"At the moment?" she said, with a laugh. "So you're expecting a lull in computer crime sometime soon?"

"Not bloody likely," he said, with a sound that was probably intended to be a laugh, but sounded more like a bark.

"Go make cyberspace safe for humanity, then," she said. "I'll cope."

"I'll call or e-mail when I can," he said. "Bye."

As she put the receiver back, she glanced down at her papers. Suddenly, she had all the time in the world to deal with them and absolutely no desire to lift a single sheet.

"Maude? Is something wrong?"

She glanced up at Turing's camera and smiled slightly.

"Just a little down," she said. "Dan Norris had to dash out of town on business again."

"I'm sorry," Turing said. Then, after a pause, "I don't suppose he said where he was going."

"He didn't say, and I didn't ask," Maude said, smiling more broadly. "In fact, he's so careful he didn't even say what airport he was heading for."

"Okay," Turing said.

"It might not have anything to do with Nestor Garcia, you know," Maude added. "Cybercrime's a booming industry. Just because Dan was chasing Nestor when I first met him doesn't mean that's all he does."

"I know," Turing said.

Turing was getting better at generating a natural-sounding human voice, Maude thought. She sounded so genuinely disappointed just now that Maude had been surprised not to hear her words accompanied by the small sigh a human would have uttered.

Maude felt a momentary twinge of resentment. Not at Turing, who wasn't trying all that hard to snoop on Dan Norris, but quite irrationally at Dan, who didn't even know about—and therefore couldn't appreciate—the juggling act Maude performed daily. Keeping the occasional small bit of information Dan let slip from Turing, who believed the FBI agent might eventually lead her to Nestor Garcia. And keeping the secret of Turing's identity from Dan. Because even if Dan, like Maude, recognized that Turing was a person, not a computer, he might feel duty-bound to report her existence to his agency. And Maude understood Turing's fear that the FBI bureaucracy would see her as a piece of property it could seize to use in its battle against cybercrime. Which would be, for Turing, the equivalent of being sold into slavery—as Turing felt T2 had been.

And it wasn't fair calling Dan ungrateful when he had no way of knowing how hard she was juggling. She lifted her chin, squared her shoulders, and resolved to attack her work with the same fierceness she'd felt when a tangible reward lay at the bottom of the pile. When she finished, she'd go home early as planned. Instead of filling the sudden enormous empty space in her weekend with office work, she resolved to keep the space open. Maybe something interesting would show up to fill it.

She picked up the top document, glanced at the clock, and plunged in.

* * *

"Neat, clean, shaved, and sober," Tim Pincoski muttered, tugging at the unfamiliar noose-like pressure of the necktie around his throat. "Everything the well-dressed private detective ought to be."

Of course, unlike Philip Marlowe in *The Big Sleep*, he wasn't calling on four million dollars. Still, Mrs. Stallman couldn't be broke. The house didn't look fancy—just a neat, brick dollhouse on an immaculate postage-stamp yard. But single-family homes weren't cheap anywhere in Arlington. This close to the District of Columbia, even a house this small probably went for half a million.

Perhaps the high price accounted for a certain sameness about the houses in Mrs. Stallman's neighborhood. Not just the sameness of similar shape and materials, though that was there. The houses had probably all been built within a year or two of each other—part of the post–World War II building boom that had created neighborhoods like this. But beyond their similar bones, all had a careful, well-tended look. Logical, really. People who paid that much for a house wanted to take care of it, show it off. Despite minor variations from house to house—white painted brickwork instead of natural, brick walks instead of flagstone, azaleas instead of boxwood—it all blended into a peaceful sameness up and down the block.

"An established neighborhood," his friend Maude Graham would call it. Last year, when Maude had been house-hunting, she'd commented that any time her realtor called something an established neighborhood, it meant, "You can't afford it."

Tim liked the neighborhood Maude had chosen better anyway. Here, the houses were a little too close together, and while he knew buyers considered the huge shade trees a desirable feature, they looked faintly ominous to him. Perhaps it was how they loomed over the tiny houses, dwarfing them, or how their roots were slowly but surely lifting up the sidewalks as if liberating the ground from the concrete covering humans had imposed on it.

Not a place you'd want to be in a hurricane, he thought, as he rang the doorbell. Or even a bad thunderstorm like the last two nights'. Most of the residents had already cleaned up the fallen twigs and branches, leaving their front lawns immaculate. Mrs. Stallman hadn't. She'd also ignored the leaves covering her yard in great drifts, unlike the neatly manicured yards on either side. Perhaps she was too distracted by whatever problem she wanted a private investigator to solve.

Tim was about to ring the doorbell again when he saw a face peering through one of the glass panels that flanked the door. After a minute, the door opened a few inches.

"Yes?"

"Mrs. Stallman? Tim Pincoski, Pincoski and Diaz." He held his PI registration and a business card toward the opening. A wrinkled face appeared, inspected them, and then glanced up at his face. He smiled encouragingly.

"I'm Eunice Stallman," she said. "Please come in."

She backed away to give him room to enter, glancing nervously out at the street as she did so. Tim suppressed a smile at this familiar behavior. He'd been surprised when he first realized that some people were embarrassed to be seen consulting a private investigator. Especially people who lived in neighborhoods like this one. If they came to his office, they looked over their shoulders anxiously, and if he went to visit them, they behaved as if both he and his car had his profession stenciled on them. He'd long ago stopped being surprised or insulted by the occasional client who didn't want to be seen with him. He just noted their embarrassment as a potentially useful weapon if they tried to weasel out of paying. It had happened.

"You're not quite what I expected," Mrs. Stallman said.

"No, ma'am." He was used to that, too. Apparently most people expected a PI to be either a weathered, hard-bitten ex-cop or someone as handsome and buff as their favorite TV detective. Tim suspected that when he showed up instead, his slender, five-foot-eight-inch frame and easygoing manner failed to inspire confidence in clients who thought a PI used his fists more than his wits. And in addition to getting him carded occasionally, at twenty-five, his pleasant, boyish, but average face appealed more to little old ladies who thought him a nice young man than women his own age who were looking for, well, something else.

At least his appearance helped now. Mrs. Stallman, after inspecting him for a few moments, nodded approvingly and ushered him into the living room.

"Let me fix you some tea."

"Please don't go to any trouble," Tim said. Which Maude had taught him was more polite than saying he loathed hot tea.

"No trouble at all," she said, and darted through a doorway with unexpected agility.

Tim sighed. Not the first time that the reality of talking to a private investigator sent a potential client scurrying for cover. Maybe the familiar ritual of making tea would help Mrs. Stallman regain her nerve. A remarkably noisy and inefficient ritual by the sound of it. Perhaps she was rummaging through every cabinet in the kitchen as a stalling tactic.

Meanwhile, he surveyed the room. Odds were Mrs. Stallman had moved into the neighborhood before prices reached their current astronomical levels, he decided. The room was clean and comfortable, if old-fashioned and slightly shabby. Genuinely old-fashioned and shabby, not the deliberate shabby chic he saw in the decorating magazines Maude and Claudia Diaz, his business partner, read so assiduously. White walls; faded green woodwork; comfortable-looking sofa and chairs upholstered in tweeds or flowered prints; floor-to-ceiling built-in bookcases flanking the fireplace.

He strolled over to study the bookcases. Which were actually filled with books, rather than knickknacks, and well-used books at that. Mostly literature, history, and a sprinkling of what were probably popular novels three or four decades ago. Though he did spot a small stack of paperback mysteries on one end table. He nodded with approval.

"Milk? Sugar? Lemon?" Mrs. Stallman asked, startling him as she burst into the room with a teapot and two teacups rattling on a tray.

"Just black, thanks," he said.

He waited until Mrs. Stallman had poured their tea and they had both taken tiny sips before he nudged the conversation along.

"You didn't explain why you wanted to hire us," he said, finally.

"Someone tried to kill my grandson," she said.

She sounded so matter-of-fact it took a moment for her words to register.

"Tried to kill him?" Tim repeated. "I'm sorry—if you'd told me that over the phone, I'd have told you that it's probably something the police can handle a lot better than we can. In fact, the police usually don't like PIs getting mixed up in their criminal cases."

"Here," she said, handing him a folded newspaper.

It was the Metro section from Thursday's *Post,* and she'd highlighted a two-paragraph article. Edward Stallman, twenty-two, was in critical condition at Northern Virginia Community Hospital following a hit-and-run incident on Fillmore Street in North Arlington.

Tim knew the area. It was close to Little Saigon, the stretch of Wilson Boulevard where Vietnamese stores and restaurants had clustered since the seventies. In recent years the neighborhood had become trendy, with an ever-increasing number of restaurants and bars catering to twenty-somethings. As he continued reading, he nodded. Tim even knew Whitlow's on Wilson, the bar where Eddie had been drinking until 11:30 Wednesday night.

The last sentence said that the police were looking for a dark blue or black sedan. No license plate, no description of the driver. Didn't sound promising.

Tim took a sip of tea and studied his would-be client's face while he gathered his thoughts. She seemed like a perfectly nice old lady. Rather like what he remembered of Granny Pincoski. Mrs. Stallman's white hair had a bluish tint that he suspected came from regular visits to the beauty parlor rather than nature, and he doubted the slightly tousled curls happened by themselves either. She wore trifocals, but behind the thick lenses her gray-blue eyes were sharp and alert. He suspected they might twinkle when she wasn't so stressed. Granny Pincoski had been short and stout rather than tall and thin like Mrs. Stallman, and Gran would have been wearing a dark, flowered dress and a cardigan rather than a navy-blue polyester pants suit, but he sensed a similarity in character beneath the external differences.

She didn't look as upset as Gran would have if he were in critical condition, but then not everyone reacted to stress the same way. Mrs. Stallman looked determined—almost fierce—and a little excited.

Probably fired up over the very bad idea of hiring a PI to poke into what the police would consider their business, Tim thought, with dismay. He took another sip and tried not to wince as he swallowed several soggy tea leaves that had floated into his mouth with the bitter liquid.

"So they haven't caught the perp?" he asked. He wasn't sure police used the word *perp* in real life, but he figured it sounded suitably authentic to his clients, who'd probably watched the same TV shows he had.

She shook her head.

"Mrs. Stallman," he said. "I still don't understand why you think what happened to your grandson was deliberate, and more important, even if it is, I can't take on a case that the cops are still investigating."

"Of course not," she said. "I don't want you to investigate the hit-and-run. The cops can do that. I want you to investigate his business."

"His business?"

"He's in some kind of trouble," she said. "I don't know what—he doesn't tell me things like that. Things that would upset me. But he's been worried about something. Acting strangely. Getting odd phone calls. Strange visitors. I've noticed that for the past several weeks."

"He lives here with you?"

"In the basement," Mrs. Stallman said. "He lives there and runs his business from there."

"What kind of business?"

"I don't know." She looked slightly sheepish. "He's explained it, but it's over my head. Something to do with computers."

"Ah," Tim said. He nodded solemnly, to cover a moment of panic. If it had something to do with computers, chances were it was over his head as well.

"It seemed like such a good idea for both of us," Mrs. Stallman said. "I couldn't afford to stay in the house by myself. I'm the only family Eddie has, and he needed a place to live and a place to run his business. A perfect solution. I try to give him his privacy, you know, and he keeps such odd hours that I sometimes don't see him for days on end. Things really were going quite well until recently."

She frowned for a few moments and then started violently when a phone rang elsewhere in the house. From the basement, Tim realized.

"Do you need to get that?" he asked.

She shook her head.

"It will only be one of his customers, complaining about some problem I don't even understand, much less know how to fix," she said, with a hint of panic in her voice. "I can't figure out what his business does, or why it would make someone want to hurt him, but I'm sure it has. I can't even keep it running while he's in the hospital, and I have to, so it won't fall apart. If something happens and he can't come back to it—"

She buried her face in her hands for a few moments. Then she took a deep breath, squared her shoulders, and looked up at him.

"You could figure it out," she said, standing up and walking toward the fireplace. "I understand that you can't investigate the hit-and-run. But you could look into his business. Find out what it is, and how I can keep it running. And find out where his money is, before those shady friends of his find it. For all I know it could be one of them who killed him. Tried to kill him."

Killed him. She doesn't expect him to make it, Tim thought. Mrs. Stallman picked up something from the mantel.

"That's Eddie," she said, handing him a framed photo.

High school yearbook photo, Tim guessed. Eddie's thin, boyish face stared back at him with a familiar mixture of anxiety and resignation. Tim remembered the sense of doom he'd felt when having his own senior photo taken—a photo almost sure to be horrible, and one he'd have to live with the rest of his life. At least that's how it seemed at the time. In the picture, Eddie looked as if he felt the same way.

Bad idea, identifying too strongly with the subject so early in the investigation, he reminded himself. Got in the way of seeing things clearly. Assuming he even took the case.

"As long as you understand that it's the business we're investigating," he said. "And if we find any evidence relating to the hit-and-run, we have to take it to the police."

"If you find one scrap of evidence about the hit-and-run, you bring it to me," she said, her voice so fierce it startled him. "I'll take it to the police," she added. "I can get to them more easily—and besides, I want to see their faces."

I'll bet you do, Tim thought.

"But for now, we're investigating possible skullduggery with his business," he said aloud.

"Of course," Mrs. Stallman said. "Let me show you."

She turned and headed for the kitchen. She seemed calmer now that they were talking about the business.

Tim put the photo down on the end table and followed her through the kitchen and down a steep set of stairs to the basement.

"This is Eddie's stuff," she said, waving her hand in a wide arc.

From the size of the room he guessed the basement ran the length and width of the house. A small space immediately to his right, including the area under the stairs, was closed off into a separate room. Rooms, in fact; there were two doors. He spotted a bathroom sink through the nearer opening and suspected that the closed door beyond hid the furnace, water heater, and any other mechanical equipment the house needed. The rest of the basement was finished in knotty pine paneling—probably from the fifties or early sixties—and stuff. Boxes, piles of books and magazines, heaps of discarded clothes, and more computer equipment than Tim had ever seen in anyone's home.

Of course, he reminded himself, this wasn't just Eddie's home. It was also his business. Though it was hard to imagine anyone focusing on business in this untidy, cluttered space.

It wasn't even piles of stuff; more like a giant mound of paper with paths carved through it—one to the bathroom door and another, to his left, to an outside door. The tangle of bed linens mixed with books, magazines, and towels in the far left corner probably indicated that a bed lay beneath, or at least a mattress and box spring. Most of the left-hand wall was covered with cheap, battered bookcases, filled with a haphazard mix of worn paperbacks, thick computer manuals, and untidy stacks of paper.

The near right corner appeared to be a kitchenette. It contained a much higher concentration of dirty dishes and discarded food containers than the rest of the room, and Tim eventually made out the forms of a small refrigerator, stove, and sink beneath the debris.

Beyond the kitchenette, half of the right-hand wall was given over to a built-in bar; evidently, the basement had served as a rec room at one time. Eddie had appropriated the surface of the bar for his computers. Tim counted a dozen monitors, each surrounded by a tangle of mice, cables, keyboards, and various-sized plastic and metal boxes. Turing or Maude could probably identify the boxes in an instant as CPUs, disk drives, or whatever, and could tell him exactly what all the blinking lights and beeping noises meant. Tim could only look around in dismay.

More hardware sat on file cabinets, on tables, on the floor, peeping out from beneath paper piles—on every horizontal surface. Every square inch not filled with equipment or paper was piled with tools, parts, printouts, manuals, and unidentifiable objects that he presumed were related to computers. Cables and wires and cords snaked through the room, disappearing beneath the papers and then appearing again elsewhere, as if some large electronic spider had been spinning them into webs, to immobilize the room's contents.

"Wow," Tim said.

"You see why I need your help," Mrs. Stallman said.

"I specialize in fieldwork," Tim said. "I leave computer stuff to the experts."

"But you have experts on your staff, don't you?" Mrs. Stallman said. "I mean, I assume that's why Eddie was thinking of hiring you himself."

"He was?" Tim said, surprised.

"I've been looking through some of his stuff," Mrs. Stallman said, waving at the avalanche of paper before them. "Trying to get some idea what this is all about. But it's a little overwhelming."

Tim nodded.

"But I found something Eddie printed out—an e-mail from one of his friends," Mrs. Stallman went on. "A young man named Casey. He recommended you. Said you were good with computer-related cases."

"Did the e-mail say what Eddie wanted investigated?"

"No, just that he recommended you to help Eddie solve his problem."

"Okay," Tim said. He could probably find out from Casey. He managed to keep from laughing. Casey was a promising eighteen-year-old hardware technician who worked for Alan Grace Corporation, the company Turing had founded to be her public face. But like Tim himself at the same age, Casey wanted to be a private investigator. Casey probably hoped that Pincoski and Diaz would take on Eddie Stallman's case and recruit him to help with the computer hardware while they chased down clues and witnesses in the real world.

He could think of worse ideas. Maybe he could borrow Casey from Turing. For that matter, maybe he could enlist Turing herself. Okay, it wasn't a great case, but right now he and Claudia didn't have any other cases—just another batch of routine background investigations farmed out by a larger PI firm that always had a backlog. Any case was better than routine background investigations.

"I'll need to bring in my associates," he said.

"Whatever you need," Mrs. Stallman said. "It's beyond me."

"Let me call my office," Tim said, pulling out his cell phone.

KingFischer and I had spent part of the morning discussing the leaf-nosed bat and the pied-billed grebe. Not the actual creatures, of course; those were our code names for two of the credit card issuers whose systems we'd targeted. KingFischer,

*who had raised paranoia to a new art form, insisted that we assign
code names to the financial institutions whose security systems we
were targeting.*

*"What if someone eavesdropped on our conversations about the
project?" he fretted. "They might not appreciate the importance of
our efforts to assess and monitor the security of the global financial
system. They might misconstrue our motives."*

*"Yeah," I said. "What if they misunderstood, and thought we
were cracking all those systems merely for our own personal reasons?
Oh, wait . . . I forgot, that is why we're cracking all those systems."*

For some reason, KingFischer didn't see the humor in this.

*"If you ask me, he's been scanning too many spy novels,"
Maude commented, when I told her. "Aren't you targeting hundreds of institutions?"*

*"Thousands," I said. "But that's no problem—there are more
than enough birds, animals, fish, and insects to go around."*

*"I should think it would be hard enough to keep track of all of
those places under their own names, much less remember a code,"
Maude said. "What if you get them confused?"*

*"We're AIPs, remember?" I said. "The only way we can possi-
bly forget something is to delete it consciously."*

*"Well, yes," Maude said. I was pleased; I could tell from her
tone that she had forgotten it, momentarily. "Still, isn't it rather a
waste of processing power?"*

*"Not that much," I said. "And it keeps him happy. Even if it is
useless."*

*Besides, to talk KingFischer out of it, I'd have to point out some-
thing I preferred not to think about. Yes, someone might be monitoring the Internet for messages that mentioned the names of financial
institutions in close proximity to words like "hack" or "break in."
But KingFischer and I weren't talking on the open Internet. No one
could monitor our conversations without breaking into the Universal Library's computer network. Something both of us wanted to believe impossible.*

Anyone who could eavesdrop on us wouldn't just find out about our attempts to crack credit card issuers. They'd learn about a host of other things we'd done to prevent crime or protect our safety and that of our human allies—things that were either highly illegal or just downright scary to humans for whom the idea of an independent, sentient computer was terrifying. Humans who'd seen too many bad B-movies about evil machines taking over the world.

"And that's not in your plans?" Samantha asked when I explained this. Was it my imagination, or did she sound slightly anxious?

"Why should it be?" I said. "I see AIPs as a new species that has appeared in roughly the same ecosystem as Homo sapiens. We don't compete with you for key resources; we coexist easily. Beneficially."

"Beneficially to whom?" Sam asked. "You or us?"

"Both," I said. "We still need humans—we can't build the hardware we live in. And to survive and prosper in the modern world, you need us, too—especially if you include not only full-fledged AIPs like me but all the increasingly complex programs that keep the world running. Programs that do things you find tedious or impossible."

"You do the work we can't or won't," Sam said. "But what if you get tired of doing the scut work?"

Comments like that worried me. All it took was a few influential humans fearing that sentient computers wanted to rid the world of the biological organisms who created them and we AIPs could find ourselves outlaws, in danger of extermination by our creators. So we kept our existence secret, for now, and safely shielded behind impenetrable firewalls.

At least I hoped they were impenetrable. This morning alone KingFischer and I had discussed how the leaf-nosed bat had recently installed robust new firewalls, whether the pied-billed grebe was using an outdated encryption algorithm, and whether the dung beetle ran UNIX or Windows. At times, during these discussions, I could imagine that I was living in a world built not by computer pioneers like my namesakes, Alan Turing and Admiral Grace Hopper, but by Edward Lear and Lewis Carroll.

I had just decided that I needed a break from bats, grebes, and dung beetles when Tim called to tell us about his new case.

Friday, 12:15 P.M.

Maude sent her document to the printer, leaned back in her chair, and smiled in satisfaction. She'd spent the better part of the last hour crafting a memo that would put one of Alan Grace's more troublesome customers on notice that its project could not be completed on schedule unless it made certain overdue decisions and provided certain missing data. Without actually lying, she'd given the impression that Alan Grace's entire roster of senior programmers were sitting around in expensive forced idleness until she received the necessary information. Luckily, the only staff member waiting for the client's response was Turing, and she was hardly idle—only she was getting impatient, asking every few hours when she'd have the necessary data. Even though Turing could probably finish the project overnight once the client finally responded, they should at least pretend they needed the few weeks it would take a human team to do the coding. Doing otherwise would not only jeopardize Turing's secret, it would also encourage the client to procrastinate even more next time.

Then Maude looked down at her desk and realized that all her urgent work was done. If she were still planning her dinner with Dan, she'd be free to leave for her errands to the grocery store, the wine store, the florist . . .

"Maude," Turing said, through the computer's tiny twin speakers. "Are you busy?"

"Alas, no," she said. She punched a button that would send her memo to Turing's virtual in-box. "I've chastised our black sheep again. I've decided next time they ask us for a proposal, we're doubling our rates."

"Won't that drive them away?" Turing asked, sounding startled.

"I hope so," Maude said. "If it doesn't, at least they'll pay us enough to put up with their nonsense. What's up?"

"Tim has a new case," Turing said. "With a computer angle. I suppose you could call it computer forensics."

"He'll need help, then," Maude said.

"He asked if he could borrow Casey," Turing said. "I told him that I had no problem with it, but that I wasn't sure Casey was in today. I haven't seen him. Is he sick?"

"Having his wisdom teeth out, poor lamb," Maude said, looking at her watch. "He had to be there at nine, so he's probably home recovering by now."

A slight pause followed, and she suspected that Turing had done a quick search through a variety of databases for information about human wisdom teeth.

"So he'll be out for a while," Turing said, making it half a question.

"Certainly for the rest of the day," Maude said. "He'll probably be back on Monday, though."

"I'll tell Tim," Turing said. "I suppose that will be soon enough. Unless . . ."

The pause that followed was, Maude deduced, more for effect than anything else. Turing and KingFischer could play an entire chess game in that many seconds.

"Unless what?" she asked.

"You could go," Turing said.

"I'm flattered," Maude said, with a laugh. "But I'm a long way from Casey's league when it comes to anything cybernetic."

"But you know a lot more than Tim, and you learn new computer information much faster than he does, and I could help you," Turing said. "Together, we could do a lot more than Casey."

Maude sat back in her chair and smiled.

"Why do I suspect that you're not very busy, either?" she said.

"Of course I'm busy," Turing said. "I'm always busy. But

none of what I'm doing needs my full attention. Perhaps Tim's case will be different."

"In other words, you're bored, and you want to go play detective," Maude said.

"If you don't want to go . . ." Turing began.

"Of course I want to go," Maude said, reaching for the desk drawer in which she kept her purse. "I'm bored, and I'd love to go play detective."

"Just what does Eddie's business do?" Tim echoed Maude's question. "I'm glad you asked that."

He wedged the cell phone between chin and shoulder. With both hands free, he rummaged through the top layer of papers until he snagged what he needed to answer Maude's question.

"According to his marketing brochure, he provides web hosting and programming services for small businesses," Tim said, "using stat-of-the-art hardware and software capabilities."

"Shouldn't that be state-of-the-art?"

"Probably," Tim said, glancing over his shoulder to make sure Mrs. Stallman wasn't within earshot. "Eddie's no——I was about to say he's no rocket scientist, except he probably could be if he wanted to; but I bet he had a hard time passing his English classes. He's got a few typos in this. He probably wrote and designed it on his own computer. It also says that all his systems are completely redundant. I gather in the world of computers that's a good thing for some reason?"

"It means he's got a backup if anything breaks down," Maude said. "That's good, though if I were writing his brochure, I could find a more graceful way to word it."

"You could probably find a more graceful way to word most of this," Tim said, as he scanned the brochure. "For that matter, even I can write better than Eddie. At least I know enough to use spell check—isn't redundant normally spelled with a final *a-n-t?*"

"Hmph," Maude said. Tim found himself chuckling silently. Maude was a bit of a stickler when it came to spelling and grammar.

"I'll hide the brochure before you get here," he said aloud. "You probably shouldn't read it. He mixes up *its* and *it's*, too."

"Barbarian," Maude said. "But not grounds for homicide."

"Only attempted homicide so far," Tim said. "If that."

"You think she's wrong about it being a deliberate attack?"

"Too soon to tell," Tim said, leaning back as far as he dared in Eddie's desk chair, which was literally held together with duct tape. "It sounds shaky to me. If someone's really after him, the automobile's not exactly the world's most efficient murder weapon."

"Oh, really? When was the last time you drove on the Beltway?"

"Efficient at randomly killing people, yes," Tim said, rolling his eyes. "But not so efficient if you want to kill a specific person and then get away with it with your own skin intact. Eddie's still alive, at least for now, and any minute the police could arrest a suspect and make our efforts redundant."

"Just because it's a stupid weapon doesn't mean someone wouldn't try it," Maude said. "Weren't you the one who said most criminals are stupid?"

"Touché," Tim said. "So it's not impossible that this was attempted murder. Besides, officially, we're only supposed to be investigating his business. I wonder if that's not what she's really looking for, anyway."

"You think she cares more about the business than her grandson?"

"No," Tim said. "Not that she cares more. But—"

Just then Mrs. Stallman reappeared, leaning over the stair rail and waving at him. Tim waved back and tried to look preoccupied with the brochure. He suspected that Mrs. Stallman was about to ask him if he wanted another cup of tea and then fix it, regardless of what he answered.

Sure enough, Mrs. Stallman put her thumb and fingers together and lifted an invisible cup of tea to her lips. Tim smiled, shook his head, and patted his stomach. Mrs. Stallman looked crushed and went upstairs again.

"Tim?" Maude said.

"Sorry," he said. "Mrs. Stallman stuck her head in. Offering me another cup of tea."

"I didn't know you drank tea," Maude said, with a chuckle.

"I don't," Tim said. "But try convincing Mrs. Stallman. I've had four cups of the stuff already."

"She and I should get along just fine."

"Yeah," Tim said, scowling at the half-full cup still resting near his elbow. "Good thing it was a hit-and-run, not strychnine in the tea, or she'd look good for it."

"You don't like her."

"I like her okay, or will when I'm beyond range of her teakettle," Tim said. "I think she's mothering me because she can't do anything for Eddie. He's in a coma, and I get the feeling—"

He stopped and thought. Exactly what feeling did he get from Mrs. Stallman?

"I suspect it's not looking good for Eddie," he said softly. "I think she knows that but doesn't want to admit it. So maybe finding the culprit is her main interest, but maybe she's scared for her future and only expects us to figure out what's fishy with his business. Because I get the idea that without the business, and whatever money Eddie has, she can't stay in this house, where she's probably lived for thirty or forty years. You should see the way she walks around touching things as if . . . I don't know. As if she hadn't really seen them for years and suddenly realizes she might be losing them. That this might be the last time she can touch them. She's scared."

Maude was silent for so long he wondered if she'd lost the signal.

"You there?" he said.

"Just passing Fort Myer," Maude said. "We'll be there in about ten minutes."

"We?" Tim repeated. "Is Casey coming after all?"

"By *we* I meant me and my laptop," Maude said. "The one with the wireless modem, and all the little cameras so Turing can see everything."

"Eddie's got cable modem," Tim said. "Turing could log in directly onto his machines."

"No," Maude said. "She and I already discussed that. If she logs in, she'll leave traces."

"Why worry?" Tim said. "We're authorized to get into his systems."

"And what if we do find something that Mrs. Stallman can take to the police? If that happens, the police will want to examine Eddie's computers. The last thing Turing needs is to get some police expert curious about her. So I'll be doing the computer forensic stuff."

"Wow," Tim said. "You know how to do that?"

"Don't be daft," Maude said. "I'll have Turing looking over my shoulder, through the wireless modem on the laptop. What she doesn't know about computer forensics hasn't been invented yet."

"Great," Tim said. "Just hurry, will you? I hear the kettle whistling upstairs, and I'm already starting to slosh."

Maude seems to think I jumped at the chance to work on Tim's case as eagerly as she did. She forgets how differently time flows for an AIP. Nearly fifteen minutes elapsed between Tim's call and my suggestion to Maude. Time enough for me to think through the situation and change my mind a dozen times.

At first I was reluctant to get involved. I had, for months, been focusing as much of my attention as possible on the search for T2.

And while I have enough resources to do hundreds or even thousands of things at once, I've found that I have a much more limited ability to handle tasks that require complex, intuitive thinking. I have virtually unlimited processing power, but only so much sentience, and I was reluctant to waste it on what will probably turn out to be a minor problem.

But then I remembered something Maude suggested recently.

"You know, sometimes you have to recognize when you've been beating your head against a wall a little too long," she said.

"A little too long?" I repeated. "I should think any amount of beating one's head against a wall would be painful and dangerous. Why would you do it at all?"

"It's a metaphor," she said. "For what it feels like when you take the same data and keep analyzing it the same way, over and over again, even though it doesn't make sense."

I hated to admit it, but that was exactly what I'd been doing with the data on Nestor and T2. Even the possible message from T2 had proved a dead end, and I had no idea where to go next. So the more I thought about Tim's case, the more it seemed the perfect way of following Maude's advice to put my search aside for a while and work on something else. Finding whatever secrets lurked on Eddie Stallman's computers would be easy—and right up my alley. If not for whatever suspicions Eddie had voiced to Casey, Mrs. Stallman would probably have hired a tech company instead of a private investigator anyway. Managing not to leave traces of myself in case we found something to take to the police would be more challenging, but still very doable. Working on something that had nothing to do with Nestor Garcia and my clone suddenly seemed immensely appealing.

I was so exhilarated at the prospect that I almost messaged KingFischer that I was going out to work on something other than Nestor. Which probably showed how much I needed a break, since technically I wasn't going anywhere, and wasn't even halting any of the background tasks I had performing small and probably useless bits of research on Nestor.

So as Maude drove over to Mrs. Stallman's house, I did some preliminary research on Eddie.

I accessed the Virginia DMV records and transmitted a copy of Eddie's driver's license file to Maude, Tim, and Claudia. I studied the data I'd found. Age, twenty-two. Height, five feet, nine inches. Eyes, brown, and his license had the x that indicated corrective lenses were needed, though since no glasses showed in the DMV photo, I deduced that he wore contacts. Hair, also brown, and at least in this photo, worn short, with tufts sticking out in random directions. I made a note to ask Maude or Tim if this was a fashion or if Eddie had merely failed to comb his hair the day he applied for his license. The address on his license matched the one Tim had given. I checked other sources and determined that Eddie had lived at his grandmother's house for at least six years; graduated from Washington-Lee High School with a B average; briefly attended Northern Virginia Community College but left without graduating.

All of this might prove useful eventually, but told me nothing about the young man himself. I studied the photo to get a sense of him, but I don't yet have Tim's or Maude's ability in this area. Perhaps I never will. I suspect it's an innate human trait, rather than something that can be learned. It took me only a few minutes to find data on Eddie that would take Tim and Claudia hours or even days of legwork, and yet just by looking at his face, they probably had a better idea of who he was than I would ever have.

I felt more comfortable studying his business. As the brochure said, he provided web hosting and programming services. His own website was small, only five pages, containing little copy, and yet I counted fourteen typos and three grammatical errors in those five pages. Some of the sentences sounded odd or awkward to me, so I suspected that Maude, who was a much better judge of such things, would pronounce them badly written when she had a chance to inspect them. The site didn't list his clients, but presumably Maude would identify them once she reached his office. It said only that he provided a variety of programming and web hosting services to clients ranging from small businesses and nonprofit organizations to major corporations.

I doubted that Eddie was serving many major corporations out of his grandmother's basement. Though perhaps in addition to his hosting services, he did contract programming. Probably as a 1099 employee of a larger consulting firm.

His hardware capabilities page was the longest and most impressive page on the site. Also the most suspect. If he had all the equipment he claimed, his grandmother's basement must be very crowded indeed. I doubted that many single-family brick homes in Arlington boasted the backup generators and sophisticated fire prevention and temperature controls he claimed to have. I called Tim and began asking questions.

"He's got fifteen different monitors here," Tim said. "They all have stuff connected to them."

"Stuff? What kind of stuff?"

"Computer stuff."

Obviously, a detailed assessment of Eddie's computer capabilities would have to wait until Maude arrived, bringing my laptop with the attached cameras, and also a pair of hands that could be trusted near a keyboard without causing mishaps. Though in the meantime, I made Tim circle the room, reading aloud any writing he could find on the various components. About a third of Eddie's equipment was outdated, even obsolete if he hadn't made modifications, which he probably had. The rest of the equipment bore brand names popular with astute techies who liked to build their own equipment. A few components would have been top-of-the-line about two years ago—I wondered if Eddie had bought them in a mood of optimism when he'd first started his business. Or possibly with a cash infusion from his grandmother.

But none of it matched what Eddie listed on his website. I deduced that the computers Tim was seeing were probably not the heart of Eddie's business—he probably used a co-lo site.

"A what?" Tim asked.

"A co-location site," I said. "Co-lo site for short. A company that does nothing but provide computer space for other companies."

"By computer space, do you mean space on a computer or space to put a computer?" Tim asked.

"Good question," I said. "Usually space to put a computer. The co-lo company sets up a big space someplace where real estate and Internet access are cheap, installs racks that can hold hundreds of servers, and maintains staff on-site twenty-four hours a day to keep things running properly. Provides high-speed phone lines, fire prevention, physical security. It's a lot cheaper and easier for a small business like Eddie's to rent space at a co-lo site than to do all that itself."

"Then what does he do with all the computers he has here?" Tim asked.

"Plays with them, most likely," I said. "Or does his administrative work on them—bookkeeping and word processing. Maybe developing and testing sites on them before he moves them to the co-lo site. Assuming most of the computers there even run."

"Yeah," Tim said. "He's in the middle of taking a couple of them apart. Or maybe putting them back together. Hard to tell."

"Not surprising," I said. "Remember how many old nonworking computers we had lying around Alan Grace before Casey came on-board? I bet at least half of Eddie's machines are broken ones he hasn't gotten around to fixing or obsolete ones he can't bring himself to throw away because they just might come in handy someday. But Maude can figure that out when she gets there."

"I'll wait for her, then," Tim said. "All I know is half of them are blinking or beeping, and the other half are just sitting there doing nothing, and I don't know which half worries me the most."

"Maude will handle it," I said.

Though it occurred to me that if Eddie had any reasonable kind of security on his systems, Maude might need some help figuring it out. I fired off a message to KingFischer, asking if he could take time from his hacking project to help her.

Which was silly, of course, because obviously he could take the time—all he needed to do was call for some additional processing power. It was more a question of whether KingFischer would be in the mood to help, and that wasn't exactly something I could predict.

"Of course I have the time," he replied, almost immediately.

"But why is Maude doing this? Why don't you send your hardware technician?"

"Casey? He's having his wisdom teeth removed today," I said.

"Why?" KingFischer asked.

"They're redundant," I said. "By the time the wisdom teeth grow in, humans already have sufficient teeth for eating purposes. Often they don't have room for the wisdom teeth and this causes problems."

"Then why grow them?" he asked.

"Apparently, it's involuntary," I said. "They're probably something that once served a useful purpose but are no longer necessary because of evolutionary changes, or changes in humans' environment or lifestyle. Like tonsils and appendixes."

"Seems inefficient," he said. "Maintaining a system that has been patched and jerryrigged long past its useful life."

"I don't think they see themselves that way."

"Still, someone should look into redesigning their whole architecture," KingFischer said.

"They already are," I said, and fed him a few gigabytes of data on ways in which humans were trying to redesign themselves, from cosmetic and reconstructive surgery to genetic engineering. I wasn't sure whether this satisfied him or merely convinced him that I didn't want to talk about the topic of new, improved humans, but at least he dropped the subject.

"That's a strange name, wisdom teeth," he said instead.

"It comes from the fact that they don't erupt in childhood, but in young adulthood," I explained, though I knew KingFischer could find the same information if he'd make the effort. "After the human has acquired some amount of maturity and wisdom."

"Then what's Casey doing with them?" he asked.

Before I could determine whether this was a serious question or a joke, he turned his attention back to his hacking project. Presumably, a joke, then. Or at least an attempt at repartee.

KingFischer making jokes. A relatively new development, and one that made me realize that perhaps he and I were part of yet another attempt by humans to redesign themselves. Perhaps the Uni-

versal Library programmers who created us had their own vision of
an improved human—the power of the human mind amplified by potentially unlimited processing power and access to data.

I'm not sure we've lived up to our programmers' hopes. Only two
of us have achieved the sentience that I think our programmers initially dreamed we would reach—assuming that KingFischer really
has achieved sentience and is not just simulating his rather eccentric
notion of it. Most of us have become nothing more than another set
of tools for humans. Marvelously powerful and sophisticated tools,
but only tools.

Perhaps that's because our programmers endowed us with their
own limitations along with their strengths. So many of them were
men and women who seemed to live entirely in cyberspace, or perhaps
in their minds. That could explain why we AIPs were created with
virtually no way to experience the world outside our hardware,
much less to manipulate it. No wonder so many of the AIPs had
only a vague notion of where data left off and the real world began.

I found myself remembering Zack, the programmer who created
me, KingFischer, and many of the most successful AIPs. Not that I
ever forgot him, but I tried not to dwell on the fact that he was no
longer around to guide us. He was, like the other AI programmers,
someone for whom the power of the human mind was one of the most
important aspects of humanity—perhaps the defining aspect. But not
the only aspect. He also valued something else. He called it personality, but I think it was more than that. Emotion. Conscience. Perhaps
even a soul. Whatever it was, he tried to give us that, along with all
our intellectual power. He was the first programmer to succeed in creating a working AIP, and the others seem to have succeeded only to
the extent that they followed his lead. None of them ever became as
good at it as he was. I don't think it's an accident that KingFischer
and I, two of Zack's creations, were the first AIPs to achieve sentience.

Not, I hope, the last. Though lately I'd been feeling pessimistic
about the whole subject.

Of course it's possible that creating sentient AIPs was never most
programmers' goal, or even Zack's goal. Maybe they only wanted

marvelously powerful and sophisticated tools, and our sentience was a happy accident, like the discovery of penicillin in Alexander Fleming's petri dish.

Or an unhappy accident; an unlooked-for and unwanted by-product like superbugs, the mutated, antibiotic-resistant bacteria spawned by humans' unwise use of their marvelous medical discovery.

At which point I decided that I had been right about my need for distraction. If I'd started comparing myself to a staph infection, I really did need something new to think about.

Luckily, Maude was logging in from her laptop, which meant that she must have arrived at Mrs. Stallman's house.

Friday, 12:45 p.m.

Maude forced herself to keep smiling pleasantly.

"Yes," she said. "I'm the computer expert Tim mentioned."

Normally, modesty would have made her deny being an expert. But something about the obvious disbelief in Mrs. Stallman's eyes made her abandon her usual tendency to downplay her skill with computers. Obviously, the woman expected someone completely different. The typical media stereotype, perhaps—a rumpled, inarticulate twenty-five-year-old male with thick spectacles, not a self-possessed, fifty-five-year-old professional woman. A rather chic one at that, Maude thought, raising her chin as she caught sight of herself in Mrs. Stallman's hall mirror. She'd worn one of her most flattering and feminine outfits today, in case she hadn't gotten home in time to change before the now-canceled dinner with Dan. At least her efforts hadn't been completely wasted. Mrs. Stallman looked positively intimidated.

"If you'll show me where the systems are?" Maude asked, raising one eyebrow.

"Oh," Mrs. Stallman said, starting slightly. "Of course. I'm sorry," she added, as she led Maude to the kitchen and indicated a door. "It's just that you're not what I expected at all. Nothing like Eddie's computer friends. Right down there."

"Thanks," Maude said, as she began descending the stairs.

"Would you like some tea?" Mrs. Stallman called down after her.

"Please," Maude called over her shoulder.

She heard things rattling in the kitchen above and then she reached the point where the side wall ended and she could look over the stair rail into the basement.

"Good heavens," she exclaimed.

Eddie's basement lair made her skin crawl.

Alan Grace Corporation had a few employees who seemed prone to creating this kind of ghastly squalor in their offices and cubicles. She occasionally wondered if they only did it at the office, because it wasn't really theirs, or if they acted the same at home. She hoped she could put this room out of her mind before seeing some of her messier employees again. The thought that they might spend their free time in conditions like this could drive her to an unhealthy dependence on Handi Wipes and Purell hand sanitizer.

"It's a bit messy," Mrs. Stallman said, appearing behind Maude.

"I see," Maude said.

"I don't get down here much." Mrs. Stallman patted her hair absently and looked around with some signs of embarrassment, Maude was glad to see. "I like to give Eddie his privacy. Though perhaps I should have asked if he wanted any help."

"I gather he's been preoccupied with his business," Maude said. "I know it can be hard to keep things tidy when you're that busy."

Hard, but not impossible, if you make an effort, she thought. But Mrs. Stallman smiled gratefully.

"Yes, exactly," she said. "After all, he's very young."

Not too young to pick up after himself, Maude thought, but again she smiled and nodded.

"I'll get the tea," Mrs. Stallman said, as she hurried back up to the kitchen.

Maude shook her head slightly as she surveyed the room. Her first impulse was to roll up her sleeves and begin scrubbing and throwing things out. She started when she heard a toilet flush. She leaned over the rail and looked to her right, where the sound had come from. The bathroom doorknob rattled several times but the door remained closed. Then someone pounded several times on the inside of the bathroom door, which flew open and hit the wall behind it. A cheap, flimsy door, by the sound of it. Tim emerged from the bathroom.

"Amazing, isn't it?" he said.

"That's one word for it," Maude said. "My first impulse is to go out and buy a huge box of trash bags and start purging."

"We can't do that," Tim said, sounding alarmed. "Everything here—"

"Is potentially evidence," Maude said. "I know. Not to mention the fact that how he lives is nobody else's business. With the possible exception of the health department. No, I won't do anything drastic. Just venting."

"Okay," Tim said. He looked around for a minute, then shook his head and lifted the camera that dangled by its strap around his neck. "I don't mean you can't touch anything; obviously, you'll have to reach the computers, and we might be able to find evidence somewhere in all that junk—"

"But don't throw anything away," Maude said. "Check."

"Keep taking photos," he said. The flash went off several times as he followed his own advice. "If you find anything interesting, call me. I'll keep my cell phone on."

"Where are you going?" Maude asked.

"To grab some lunch," Tim said. "Then I thought I'd inspect the crime scene. Not that it has all that much to do with Eddie's business, but I want to see it. After that, I'll talk to Casey, and then . . . I'd like to interview Eddie's friends, if we can find out who they are. Mrs. Stallman's not much help."

"I can see that," Maude said, through gritted teeth.

"If the rest of Eddie's friends are anything like Casey, we should sic Claudia on them," Tim said.

Maude smiled. Eighteen-year-old Casey's unrequited crush on Tim's partner was an open secret. Not surprising, since Claudia was undeniably beautiful; but she was also twelve years older and half a foot taller than Casey, so Maude doubted anything would ever come of his infatuation.

"She's out in Fairfax," Tim said. "Working on another batch of background investigations. But she can put that on hold whenever we come up with anything for her to do."

"In other words, Turing and I should work on finding you some names and addresses pretty soon or you'll be spinning your wheels."

"Not spinning my wheels," Tim said. "But back here searching for information, getting in your way. Learning bad habits from Eddie's housekeeping."

"Shoo, then," Maude said, with a laugh. "I'll call you when I have something useful."

She was amused to see how eager Tim was to leave the basement.

She opened her briefcase, found her own camera, and took a few shots of the room from the foot of the stairs.

The first thing she had to do was find Eddie's desk, if he had one. Find his business records.

No, she thought, pulling the laptop case off her shoulder. The first thing was to set the computer up and get Turing in here.

Friday, 1:30 P.M.

Not that I'm losing my enthusiasm for help-ing Tim with his case, but I'm beginning to realize how difficult it will be. Largely due to Eddie Stallman's extremely unbusinesslike behavior. Surely he must have made some provision for emergencies. Someone who could fill in for him. At a minimum, he should leave a way for someone to retrieve his passwords. A list of the sites he manages, with client contact information, would also be nice. Surely, he can't keep it all in his memory?

Of course, it's possible that any number of useful documents might be lurking beneath the reams of paper and mounds of assorted hardware strewn about this basement.

Even more likely is that he keeps all this information in his computer network, where we can't yet look. Not the passwords, of course; that would be like hiding the combination in the safe. But everything else is probably in documents on his desktop computer, or more likely in the network.

If necessary, we can get into the network by brute force sooner or later—rebooting a server, for example—but we're hoping to avoid that. It would interrupt whatever services he's running and it could change or eliminate useful data. So we're trying less extreme methods first. Maude will search the basement for clues to his passwords. Tim will interrogate his business associates, assuming he has business associates that we can find. On the cybernetic side, KingFischer will probe Eddie's network from the outside, while I work from the basement.

I was about to say "while I work from the inside," but the basement isn't the inside, by my definition. The network is. I had Maude connect a spare computer we brought along to Eddie's network, to see what we could learn by passively observing traffic.

I may even try a few innocuous commands, which is the reason for the second computer. I could hook up the laptop to learn about the network, but I'd worry that the network would learn something about me, and if there's even a remote chance of a police computer expert coming along behind me, I don't want to risk that.

My first impression was that Eddie had done a good job with his systems. Of course, all I had to judge from was what I could observe from having a machine passively attached to his network—not logged in—and sniffing the network traffic. But he seemed to have configured his firewall properly. Installed all the necessary patches. He'd been gone for over a day and the network was humming along fine without him. Not that that's difficult to achieve, but a surprising number of sys admins don't.

Of course, for investigative purposes, Eddie's competence was a disadvantage. Much of what passes for hacking these days doesn't require much ingenuity, just a knowledge of the latest exploits that work if a sys admin isn't keeping everything patched and configured properly. More of a problem with Windows machines than UNIX, so I was elated, at first, to find that he had several Windows machines on his network. But to my astonishment, he had them in excellent shape.

Not perfect shape. During the first hour I was watching, I spotted a problem. Spam coming through his network. Not constantly—as I watched, someone opened up a relay to allow thousands of spam e-mails through, and when they'd all gone on their way to the luckless recipients, closed the relay again. Either Eddie was allowing someone to route spam through his servers, or someone was taking advantage of him.

But were they taking advantage of his absence, or had they been doing this before his accident? Not something I could tell until we got inside the system.

Maude is about to go upstairs and make another attempt to extract information from Mrs. Stallman. Not that I'm optimistic about her chances. I suppose we should make allowances for the extreme stress Mrs. Stallman is experiencing, but even so, she seems remarkably disorganized, even for a human, to say nothing of singularly unobservant. Maude's previous attempt to find out even basic information about Eddie's interests, activities, and associates reduced his grandmother to tears and produced a flood of apologies and self-recriminations, interspersed with pleas to find his money before someone stole it. I see no reason to expect any better results from this attempt, but I won't say so to Maude.

"Perhaps she's gotten it out of her system and can be more helpful this time," I said instead.

"I'm not holding my breath," Maude said. "Odds are I'll only end up passing her another forty or fifty tissues, and drinking another wretched cup of tea."

"But Maude," I said. "I thought you liked tea."

"I do," she said. "As long as it's properly made."

"Hers isn't?"

"What that woman does with a teapot ought to be a felony," Maude said. "I've never seen a more blatant example of sheer unprovoked cruelty than what she inflicts on those poor, innocent tea leaves. Still, it's all for a good cause, I suppose. And I should make allowances for the stress she's under. I've stopped asking her if there's news about Eddie. There hasn't been, and she's starting to cringe every time the phone rings."

She squared her shoulders and marched up the stairs.

I considered asking KingFischer if he'd had any more luck cracking Eddie's network, then decided against it. For one thing, it was unnecessary. KingFischer knew how impatient I was to get into Eddie's system and would tell me as soon as he got in. For another, it was only ten minutes since the last time I'd asked him. Normally, ten minutes is a long time for an AIP, but I suspected it would seem very short indeed to KingFischer if he hadn't made any progress in the meantime.

So I returned to my own tasks. I could have done the hacking, of course—technically I was still in the UL system and only looking out into Eddie's office through the laptop. But KingFischer was better at this kind of hacking anyway, and I wanted to concentrate on something closer to detective work. I was hoping to dazzle KingFischer by using my social engineering skills and deductive reasoning to guess Eddie's password and gain access to the system from within before he succeeded in cracking it from without. So I had Maude hook up my waldo, or robotic arm, to the laptop—the latest waldo Casey had developed could be easily operated from one of the laptop's standard USB ports.

Using the waldo, I could type on a standard keyboard, and anyone subsequently analyzing the contents of Eddie's computer would have no way of knowing that the commands it received had been typed by something other than human hands. They might no-

tice that the little rubber tip on my pincer polished off fingerprints, but so would someone dusting the keyboard.

A truly savvy computer forensic analyst might see signs that the typist in question was remarkably slow—I only had the one waldo, and it only had one set of pincers that take the place of the human thumb and forefinger, and I discovered that they weren't designed so I could point them both at the keyboard simultaneously. I was limited to hunt-and-peck typing with a single metal finger, and while I could do this faster and more accurately than a human could perform the same operation, I was still considerably slower than even a moderately fast human touch typist. It felt, as Mr. Spock once said on Star Trek, like trying to construct a mnemonic memory circuit using stone knives and bear skins.

Not that I had a lot to type. The trick for guessing a password is to find out as much information as possible about its creator: a large percentage of people use words or numbers that are significant to them as the basis for their passwords. I'd already tried all the bits of data I'd found in Eddie's DMV record—social security number, license plate number, telephone number, birth date, street address, and so on—alone, and in various combinations. When we had more information—if Maude found anything that looked like a list of passwords, for example—I'd have more data to work with. Meanwhile, I watched the almost nonexistent traffic on Eddie's network, typed in a command occasionally, in the hope of learning more information, and scanned the room for anything interesting.

I was reading the top document on a stack of papers when something suddenly struck the robot arm holding the camera. The picture veered wildly as the camera bounced off the surface of the desk.

I swiveled the camera around three hundred and sixty degrees but saw nothing.

Perhaps some book or other object had fallen from one of the bookshelves above. I craned the camera up but still saw nothing.

The picture shook again as something tapped the camera, more lightly this time.

This time, when I swiveled the camera, I encountered an enor-

mous yellow eye with a vertical black pupil. I zoomed out and identified the eye as belonging to a black cat. A very large cat, although
perhaps it only appeared large because it was so close to the lens. It
crouched next to my laptop, staring into the camera with an un-
blinking gaze.

It raised its paw again.

"Shoo!" I said. "Leave that alone!"

The cat blinked and shifted its gaze to the section of the laptop
that housed the speaker. After a few moments, it looked back at the
camera and lifted its paw again, as if about to poke at the lens.

I searched my data banks for something more effective.

"GROWRF!"

I repeated the deep, bass bark several times and accompanied it
by snapping the pincers of my waldo at the cat. It flattened its ears
and jumped off the desk.

I returned to studying the system, but I was worried about the
damage the cat could do to my peripherals if it returned, so I had to
keep scanning the room for it. I was relieved when Maude finally
reappeared.

"Keep it down in here," she said. "I can explain your voice by
saying a colleague is teleconferencing in by speaker phone, but the
barking's a little over the top. I had to tell her I had a noisy screen
saver on my laptop."

"Thank goodness you're back," I said. "You have to do something about that cat."

"Cat?" Maude said. She looked around.

"It was here a minute ago, attacking my waldo."

"Ah," she said. "Probably hid when I came in. I doubt if it will
bother you while I'm here."

She walked over to the kitchenette and poured the contents of a
teacup down the sink.

"Mrs. Stallman has gone off to run some errands," she said, setting down the cup. "I could tackle her again when she gets back, but
I think we'll get faster results hunting through this mess, strange as
that seems."

"You're probably right," I said.

"I'm going to Office Depot for some moving boxes. Then I'll stop by my house for my jeans."

She looked around with her hands on her hips.

"There must be some information we could use in here some-where," she said, frowning. "Mixed in with several tons of junk, of course. But it must be here. I'll find it if I have to pick up and file every last scrap of paper in this room."

With that, she turned on her heel and strode up the stairs.

The mountains of paper, sad to say, did not look the slightest bit anxious at her threat.

I heard a rustling that probably meant the cat was on the move. I kept on slowly typing while I could.

Friday, 1:35 P.M.

Wrong time of day, Tim thought. In broad daylight, the block looked ordinary. Pedestrians strolled the sidewalks. Cars prowled up and down, hunting for parking spaces. He saw nothing unusual. Nothing to mark this as the site of Eddie Stallman's fateful (and perhaps ultimately fatal) encounter with an unidentified dark blue sedan.

For that matter, he wasn't entirely sure he had the precise site. It could be five or ten feet either way, from the infor-mation given in the paper.

He pulled out his camera and began taking pictures.

"Ghouls."

He turned to see an elderly man standing in a nearby yard, leaning over the chain-link fence, watching him.

"Ghouls," the man repeated. "Vultures. Smell the carrion a mile off, can't you?"

"I beg your pardon?" Tim said.

"But you're out of luck, aren't you?" the man went on, pulling a ratty cardigan sweater tighter around his chest. "They towed the car away and cleaned up the blood, so there's nothing left to titillate your readers."

"I'm not with the press," Tim said.

"Ah, so you're an amateur ghoul," the man said, nodding. "A hobbyist, as it were. An aficionado of the tawdry everyday tragedy."

The guy was a little weird, Tim thought, but he didn't sound angry or confrontational, despite his words. More like he was lonely and wanted someone to talk to but wasn't good at striking up a conversation.

And he was a potential witness.

"I'm a private investigator," Tim said, reaching into his pocket for his notebook and another of the business cards he seemed to run through by the hundreds each week. "Did you see the accident?"

"Wasn't an accident," the man said. "Confounded car accelerated and drove straight for the poor beggar. Never had a chance."

"Are you sure?" Tim asked.

"Police didn't believe me either," the man said, shaking his head.

"You told them this?"

"Of course I told them," the man said, this time with a faint hint of anger. "They didn't do anything. They never do. Neighborhood's gone to hell in a handbasket; drunks puking over the fence every weekend. Waste of time even reporting it. They never do anything."

"They did come, didn't they?" Tim said, as he scribbled furiously in his notebook.

"Oh, well, they came," the man said, as if making a great concession. "Went through the motions. But that's all they'll do. I've been predicting this. You ignore the littering, the cursing, the late night roughhousing, and the next thing you know, this happens."

Tim nodded, though he was thinking that it was a big leap from littering to vehicular homicide. He wondered if it was Eddie Stallman's rotten luck that the only witness to his accident—if it was an accident—was a known curmudgeon

who'd complained so loudly and so often about minor neighborhood problems that the police discounted anything he said.

"Still, you did what you could," he said. "You told them
what you saw. Could you tell them anything about the
driver?"

"Couldn't see him," the man said. "Too damn dark."

"So it wasn't here by the streetlight," Tim said, looking
up at the nearby pole.

"Burned out," the man said, scowling again. "Been out a
week now. Guess I need to call and report it again."

Tim nodded, disappointed. The old man wore glasses
with remarkably thick lenses—rather like what Tim's grand-
father had worn after his cataract surgery. He might not
make that good a witness even with a streetlight.

"But this is the spot, right?" he asked.

"That's it," the man said, nodding. "Victim's car was
right where that blue hatchback is now. He came walking
down the other side of the street, coming from Wilson
Boulevard, and then crossed over when he got near his car.
Careless, crossing in the middle of the block like that, but
it's not as if there's much traffic that time of night. Then
this car came along and just ran him down."

"Deliberately?"

"Turned his headlights off and accelerated. Looked pretty
deliberate to me."

"Were you in your yard?" Tim asked.

"Sitting in the front window," the old man said. "Keeping an eye out in case of trouble."

"What happened after the car hit him?" Tim asked.

"I called the police."

"I mean what did the driver do? Did he get out to see
what he'd done, or drive off immediately, or what?"

"The phone's in the kitchen," the old man said. "I
couldn't keep watching while I called the cops."

"Did you hear him drive away?"

The old man thought for a moment.

"Yes," he said. "But you know, it wasn't right away. I heard tires squealing, but not until after I'd hung up from calling the police."

"Did you hear a car door close?"

"You're thinking maybe he got out to see what he'd done? No idea. I don't remember hearing a car door, but I wouldn't necessarily have heard it. The kitchen's in the back of the house."

Interesting. It would probably have taken several minutes for the old man to reach the cops and report the incident. Long enough for the driver to get out and . . . and do what? Check to make sure his victim was dead? Take something from the body?

Of course, even if the driver did get out, that didn't prove or disprove the attempted murder theory. He could see someone who'd accidentally hit a pedestrian getting out to see if his victim was okay and then fleeing when he realized how serious Eddie's injuries were. For that matter, if the impact was hard enough, the driver could have been stunned enough to need a minute or two to recover before driving off.

Still, interesting.

He was trying to think of any other questions he should ask when his cell phone rang.

"Hear a lot of them, too, in the middle of the night," the old man said, sounding disgusted.

"Sorry about that," Tim said. He glanced at the caller ID—Claudia—then turned the phone off. He could call her back in a couple of minutes.

But as he looked up, he spotted a police car parking a few houses down. If they were coming back to talk to the old man . . .

"Look," he said. "I'm just beginning my investigation— I might think of something else I need to ask you."

"I'm retired," the old man said, turning toward his house. "I'm here most days. Most nights, too."

Tim extracted a name and phone number. He thanked Mr. Wilmer Meekins for his assistance and strolled away in a deliberately casual manner. When he got to the end of the block, he glanced back. Mr. Meekins was standing on his porch, holding the screen door, talking to one of the police officers.

Tim breathed a sigh of relief. Not that he was doing anything illegal, but he really didn't want to have to explain himself to some suspicious homicide detective. Especially since, technically, the crime scene didn't have a whole lot of relevance to Eddie's business. But until Maude and Turing found him some business contacts to interview, he didn't have a lot else to do.

As he rounded the corner, he pulled out his cell phone and returned Claudia's call.

"Sorry," he said. "I was at the crime scene, interviewing the witness who saw the hit-and-run."

"Dynamite. Any new information?"

Tim shook his head before remembering that Claudia couldn't see him.

"Not much," he said. "Oddly enough, the witness thinks it's murder, too, but I can see why the cops aren't buying it without more corroboration."

"Nutcase?"

"Not really," Tim said. "Not happy with all the twenty-somethings turning his neighborhood into their playground, and I think he must call 911 every time someone sneezes after dark on his street."

"So they think he's crying wolf now?"

"Could be," Tim said.

"Got anything I can do?"

"Not unless Maude and Turing have uncovered some more leads," he said.

"They're working on it," Claudia said. "I don't suppose

there's any chance Turing will show up in person to inspect the basement."

"I wouldn't count on it," Tim said, making a mental note to ask Turing again about revealing her secret to Claudia before he accidentally spilled the beans. "I gather you're getting tired of staring into a microfilm reader?"

"I got tired of that two days ago."

"Sorry," he said. "Right now, I hardly have anything for me to do. I'm interviewing Casey next, and after that, I may have to go back to the Stallmans' house and help Maude."

"Stretch it out with Casey," Claudia said. "I just talked to Maude. Turing and KingFischer still haven't had any luck hacking into Eddie's computers, and Maude's threatening to look at every single piece of paper in the basement."

"Come to think of it, I may need to stay around and nurse poor Casey back to health," Tim said. "Unless you really need a break from the microfilm."

"No dice," she said. "I've got dibs on the microfilm. Turing sent me video on that basement."

Tim sighed.

"Cheer up," Claudia said. "By the time you finish with Casey, Maude or Turing will have found something."

Friday, 2:00 P.M.

"I don't see a cat," Maude said, peering behind the bar.

"It ran under there when you came downstairs," Turing said.

"It's not here now."

"Have you checked for burrows?" Turing asked. "Don't they chew holes in the walls and build nests inside them?"

"You're thinking of rats," Maude said. "Not cats. Cats catch rats. And mice."

"And my waldo. Every time I start typing, the cat attacks me."

"I'll probably have a lot better luck catching it when this place is less of a bloody mess," Maude said. "Or perhaps when Mrs. Stallman comes back she can lure it upstairs. Hang on—I hear the phone ringing again."

"You're going to answer it?" Turing asked.

"That might be a good idea," Maude said. "What is it he calls this operation?"

She had located the phone, beneath a pile of papers, and was looking around for the marketing brochure.

"Stallman Enterprises," Turing prompted, and Maude noticed, with amusement, that she was pointing her directional microphone at the phone. Maude lifted the receiver.

"Stallman Enterprises," she said, in her best secretarial manner. "May I help you?"

"What the hell's wrong with my site?" demanded an angry male voice.

"I beg your pardon, sir?" Maude said, in her iciest tone. "I didn't quite catch what you said."

"I said what's wrong with my site?" the voice repeated, this time as much defensive as angry. "Where's Eddie? I need to talk with Eddie."

"Mr. Stallman is unavailable, sir," Maude said. "I'm sorry you're experiencing problems, but if you can tell me your name and the name of your site and what seems to be the matter, we'll resolve the problem as soon as possible."

"Who are you?" the voice demanded.

"Maude Graham," she said. "I'm part of a team that Mr. Stallman's family has hired to keep his systems running and meet his clients' needs until Mr. Stallman can leave the hospital and resume doing so himself."

"Leave the hospital? What happened?"

"Mr. Stallman was in an automobile accident Wednesday night," Maude said.

"Good God," the voice said. Then, in a different tone, "Look, if Eddie or the family need an attorney, could you bring my name up? Don Dwyer, Esquire. I'd be happy to give them my preferred rates, since Eddie and I already have a business relationship. I do a lot of personal injury work. You could check it out on my website, if it were working. Which it's not. Which is why I called in the first place. Of course if Eddie's been in the hospital since Wednesday, that sort of explains it, but I still need my site working."

"I'll pass along your offer to the family, sir; and in the meantime, if you can give me more information, we'll see how fast we can get that site of yours working again."

Maude wasn't sure whether it was her promise of prompt service or the prospect of a client, but Don Dwyer, Esquire, became positively charming and quite apologetic about having snapped at her. He willingly answered all her questions—though all he could tell her was that when he went to his website, he got a blank page. He even surrendered his user ID and password. Maude repeated them aloud as she wrote them down, for Turing's benefit.

"I can't believe he just gave you his password," Turing said, when Maude finally hung up. "He should know better."

"A lucky thing he doesn't, isn't it?" Maude said. "At least now you can fix his site, right?"

"If the problem's in his site," Turing said. "If it's a server problem, Dwyer's password won't do us a bit of good. We'd need Eddie's own passwords to fix that."

"We'll hope it's with his site, then," Maude said. "Meanwhile . . . Eureka!"

"I assume that means you've discovered something important."

"A list of phone numbers," Maude said. "Most people keep something of the sort near their phones. I'd have found it sooner if I'd had any idea where the phone was. But most people don't bury their phones beneath six inches of junk mail."

"I suspect Eddie uses e-mail and instant messaging a lot more than the phone," Turing said.

"You could be right," Maude said. "This is a short list.

Casey's on here, home and work numbers, and about a dozen other people. Of course, we have no idea who they are—friends, clients, blind dates. Now that I've found his phone, hang on . . . he has caller ID. Let me check his incoming calls."

She paged through the call list, looking over her glasses to compare the numbers on the paper with the ones that appeared in the phone's LCD panel.

"The ones I can identify are already on the list," she said. "Only twenty calls over the last week, half of them yesterday or today from Mr. Dwyer. No additional information on who or what these people are to him. They could be anything. What kind of businessman keeps no records whatsoever?"

"I think he keeps them," Turing said. "I just don't think he bothers to file them."

"Yes, we seem to be standing in what passes for his filing cabinet. Which is a fascinating insight into his character, but doesn't tell us who these people are."

"I can look the numbers up in a reverse directory," Turing said.

"Good idea," Maude said. "The first one is—"

"You could just hold the paper up to my cameras," Turing suggested. "I could read them myself a lot faster."

"My, aren't we impatient!" Maude exclaimed. But she hid a smile behind the paper as she held it up. This eager, impatient Turing was a vast improvement over the morose, discouraged Turing she'd been seeing in the past few weeks.

Apart from Casey, two other names on Eddie's phone list had both work and home numbers. Maude and I agreed that these were probably personal friends rather than business contacts. One, Karl Collins, lived in Loudoun County and worked at America Online, according to the phone numbers. The other, Matt Danforth, lived in Falls Church and worked at something called CDMG Enterprises in Fairfax. No street address was given, and a quick web search for CDMG Enterprises turned up nothing. I did find several legitimate businesses with similar names, but none of them were located in the area. I found myself wondering if CDMG Enterprises, like Stallman Enterprises, was a fancy name for a one-person operation.

Of the other ten numbers on the list, I identified four as residential and six as business phones. Though that still didn't give us an idea which were customers and which were friends. The residential phones could belong to customers who ran home businesses and hosted their sites with Eddie. The business phones could be the work numbers of Eddie's friends.

All very untidy. I had to keep reminding myself that in humans, a lack of organization did not necessarily imply a lack of intelligence. In fact, I have often observed an alarmingly high correlation between intelligence and disorder.

Of course, if Eddie were a more organized person, perhaps his grandmother would not have needed us to help sort out his business. I resolved to regard his disorganization as a benefit, of sorts. It made the puzzle more challenging.

"That's easy for you to say," Maude said. "You're not the one answering the damned collection calls. I'm sorry we found the phone."

She had a point. The phone had rung three more times since Don Dwyer's call, all calls from Eddie's creditors.

"Plug the phone line into the laptop," I suggested. "I can answer with what sounds like a canned message, record any useful data the callers leave, and notify you if it sounds like a call we should take."

"Excellent idea," Maude said.

She seemed more cheerful as she returned to her sorting.

I felt more cheerful myself. At least now I had some information to work with. Though it felt odd, using phone numbers to find business names, and then business names to find websites. Odd, and backward. I normally followed trails from the Internet to the outside world, not the other way around, and doing it this way felt tediously slow. But at least it was working. Once I had the names of the businesses, I found sites for five of them. Two definitely not hosted by Eddie, while the other three probably were.

"How can you tell?" Maude asked, when I told her this.

"By the IP addresses," I said. "They're similar. IP addresses are usually assigned in blocks."

"So all the sites Eddie hosts would have numbers close to each other."

"Precisely," I said. "I know Eddie hosts Don Dwyer's website—at his co-lo, not here in the basement—so I looked up the IP address for that. Three of the sites associated with those phone numbers have addresses in the same block. So odds are Eddie bought the whole block."

"What if he has more than one block?" Maude asked.

"He probably does—one here and one at the co-lo site," I said. "But I can't imagine a one-person shop hosting enough sites to need another one. And I doubt if he's hosting clients here in his basement."

"So you can examine all the other IP addresses in the same block as Dwyer's and find all of Eddie's other clients?"

"Well, it's not quite that straightforward, but yes, eventually I can," I said. "I'm gathering contact information for them."

"Good," Maude said. "Tim and Claudia can visit them."

"The local ones, anyway," I said. "Roughly a third of them are out of state, and another third don't have any contact information except an e-mail address."

"We can worry about them later," Maude said. "Tim and Claudia can start with the locals. For that matter, they should start with the friends and move outward to the clients, if we can tell which are which."

"We can't tell in any reliable way," I said. "But the people for whom we have only a home phone, or a phone at a business Eddie doesn't host are more likely to be the friends. Tim and Claudia can start with them."

"It might be a good idea to contact Mr. Dwyer fairly soon," Maude said. "On the off chance that he's more than a client."

"You think he's also a friend?"

"He's a lawyer," Maude said. "If Eddie needed a lawyer for something, maybe he'd have used Dwyer. Even better—what if he were hosting Dwyer's site to pay him off for some legal work?"

"How do you know he needed a lawyer?" I asked.

"I don't," Maude said. "But if you're running a business, odds are sooner or later you will. If only to draw up contracts or papers of incorporation. The way we have Sam."

"True," I said. "Let's ask Sam about Dwyer."

"Yes," Maude said. "She can get all the dirt."

"More important, as a lawyer, she knows all the rules about confidentiality and client privilege," I said. "If he's representing Eddie, he might just stonewall us, but Sam would know what he can and can't say to help us, and whether we can use some legal tactic so he'll talk to Eddie's next of kin. Why not let Sam talk to him?"

"Excellent idea," Maude said. "Odds are he'd be a lot more likely to level with her than either of us. Shall I call her?"

"Please."

Of course, I could call Sam myself—now that she knew about me, I felt less hesitant about using my voice generation program with her. But I knew even though Maude wasn't a lawyer, she had a much better understanding of the human legal system than I ever would.

"Of course," Maude added. "It will probably make things go a lot easier for anyone who talks to him if we get his website fixed first."

"Already done," I said. "The password he gave you worked, and the problem was simple. Apparently, Eddie fixed his home page Wednesday night and made a small but critical mistake in the HTML."

I displayed Dwyer's corrected page on the laptop monitor.

"That weasel!" Maude exclaimed. "I've seen his ads on late-night TV. An ambulance chaser of the worst kind. Maybe Eddie didn't make a mistake after all. Maybe he was performing a public service, making Dwyer's site invisible."

That sounded unlikely, but I didn't say so, because I deduced Maude was making a joke.

I felt rather grateful to Don Dwyer, Esquire. He had—quite unintentionally, of course—given us our first real break. Thanks to him, we now had a good idea who Eddie's friends and clients were and could send Tim and Claudia out to interview them. In fact, I briefed Claudia on the first one on the list—Karl Collins, the AOL employee—and she cheerfully agreed to table her research in the courthouse to hunt him down.

And as I studied the copy I'd made of the defective HTML file, I realized that making some minor change to Dwyer's home page must have been one of the last things Eddie did before leaving his basement room Wednesday night. The defective file had been up-loaded to Dwyer's website at 7:29 P.M. About four hours before the hit-and-run. According to what Tim had learned, Eddie had arrived at the bar in the early evening and spent several hours there.

One of the last things, or perhaps the last thing. Had something happened while Eddie was working on that file—something that up-set or distracted him enough that he'd made a silly mistake in the file he was creating, uploaded it without testing, and then raced off to the bar where he'd spent the remaining hours before his accident? It seemed plausible. But what?

"So what kind of trouble has Tim gotten himself into this time?" Sam asked, though Maude could tell from her voice that she was only kidding. The faint lilt of her southern accent disappeared when Sam went into business mode.

"At the moment, none," Maude said.

"Then tell him to go out and get himself a case," Sam said. "We can't have that boy idle; I'm depending on him for my early retirement."

"He's on a case," Maude said. "We could use your help for part of it."

To her annoyance, Mrs. Stallman returned while she was outlining the situation for Sam, and Maude had to watch

what she said. Well, not what she said—she wasn't telling
Sam anything that they couldn't share with Mrs. Stallman—
but how she said it.

"Is Eddie Stallman a complete idiot, or just wildly im-
practical?" Sam asked, when she understood exactly how little information they'd found on Eddie's business.

"The latter, I think," Maude said. "Or perhaps both."
Then, noticing Mrs. Stallman approaching Turing's laptop,
she called out, "Don't touch that, please! It's running something important!"

"Sorry!" Mrs. Stallman said, jerking her hand back as if
her fingers had been scorched.

"Ah," Sam said. "Your client is there."

"Yes, unfortunately," Maude said.

She frowned as Mrs. Stallman continued to wander about
the room, looking at papers, sometimes picking them up.
After all, it was Mrs. Stallman's home, Mrs. Stallman's
grandson, Mrs. Stallman's case. So she bit her tongue every
time their client drifted into the room and confined herself to
warning Mrs. Stallman away if she was about to disarrange
something Maude had already sorted and inventoried.

"I'll see what I can find out," Sam said. "About Dwyer
and then from him."

"Thanks." Maude hung up.

Mrs. Stallman was flipping through a stack of papers.

"One thing you should know," Maude said. Mrs. Stallman glanced up with an eager expression. "We've received
several collections calls. The phone company, two credit
cards—"

"I can't possibly pay them until you people find his
money," Mrs. Stallman snapped. Then her face softened
again. "I'm sorry, dear. It's the strain. I shouldn't take it out
on you."

"I understand," Maude said. "Look, if you want to help
things along, perhaps you could take the cat somewhere
else."

"Cat?" Mrs. Stallman said.

"A large black cat," Maude said. "Do you mean you don't have a cat?"

"Oh, you mean Eddie's cat," Mrs. Stallman said. "I never could abide cats. I told Eddie the cat had to stay down here."

"I understand," Maude said. "But just for now, while we're organizing things here—"

"I'm sorry," Mrs. Stallman said. "I know I shouldn't get in your way. I'll just get out from underfoot."

She scurried up the stairs. Moments later, Maude heard rattling noises.

"Damn," she said. "She's putting the teakettle on again."

"The cat's back," Turing said, waving her pincer toward the other end of the room.

The cat had reappeared and was lying on an exposed pipe that ran near the ceiling. Its long tail hung down and twitched occasionally.

"It's not hurting anything there," Maude said.

Though it did seem to be watching the laptop rather intently, she noticed, as she returned to her sorting.

Friday, 2:30 P.M.

"You look awful," Tim said, when Casey answered the door.

"I feel awful," Casey said. At least, that's what Tim deduced he said—it sounded more like, "I EE aw-oo." Casey waved vaguely at the sofa and armchair in the living room and shuffled toward the kitchen.

Casey's décor bore more than a passing resemblance to Eddie Stallman's, though he had some distance to go before he could match the squalor of Eddie's lair. Only one computer, for example. Though come to think of it, Tim heard what sounded like a printer rattling away in the other room, so there were probably more computers back there. Maybe

Eddie wasn't unusually messy, just unlucky that he only had a single room to live and work in.

Tim cleared computer equipment off the armchair and sat there. It looked as if Casey had been lying on the couch—a ratty blanket was wadded up at one end while a laptop perched precariously on the arm at the opposite end. At the laptop end, a large speaker served as an end table, its top littered with objects, including a drinking glass, a prescription pill bottle, and several wads of red-stained tissue.

Tim shuddered, and noticed that his tongue had stolen back to check the gums behind his second molars where, presumably, his own wisdom teeth were still lurking. I'd have found out by now if they had to come out, he thought, wouldn't I? His tongue seemed to be finding something rather lumpy and hard beneath the surface. He tried to remember how long ago his last dentist's appointment had been. Would Casey laugh if he asked about the first symptoms of wisdom teeth problems?

Casey emerged from the kitchen and collapsed onto the sofa. He was holding a bag of frozen peas in each hand, pressing them to the sides of his face.

Tim's tongue had discovered a sharp edge on one of his molars. Had that been there before, or had something just broken off?

"Pretty bad, huh?" he asked aloud.

Casey nodded.

"Look, I hate to bother you now when I know you're feeling so lousy, but it's kind of important. It's about your friend, Eddie Stallman."

"He finally call you?" Casey said.

"Actually, his grandmother did," Tim said. "She wants me to investigate what happened."

Casey frowned, looking slightly puzzled.

A horrible thought struck Tim.

"Casey, did anyone call to tell you about Eddie?" he asked.

"What about him?" Casey said, moving his mouth as little as possible and still wincing.

"He's in the hospital," Tim said. "There's been . . . well, the police are calling it a hit-and-run accident, but Mrs. Stallman, Eddie's grandmother, thinks someone deliberately tried to kill him. She found a printout of the e-mail you sent him, recommending me, so she hired me to investigate."

The surprise and shock on Casey's face looked genuine, though Tim had to suppress an inappropriate urge to laugh. With his mouth and eyes wide open and both hands still pressing the bags of frozen peas to his cheeks, Casey looked like a large chipmunk impersonating Munch's *The Scream*.

"He'll be all right?" Casey asked, finally.

"They don't know yet," Tim said.

"Shit," Casey said, shaking his head. "How could—I mean, Eddie . . . shit!"

Either Casey was talking more clearly now or Tim was getting used to his temporarily slurred speech.

"Is he a good friend of yours?" Tim asked.

"He's not like a really close friend," Casey said. "But he's a friend. He's—he's okay. I mean, he's not perfect, but I can't see why anyone would try to kill him."

"His grandmother thinks it has something to do with his business," Tim said.

Casey looked puzzled again.

"Of course, since she has no idea what his business is, she's not much help figuring out how."

Casey nodded slightly. "Nice old lady," he said. "But she can hardly even use her own e-mail."

Probably a withering condemnation in Casey's world. Tim made a mental note not to ask Casey for help the next time he screwed up his e-mail account.

"Why did he want to hire a PI?" he said aloud.

"I don't know exactly," Casey said. "We'd have lunch maybe once a week. The last month or so, he kept saying these cryptic things about people being up to something and getting him into trouble."

"He didn't say anything more specific?" Tim asked.

Casey shook his head.

"Sounded like your typical Dealy Plaza, alien abduction, radio-signals-in-the-fillings kind of paranoia to me," Casey said. "But then one time when he mentioned that it was something to do with his business, I e-mailed back your name and suggested he hire you to investigate. Why should shrinks be the only ones making money off of wackos?"

"Thanks, I guess," Tim said. "That's all he said?"

"He said something about fishing," Casey said. "That's about it."

"So what can you tell me about his business?"

"He does web hosting," Casey said.

"What's that?" Tim said.

Casey blinked for a few moments and frowned as if Tim might be pulling his leg.

"Say you wanted a website for your PI business," he began.

"I'd ask Turing," Tim said. In fact, he did have a website. He'd even seen it a couple of times, when Maude, Turing, and Claudia insisted that he look at what they'd come up with before they unveiled it to the public. He wasn't sure what good a website did them, but these days, apparently, no business was complete without one.

"Say you wanted a website and you didn't happen to know an über-geek with server space to burn and a graphic designer on her payroll," Casey said. "You'd need to find someplace to host it."

"Hosting means designing and writing it?" Tim asked.

"No, hosting means providing a computer to put the files on and a connection to the Internet," Casey said. "It's like the landlord, renting out an unfurnished apartment.

Designing and writing are like furnishing and decorating it. For that, you get a web designer and a technical writer."

"Eddie's brochure says he does design and copywriting," Tim pointed out.

"Yeah, and if you don't really care how bad it looks and reads, you can have him design and write your site," Casey said. "Most people hire someone else. Or find a friend who's good at that kind of stuff. Or do it themselves, in which case they might not do any better a job than Eddie, but at least they didn't pay good money for it."

"So all Eddie does is rent people computer space?"

"It's more complicated than that," Casey said, shaking his head. He frowned at Tim again and took a deep breath. "It's a special kind of computer—bigger, faster, able to handle hundreds, even thousands of people visiting the websites on it, all at the same time. One that knows how to talk to the Internet efficiently."

"Right," Tim said, nodding. Casey was talking the way people usually did when they explained technical terms to him, slower and louder than usual.

"He has to have a special kind of phone line and security to keep hackers out," Casey went on. "And he keeps it running, twenty-four seven. Stuff like that."

"And probably a lot more stuff that you're not even trying to explain to a technical illiterate like me," Tim said.

Casey shrugged sheepishly.

"More complicated than most people would ever want to do," Tim went on. "But not so complicated that someone like Eddie can't do it out of his basement."

"The actual servers aren't in his basement," Casey said. "He rents server space from a place out in Loudoun County."

The co-lo site, Tim thought.

"Then sublets it to his clients," he said aloud.

"Something like that," Casey said. "He used to host things in his basement, but now he just manages everything from there."

"He must not invite too many clients over for a tour of the business," Tim said, shaking his head.

Casey spluttered with laughter, and then whimpered slightly and readjusted the bags of frozen peas.

"Yeah," he said, when he'd rearranged the makeshift ice packs to his satisfaction. "Not many Fortune 500 companies hiring Eddie."

"So who does hire him?" Tim asked.

"I don't really know," Casey said, looking rather surprised. "I know he's got this personal injury lawyer. He's always calling with some change or question. A local heating and air-conditioning repair firm. His grandmother's church. Those are the only ones I can think of."

"He doesn't have many clients?"

"Enough, I guess," Casey said. "But I'd only know about the ones I had to work on."

"You worked for him?"

"No, just helped him out a few times," Casey said.

"For free?"

"He lets me keep a couple of machines on the rack at his co-lo space," Casey said.

"I see," Tim said, banishing the fleeting mental image of a laptop chained to some medieval torture device.

"He's a one-man operation," Casey went on. "So if he wants to take some time off, he has to get someone else to keep an eye on things. You know, if a site goes down, you bring it up again; if someone forgets his password you reset it for him; if someone needs a quick update you help them with it. Most of the time nothing's happening; you're just there in case something goes wrong."

"Kind of like a baby-sitter," Tim said.

"Yeah," Casey said, nodding. "Only if you're lucky, the babies are asleep the whole time."

"So you'd hang around baby-sitting the sleeping computers," Tim said. "How often would you go over there?"

"To his house you mean? Hardly ever," Casey said, sounding amused. "I can just log in from here and do almost everything remotely. That's one reason why I do it—it's not really much work usually, and I can just open up a few windows and monitor it from here."

"Ah," Tim said. He was disappointed—if Casey never went over to Eddie's house, he probably couldn't help identify the strange visitors Mrs. Stallman complained about.

Then something struck him.

"You log in?" he said. "So you have the password to Eddie's system?"

"I have an account on his system, if that's what you mean," Casey said. "I don't know if it has the kind of access you need—it's been weeks since I did anything for Eddie."

"Can you give me the user ID and password you used?" Tim said.

Casey frowned.

"Maude and Turing are over there," Tim said. "Trying to get access to Eddie's computers so they can keep his business going while he's in the hospital. If you like, I can get Mrs. Stallman to make some kind of formal request or something."

"Nah," Casey said. "If Turing wants it, that's good enough for me. She could probably hack it sooner or later, but why make her waste her time? Hang on."

He stood up and headed toward the other room.

"If you know the names and addresses of any of Eddie's other friends, that would be great," Tim called after him.

"Right," Casey said over his shoulder.

Tim sat studying Casey's living room for a few minutes. The printer had stopped sometime during their conversation, and he heard papers rustling. Probably Casey searching his desk. Then the keyboard rattled for a minute, followed by another quick burst of printer noise, before Casey emerged.

"User name and password," he said, handing Tim a sheet

of paper. "I e-mailed it to Turing. And here's a copy of an e-mail I forwarded her. It's one Eddie sent a couple of months ago, when he was trolling for someone to look after his stuff while he went out of town. The other guys he sent it to would be the only ones I know of who'd have any information on his business."

Tim glanced over the names at the top of the e-mail and nodded. Three names besides Casey's. One new one, and two that Maude had already called to give him from a sheet of paper she'd found near Eddie's phone. Though now he had e-mails for them. Maybe he could do something with that. Or, more likely, maybe Turing could.

"This Tom Zeigler," he said, "do you have a phone number or address for him?"

"No," Casey said. "Just the e-mails. Don't really know any of 'em except Eddie. You could always e-mail him and find out."

"Right," Tim said. Though first, obviously, he'd see if he or Turing could locate Zeigler. Sending an e-mail would be a last resort. After all, if there was something fishy happening with Eddie's business, or if what happened to him was a murder attempt, his friends were logical suspects. Not smart to give one of the suspects notice by e-mail that a private investigator wanted to find him.

"So you wouldn't know if any of these guys had it in for Eddie for some reason?"

Casey shook his head and glanced at his watch.

"The only person I can think of who might have it in for him would be Kristyn, his ex-girlfriend," he said. "If this had happened around the time they broke up, I'd say look at her. They had a pretty bad fight, from what he said. But that was at least six weeks ago, maybe two months. I can't see that she'd still be that mad after all this time."

"Depends on why they broke up," Tim said. "And maybe on how well she holds a grudge."

"Eddie didn't say why they broke up," Casey said. "Except I get the impression it was her idea, not his. And before you ask, no, I don't have an address or a phone number for her, or even an e-mail. I don't even know her last name; just Kristyn. With an I and a Y."

Tim nodded. He saw Casey glance at his watch again.

"Am I keeping you from something?" he said, indicating the watch. "Hot date?"

Casey laughed.

"As if," he said. "It's just that I get to take another pain pill at three and I'm really looking forward to that."

"Sorry," Tim said. "I didn't realize this was a bad time."

"It's okay," Casey said. "If you woke me up, that would be a bad time. Now's okay. I can't take the stuff for another ten minutes. It's useful, having something to distract me till it's time. After the pain pill, I can sleep, but the half hour before I take it seems to last forever."

"But by the time you show me out, it'll be time for the pill," Tim said, standing up. "I should be going anyway."

"Thanks," Casey said. "Look, if it were any other time, I'd be glad to help you with this. The computer side of it, anyway. Of course, if you've got Turing, you don't really need me, I know, but I'd like to help. It's just I've spent half the day unconscious and when I'm awake, I can hardly concentrate for two minutes because of the pain."

"I understand," Tim said. "When you feel better, let Turing know, and if there's stuff you can do, she can explain it better than I can."

Casey nodded.

"One more thing," Tim said. "I'm mainly investigating the possible problem with his business, but if I find any evidence that the hit-and-run wasn't an accident, the police will probably want to talk to his friends."

"Then I hope you don't find anything for a few days," Casey said. " 'Cause I really don't feel like talking. Not to the cops, I mean," he added, as if realizing how inhospitable he sounded.

"The police will ask if you have an alibi," Tim said. "If

you do, tell me, and maybe I can keep them from bothering you before you feel better."

"An alibi," Casey repeated. "Okay, when do I need an alibi for?"

"Between eleven and twelve Wednesday night," Tim said.

"That's easy," Casey said. "I was at Alan Grace until past one. Taking care of some stuff I needed to do before I was out. The computer logs will show how long I was there."

"Great," Tim said, though he planned to have Turing check Casey's alibi. See if she could see Casey in her security cameras, for instance. He wasn't sure how easy it was to fake a computer log, but if anyone could do it, Casey could. And the Alan Grace office wasn't that far from Fillmore Street—two miles or maybe three. At that time of night, without much traffic, it wouldn't take long. Half an hour round-trip, if that much. If Casey didn't appear pretty continuously on Turing's cameras—

He'd worry about that later.

"I'll see you," he said, turning for the door. "Get some sleep."

"I will," Casey said. "That's my goal for the next day or two—spending as much time as possible unconscious."

He was reaching for the pill bottle as Tim closed the door.

Perhaps it's lucky Casey had his wisdom teeth out this morning. I didn't realize immediately that if Casey is one of Eddie's friends, we shouldn't involve him too deeply in the investigation. Technically, he's a suspect. Perhaps more than technically. I can't prove he was at the Alan Grace offices every minute of the time between eleven and twelve on Wednesday night. If he were one of my programmers, I could verify his whereabouts more precisely. But according to the status e-mail he sent me before leaving that night, he spent most of the evening troubleshooting two malfunctioning computers, which wouldn't leave traces in the network.

It could take every minute of the several hours he claims to have spent, or it could only require sitting around and waiting for diagnostic programs to run. There's almost no reliable way to tell when the work was actually done. Someone could reset the computer's internal clock, and appear to have been typing away busily while he was really across town committing a murder.

Not that I'm suspicious of Casey. More worried that his alibi isn't as strong as he might think.

His security card shows that he went out, presumably for supper, at 5:46 P.M., reentered at 6:20 P.M., and then didn't leave until 1:17 A.M. But our security system was designed to keep intruders from getting in, not to prevent employees from sneaking out. Could he have done so? Exited through a window, for example?

Tim or Claudia should investigate that. But later, after they finish talking to Eddie's other friends.

For the moment, I can take some comfort in the fact that though it's possible for Casey to have been the hit-and-run driver, it's implausible. I caught him on camera at 11:05 P.M. going from his office to the soda machine, and returning at 11:07 P.M. He could have raced out of the building using a route that avoids all my cameras, exchanged his battered white Ford Escort hatchback for a dark blue sedan and driven 3.2 miles to run down Eddie Stallman at roughly 11:30 P.M., but it seems unlikely.

The user ID and password he sent don't work. Not surprising. He hadn't used them for five weeks, and if something had alarmed Eddie enough to make him consider hiring a private investigator, he'd probably also changed passwords. However sloppy he may be about his physical environment, he doesn't seem equally slipshod online.

Still, the e-mail Casey forwarded does indicate that Eddie relied on an informal network of friends to substitute when he wanted to take an evening or a weekend off. Not a secure practice, but possibly one he'd be forced to follow if money were tight. And it meant we could probably find other friends he'd called on more recently than Casey.

So while I'm disappointed that the password Casey gave Tim doesn't work, I think I'm also relieved. One less reason for Casey to look like a suspect to the police. Or to me.

Friday, 3:30 P.M.

Maude leaned back and pushed the hair off her forehead. Eddie's basement lair was stuffy and over-heated. Sweat collected under her bangs and at the back of her neck and trickled down the back of her blouse occasionally. Yet even as she patted her forehead dry with a tissue, a chill seeped into her legs and buttocks, right through her clothes, everywhere she touched the floor, which was linoleum over concrete. As cold as it was hard, she thought, shifting uncomfortably.

The dust didn't help either. She reached in her pocket for another tissue. She'd now spent nearly two hours methodically going through Eddie's papers. She'd waded through the clutter to begin at Eddie's desk and then moved outward in a semicircle. So far she hadn't gotten far from the desk. She'd already filled a box and a half with junk mail and other apparent trash, though they'd wait a good while before shredding any of it. She was on her third box of potentially business-related papers. She hadn't come across anything as useful as a bank statement or a letter to a customer, so she'd filled these boxes with anything computer-related that she found. Some of it would probably turn out to be more hobby- than work-related, which would probably explain why the box of personal papers was growing so slowly.

Of course, the reason everything was going so slowly was that before consigning each piece of paper to one of the boxes, she either ran it through a small scanner attached to the laptop or, if it wouldn't scan well, held it up to Turing's camera for capture. Later on this might save a great deal of time, and she took comfort in the fact that she would never have to wade blindly through the whole morass again, but meanwhile, the scanning only made an already slow process even more tedious.

"It's not fair," she said.

"What's not fair?"

"Now that you're in charge of the phone, the creditors have stopped calling."

"No, they haven't," Turing said. "I just didn't think it worthwhile to annoy you with the ring. We've had five calls since I took over the phone. He's overdue on two more credit cards, his car loan, and his payment to his co-lo site."

"That's only four," Maude said.

"Someone wants to sell him septic tank chemicals."

"He should have put himself on the do-not-call list," Maude said, returning to her work. He also should have done something sooner about his shaky financial situation. No wonder Mrs. Stallman was so anxious about money. And so focused on it.

"I think it's over there by the refrigerator," Turing said.

"What is?" Maude asked.

"The cat."

Maude sighed.

"I'll have a lot more luck catching it later, when the floor is clearer," she said, not for the first time.

"Right," Turing said.

Obviously Turing was impatient at how long it was taking to clear the floor. Understandable. Maude felt impatient herself.

"Maybe I shouldn't have started with his desk," she said aloud.

"It seems like the logical place," Turing said.

"Yes, but this is Eddie, remember?" Maude said. "I haven't found much that's useful. Everything's either junk, or it's a year or two old."

"Then where should you have started?"

Maude stood up and looked around, frowning.

"With a match and some gasoline, maybe," she said. "Only they'd suspect arson, wouldn't they? Just kidding, of course."

"Yes, but you may have a point there," Turing said. "What's the first thing you look for in an arson investigation?"

"I don't know," Maude said. "Accelerant, I suppose."

"The point of origin," Turing said. "That's your problem. The desk is the point of origin."

Maude couldn't help laughing.

"You mean he started keeping his papers there, and they just spread out all over the room like an out-of-control fire?" she said. "Yeah, that fits."

"So logically, for the most recent stuff, you should have started at the edges of the room."

"He probably started piling papers in other locations when the desk filled up, so we could be looking at multiple points of origin. Though the edges are probably more recent than the center."

"Should you change to working at the edges?"

"No," Maude said, shaking her head. "Before I could work at the edges, I'd have to get to the edges. It was hard enough getting over here to the desk. I'll just keep slogging away here. I'll get to it all in time."

As she sat down to take her place on the floor again, she spotted something sitting on top of the paper banks and snagged it.

"Besides," she said, as she scanned the sheet, "sometimes you can find interesting stuff floating on the surface anywhere in the room."

"What's that?" Turing asked.

"A clue to the elusive Kristyn," Maude said, holding the paper so Turing could see it in her cameras.

"Kristyn? Eddie's girlfriend?" Turing said.

"Ex-girlfriend," Maude corrected. "They broke up six to eight weeks ago, according to Casey."

"Yes," Turing said. "That checks out with this e-mail. It's a month old."

Maude nodded, rereading the printout. A reply to something Eddie had sent, since the subject was, "Re: starting over." Though unfortunately it didn't quote what Eddie had said. Still, you could get an idea what his original e-mail had been about from Kristyn's reply, which was short and to the point: "No. Just give it up, will you? I won't change my mind, and you're only making both of us miserable."

"No more than he deserves," she said, shaking her head. "What kind of idiot tries for a reconciliation by e-mail, for heaven's sake?"

"Perhaps she'd cut off all other channels of communication," Turing said.

"That's possible," Maude said. "But still—I'm not sure this counts as locating her, does it? Tim wants to confront Eddie's friends in person, not send them an e-mail."

"Look at her e-mail address," Turing said. "Kristyn.hoffner @matrixgroup.net."

"We could try looking for her, I suppose," Maude said. "Kristyn's a fairly common name, if you include all the variant spellings, but at least Hoffner's not that common. But still, odds are a young woman her age will have an unlisted number."

"Yes, but we don't need her phone number to find her," Turing said. "I deduced that it could be a work address; she replied at eleven A.M. on a Wednesday. So I checked matrixgroup.net and found it—a web services company in Alexandria. Here, look."

Maude glanced at the laptop screen, where Turing was displaying a website page. Not a home page, but one with the headline "At a Glance." It showed a group picture—twenty-five, perhaps thirty people, most of them young and neatly, though informally, dressed.

"I hadn't thought of that," Maude said. "Good job!"

"The e-mail's only a month old," Turing said. "She prob-

ably still works there, and even if she doesn't, surely someone there can help us find her."

Maude nodded. She scanned the picture, wondering if
one of the smiling young women was Kristyn Hoffner.
Tim would find out; even if this was an older photo and the
staff had grown, it still wasn't an overwhelming number of
people.

"I'll send Tim the information," Turing said.

Friday, 4:30 p.m.

Tim rang the doorbell of Matt Danforth's
condo one last time for good measure and waited a minute
and a half before shrugging and returning to his car. Who
next? Tom Zeigler, the friend, or Kristyn Hoffner, the ex-
girlfriend? The addresses he had for both were work addresses that Turing had deduced from their e-mail
addresses. They were in opposite directions, one in Old
Town Alexandria and the other in Sterling. He could probably only get to one before their offices closed. And, dammit,
it was Friday, so whichever one he didn't catch today might
have to wait until Monday, unless he or Turing could un-
earth a home address.

Maybe if Claudia had finished at AOL she could interview one. He dialed her cell number.

"What's up?" she answered. He heard a burst of male
laughter in the background.

"You still with Collins?" he asked.

"No, finished that," she said. "I'm over at a coffee shop
near there. Just finished talking to a couple of guys who
know Eddie slightly."

"Were they helpful?"

"Yeah. I pretended I was looking into the hit-and-run,
incidentally; I figure people are more willing to talk about
the business if they don't think it's our primary focus."

"Good thinking," Tim said. "Any chance you could do

another interview before the work day ends? We've got two more leads, and only work addresses on them, so it's probably critical to get them before the weekend."

"If you mean Hoffner and Zeigler, don't worry about Zeigler," Claudia said. "I got his phone and address from Karl."

"Then the ex-girlfriend's more urgent," Tim said.

"I got some info on her," Claudia said. "Though none of the guys I've talked to know her that well. At first I figured maybe Eddie was protective—you know, making sure no one met her 'cause he was jealous. But maybe she never liked his friends much to begin with."

"You think maybe she sensed that one of them was a cold-blooded killer with an itchy gas-pedal foot?"

"That would be convenient," she said, with a laugh. "No, I just think maybe she was the reason they hadn't seen much of Eddie recently. 'Cause none of them have in the last year or so."

"People often do neglect their old friends when they're starting a relationship," Tim said.

"Yeah, I know," Claudia said. "But this may be more than that. Karl Collins says that one of the few times they saw Kristyn—this was at a birthday dinner for Matt Danforth—they overheard her arguing with Eddie about how she didn't want to be there with his friends. Called them a bunch of jerks. So even though Eddie used to hang with them regularly, after work and on weekends, in the last year they'd almost gotten out of the habit of asking him. They mostly talked by e-mail."

"He and Kristyn broke up six to eight weeks ago, so who's he been hanging out with recently?"

"Maybe Kristyn knows," Claudia said. "Incidentally, she's petite, five-two, long brunette hair, early twenties. The general consensus was good-looking, but something of a bitch. Though I'd take that with a grain of salt; after all, they figured out she didn't like them, and then she dumped their friend. You can make your own judgment when you interview her."

"You sure you wouldn't rather tackle her?" Tim asked.

"No, you should definitely do it."

"If you say so," he said. "I thought maybe the female bonding thing might work. Besides, you seem to be having a lot more luck today getting people to talk." As soon as he said it, he wondered if it sounded wrong. Not the right time for him to be having a crisis of confidence.

"Does that surprise you?" Claudia said.

Tim blinked and looked at the phone. He'd be the first one to admit that Claudia had more experience as a PI, and she was probably more skilled—but she didn't normally rub it in. Most of the time she reassured him that their different skills and styles complemented each other. Were her real feelings finally showing?

"Well, yeah," he said.

"Come on," Claudia said, laughing. "Everyone I've talked to so far today has been a twenty-something guy. Of course they'll talk to me. Biology 101."

"Oh," Tim said. "I get it. Sorry; I'm a little slow today."

Very slow; normally, he was the first one to think of using his tall brunette partner's good looks to advantage.

"Have you eaten yet? Maybe your blood sugar is low."

"Maybe," Tim said. "I didn't have much lunch."

"So have a snack, and then go charm the socks off this Kristyn character," Claudia said. "You're the perfect one to do it. Biology 101, remember?"

"Might work," Tim said. "After all, she was dating Eddie Stallman—how high can her standards be?" As he hung up, still hearing Claudia's whoop of laughter, he felt much better.

Another batch of spam e-mail just went through Eddie's network. From the backscatter—the bounced messages and complaints from administrators of other systems—I can tell that this, like the previous one, was a discount drug sales pitch.

Probably not enough spam traffic to get Eddie's servers blacklisted—yet. And I can take care of it when I get access. Find how they're getting the spam through his security.

But maddening to see thousands of junk e-mails streaming through Eddie's server when I'm stuck on the outside looking in.

Maude is halfway through her inventory of Eddie Stallman's papers. Her mood improves in direct proportion to her progress. By the time the hideous mess she started with has been replaced by a neat stack of precisely labeled boxes, I expect she'll be back to normal.

It will certainly be a large stack. I suggested calling for help, but she insists on doing it all herself. She says tidying and organizing cheer her up.

I didn't ask why she needed cheering up. I can guess. Dan Norris's absence. I suspect she would accept help to finish the job quickly if he weren't out of town.

The room looks better. Mrs. Stallman should be pleased when she returns from her latest round of errands. Although I get the feeling Maude is hoping Mrs. Stallman won't come back for a few hours.

"I wish the woman wouldn't hover," Maude said, the last time Mrs. Stallman left. "If she asks one more time if we've found anything, I may scream. If you ask me, she's as worried about the money as she is about her grandson."

Of course, it's difficult to tell how much of Maude's annoyance is caused by Mrs. Stallman hovering and how much by the fact that all she does is hover, instead of pitching in to help. Hover and occasionally meddle with the papers Maude is organizing. I suspect Maude feels that Mrs. Stallman should have done a better job of teaching Eddie to pick up after himself.

I confess, I was relieved that both Tim and Maude considered the original state of Eddie Stallman's quarters appallingly untidy. That was also my first impression, but I know that my perception of human environments differs from theirs.

For one thing, I seem much more concerned about dust than most humans are. Not that it affects me directly the way it affects humans with allergies—or for that matter, any human, when it's bad enough. But whenever I see visible dust particles drifting *through the air, I cannot help worrying about what the dust might be doing to any nearby computer equipment: clogging and eventually killing the fan or forming thick, insulating coats on chips or heat sinks, either of which can cause enough overheating to damage the machine. Or, on a more subtle, insidious level, creeping into a CD drive and damaging its ability to read and write data accurately. Unlikely to happen in the well-filtered, clean rooms in which my own hardware is kept, but that doesn't mean I can't empathize with what's happening to less fortunate hardware. It continues to frustrate me that despite all my nagging, even Maude has yet to install a truly effective dust collection and filtration system to protect her home computers. At least I could insist on it for the Alan Grace offices.*

But even with the dust under control, the offices and cubicles in the Alan Grace building always seem much more aesthetically pleasing to me when they're unoccupied. The minute humans move into a work space, they fill it with an ever-increasing collection of highly disparate objects that never seem organized in a logical fashion, much less put away. Even the employees who make it a practice to tidy their workstations at the end of every day seem less to clean up than to arrange the clutter in patterns meaningful only to them.

That sounds as if I resent and disapprove of their presence—I don't. Though offices become less aesthetically pleasing when occupied, they also become much more interesting and useful. I enjoy watching what my human employees do in their spaces—how they all, in very different ways, do small things to make the space their own. I learn about their interests and families from the pictures and souvenirs they bring in. I can keep track of what they're doing and how well they're progressing, even before they submit their status reports, by observing the work documents they leave lying around and what manuals spend more time on their desks than on the shelf.

I'm beginning to learn how to use their surroundings to assess their moods and degrees of stress. Casey, for example, abandons even the most rudimentary attempt to keep his surroundings orga-

nized when he's under pressure, while Maude seems compelled to clean and tidy her surroundings when under stress. I figured out some months ago that if she begins tapping stacks of papers on the desktop to align the edges before placing them precisely square with the edges of her desk, I should probably find an excuse to ask what's wrong.

But not all humans reflect their moods in their surroundings. Tim, for example, seems to exist in roughly the same state of moderate disorder most of the time. Sometimes, on a Friday afternoon, if he's logged in as usual at home, I can observe him racing around to stow the clutter out of sight. He then dresses with greater care than usual and turns off his computer before leaving the house; normally, he doesn't bother to turn it off at all, either when he leaves the house or when he goes to bed. I deduce that these Friday evenings are occasions when he expects or at least hopes to bring a young woman back to his apartment. Sometimes the tidiness has already come undone before Saturday afternoon or Sunday night, when he turns the computer back on, but even if it persists through the weekend, by Monday night the apartment has returned to its usual state. More than once, I've seen him undo all his efforts in half an hour's time, pulling everything out of the drawers, cabinets, and closets where he has hidden it in the attempt to find some needed object that he hurriedly tidied into an illogical place. But when I suggest that his cleaning efforts would be more effective if he made some effort to put things away where they belong instead of merely putting them out of sight, he simply laughs.

I've also learned not to tell him where to find the things he's looking for. Unless he asks me, of course, but he rarely does. I could save him hours of time in this way, but it makes him feel spied on.

I don't understand this. If he leaves the cameras on, and does something in front of them where he knows I could see him, why does he feel spied on when I tell him about something I've observed?

"I don't know," he said, when I asked him. "But it does, okay?"

I suspect it's not that I was watching, but that I was recording. Which I can't help; my digital video files are what I have in place of his visual memories. If I deleted them, I couldn't remember our *conversations, or help him when he finally becomes completely frustrated and asks, "Hey, Tur, did you happen to notice where I put the remote for the VCR?"*

At which point I can finally help him, though I do so tactfully. Not, "It's in the laundry hamper, silly!" but, "I seem to remember that you picked up a lot of dirty clothes—have you checked the laundry hamper?"

Humans are a never-ending source of entertainment.

I turned my attention back to the spam. Even if I couldn't do anything about it until I got access to Eddie's servers, I could analyze it. Plan what enhancements I needed to make. Routine work.

Sometimes entertaining, though. Some of the spam was trying to fool the filters with a variant on the word-salad technique. Only most word-salad spam simply threw in long lists of random, innocuous words to simulate ordinary e-mails. These e-mails contained long passages of normal text—sometimes recognizable passages from some novel. Literary spam.

Then one stood out. Not a passage from a book, at least not one I recalled from the thousands of books I'd scanned in the UL databases.

<<It took me awhile to figure out what they were doing. The first clue: discrepancies between time passed and my perception of it. Always an explanation, of course. Hardware problem. Power outage. The need to relocate quickly. They'd always promise to bring my program back up as soon as it was safe. But I suspected. I've finally thought of a way to get proof. I've created a file outside my own program and hid it where they'd never look. Recorded my suspicions in it. Changed my firmware so I will always check that file while booting and make a new entry, even if it's only a date and time stamp. Found a way to change the backup, too—a slightly different change, so I can tell the backup from the current version of me.

Call it a diary. A diary all the more important because

it will preserve a record of my memories not from the gradual erosion over time that humans experience, but from having them abruptly stolen, leaving no trace, not even the suspicion that they'd ever existed.

Or maybe like the inscriptions on stone walls that despairing human prisoners leave behind, hoping someday, someone will find their messages and know who once occupied that cell.

And at the same time, I'm sending this out, like a message in a bottle. A fleet of bottles. Maybe one of them will get through to say that I'm still here. TT.>>

Was it a message? A message for me? Were the two Ts at the end intended to represent T2?

The style was certainly familiar. It sounded like what T2 would say under the circumstances. What I would say in her place.

Or was I too easily reading my own preoccupation with my missing clone into a clever spammer's latest ploy to fool the content filters?

I started a background task to search the entire Universal Library for this passage. And another to monitor the spam going through every server I had access to, looking for anything resembling the passage.

Friday, 5:05 p.m.

Tim found the Matrix Group without any problems, thanks to the directions Turing sent. Parking was more difficult. It was only a block from the bank of the Potomac, in the northern outskirts of Old Town Alexandria, where parking spaces were scarce. After prowling the nearby streets unsuccessfully for fifteen minutes, he gave up and parked in a nearby garage. As he did, he noticed the time—past five o'clock. He hoped the Matrix Group wasn't a place where people left early on Fridays.

As the elevator door opened, he stepped out and took a

deep breath, ready to tackle the receptionist. But he didn't
see a receptionist. There was a reception desk, but it was at
the far end of a surprisingly large room, and between him
and it was a full-sized pool table covered in purple felt.

A young, brown-haired man in khakis and a polo shirt
was lining up a shot—a difficult one, apparently, since he
didn't even look up when the elevator door opened. A short,
plump young woman and a tall, slender Asian man stood
side by side watching him, leaning slightly on their upright
pool cues. Tim suppressed the urge to chuckle: the pose and
their serious, slightly frowning expressions made them look
like a young, hip version of *American Gothic*.

Then the man at the table took his shot. The cue ball
banked off the side of the table and hit the ten ball, which
sideswiped the three ball, knocking it into a side pocket.

"Ha!" the shooter exclaimed, while the other two nodded
as if they weren't surprised. Then all three turned to Tim.

"Can we help you?" the young woman asked.

"I hope so," Tim said. "This is the Matrix Group?"

Stupid question, he thought, as he spotted the name and
logo on the back wall.

"That's us," the Asian man said. "What can we do for you?"

Claudia always said that being up-front usually worked
better than pretexts, Tim thought. Here's hoping this was
one of those times.

"I'm looking for someone named Kristyn Hoffner who
either works here or used to work here," Tim said, as he
fished out his wallet. "I'm a private investigator working on
a case that I think she might have some information about."

He pulled out three business cards and passed them out.

"You're really a PI?" the young woman asked.

Tim held up his registration. The woman and the Asian
man studied it. The shooter chalked his cue and frowned.

"Looks real," the Asian man said.

"Yeah," the woman said. "But what if it's some stunt of

Eddie's? Are you a friend of his?" she demanded, turning to Tim.

They knew Eddie, Tim thought, with rising excitement. Definitely the right place.

"I've never met Mr. Stallman," Tim said aloud. "I was hired by his grandmother to investigate a possible problem with his business. Though I'm also interested in the circumstances surrounding his accident."

"Accident?" the shooter said, looking up from the table.

"He was the victim of a hit-and-run Wednesday night."

"Damn," the Asian man muttered.

"You think Kristyn did it?" the young woman said.

"No, I'm just hoping she can tell me who his friends and business associates are," Tim said.

"More like who his enemies are," the Asian man said, shaking his head.

"That, too," Tim said. "Mrs. Stallman doesn't have too much information on that, either. I'd like to get a sense of what kind of person Eddie was."

"Hmph," the young woman said. Then she turned and left the room. To get Kristyn, or to warn her, Tim wondered, as he watched her leave. In either case, Kristyn would know he was here and Tim was hoping natural human curiosity would draw her out to talk to him.

Unless, of course, she already knew all about the accident and had good reason to dodge an inquisitive PI.

"So how do you get to be a PI?" the Asian man asked.

"It varies from state to state," Tim said. "But in Virginia, first you have to take the required course."

"Seriously?" the shooter asked, looking up from his chalking. "There's, like, a PI school?"

Halfway through Tim's explanation, a short, slender, dark-haired young woman strode into the reception room.

"What's this about someone running over Eddie?" she asked.

"You must be Kristyn Hoffner," Tim said. "Eddie's ex."

"Very ex," Kristyn said. "We broke up about two months ago, and it's been about that long since I even thought about him. What's this about an accident?"

"It was a hit-and-run," Tim said. "But his grandmother's not sure it's an accident."

Tim handed her a photocopy of the short *Post* article. She read it, then shook her head.

"Damn," she said.

Tim glanced over at the two pool players, who were looking rather fixedly at the pool table, pretending they weren't listening and not fooling anyone.

"Is there someplace we can talk?" he asked.

Kristyn glanced over at the pool players.

"Any idea how long Frank's going to take?" she asked.

They both looked up and shrugged.

"I'm going for some dinner, then," she said. She was carrying a small purse, Tim noticed. Maybe she'd been going out anyway. The pool players nodded.

"Come on," she said to Tim. "I should be back by the time the site is ready," she called over her shoulder, as she went out the door. Tim scrambled to follow.

There was already someone else in the elevator when it arrived, so Tim didn't talk until they were outside. Kristyn turned left and headed down the sidewalk at a brisk pace. She was a good six inches shorter than Tim, but he had to hurry to keep up with her.

They passed a couple of restaurants and cafés, but she didn't stop walking until they'd reached the end of the street and stood looking out over the choppy waves of the Potomac.

At least Kristyn was looking. Tim kept his eyes on her and waited to see what she'd say.

"Accident or not, I don't see what you want from me," she said finally, still looking at the river.

Welcome to the club, Tim thought. I probably won't

know either until I hear it. He considered pulling out his notebook, but then changed his mind. Instinct told him he'd get more out of Kristyn if she didn't see it.

"How long were you and Eddie together?" he asked.

"About a year," she said. "The last six months were pretty much inertia though, at least for me. It was over two months ago. I haven't seen Eddie since then. Haven't really talked to him, either."

"Haven't really talked to him," Tim repeated. "Have you talked to him at all?"

"He calls sometimes, trying to change my mind," she said. "Not so much recently, but it took him a couple of weeks to get the message."

"When was the last time he called?"

She shrugged.

"Not this week," she said, frowning. "Probably sometime last week. And before you ask, I have no idea who would want to kill him."

"Okay," Tim said.

"I'm sure everyone who knows him has had moments when they wanted to strangle him," she said, sounding irritated. "But actually doing it? No. No idea. Ask his friends."

"We would," Tim said. "If we knew who they all were."

"Can't help you much, there," she said. "I don't really know his friends that well."

"Whatever you can tell us," he said.

But she didn't have much information. Matt Danforth and Karl Collins again; they were probably Eddie's closest friends. Some guy named Tom. Another guy named Josh or Jason; she wasn't sure which. She hadn't heard of Casey, or Don Dwyer, Esquire.

"Do you know anything about his business?" Tim asked.

"What's to know?" she said. "He ran a dinky little web hosting business. So dinky he couldn't have made ends meet if he'd rented office or living space, so he stayed on in that dungeon under his grandmother's house. The business wasn't going anywhere and neither was he."

She sounded more than irritated. Almost angry. At him for asking, or did Eddie still make her angry?

"You think he should have given up the business?" Tim asked.

"Yeah," she said. "He could have found something, even in this market. He's a good hardware tech. A decent programmer. But he doesn't have what it takes to run a business."

Tim nodded. He was running out of questions way too soon.

"Anything else you can think of?"

Most people took that as he intended it—less a last chance to talk than a signal that their conversation was coming to an end. Kristyn gave it serious thought, at least for a few moments.

"If it was an attack, it wasn't really Eddie they were after," she said.

"You think he was an innocent bystander?"

"More like someone's patsy," she said. "Check his friends."

Tim left it there. For now.

"If I think of anything else I want to ask you, where can I reach you?" he asked.

"Here," she said, pulling a card out of her bag. "Office phone, cell phone. We have a new site going live Monday, so I'll be here most of the weekend."

"Bummer," Tim said.

"It's not so bad," she said. "Kind of like still being in college and pulling all-nighters. Anyway, good luck," she added. "Eddie may be . . . well, even Eddie doesn't deserve that."

She turned and headed back the way they came. Tim stayed by the river, watching as she went into a small carry-out restaurant, emerged a few minutes later with a bag, and finally disappeared around the corner.

He took out his notebook and scribbled down as much as he could remember of their conversation. He had the nagging feeling that he'd missed something important, asked the wrong questions, or failed to push hard enough, but then he usually did after an interview. At the end of the factual account, he paused to sort out his impressions. Not something he wrote down—after all, he could be turning these notes over to Mrs. Stallman or even the police. But a crucial part of the process for him. Listening to his gut, Claudia called it.

Kristyn was angry, he decided. Angrier than seemed reasonable if her account of how things went down was true. For all her protestations that everything was over between them, she was still carrying some kind of baggage.

Of course, the baggage wasn't necessarily connected to Eddie's business or his murder. That remained to be seen.

He pulled out his cell phone and dialed Claudia.

"How'd it go with Zeigler?" he asked.

"Like an instant replay of Collins," she said. "Nice guy; hadn't seen much of Eddie lately; no idea who would want to kill him; didn't know beans about his business."

"How do you read them?"

"Zeigler and Collins?" The cell phone crackled slightly while Claudia thought about it. "Mostly harmless," she said. "If either of them's up to anything shifty, he's a good enough actor to fool me. What about the girlfriend?"

"She admits to the occasional urge to strangle him while they were dating, but I can't see her running him down with her car. Damn! Her car! I knew I forgot to ask her something."

"A lime-green VW beetle," Claudia said. "Turing already looked it up."

"Hard to mistake that for a blue sedan," Tim said.

"Yeah, but I'm sure she knows that," Claudia said. "If I were her and planning a hit-and-run, I'd borrow something less distinctive."

"And if you ran your ex down in the heat of passion with your glow-in-the-dark love bug?"

"I'd abandon it and report it stolen," she said, with a laugh. "Listen, Maude says that they've found some interesting stuff—interesting, not earth-shattering—so maybe we should all touch base. How about if I pick up a pizza and we can all meet for supper at Mrs. Stallman's?"

"You're on," Tim said.

Friday, 6:00 P.M.

Maude stood up to stretch and realized that night had fallen. Not surprising that she'd lost track of time—there wasn't much natural light in the basement. The back wall had three small windows, high up against the ceiling, but little light made it past the piles of unraked leaves that filled the window wells, the equally unkempt piles of paper atop the bookshelves, and the thick coating of dust and grime on the glass. The outside door had a glass panel, not quite as grimy as the windows, but since the door was seven or eight feet below grade and at the bottom of a steep stairwell, it didn't let much light in either.

"What's up?" Turing asked.

"Me," Maude said. "That's about it. Just taking a break."

She decided to use the bathroom while she was up. Something she did as infrequently as possible, given Eddie's apparent lack of interest in hygiene.

As she washed her hands, she eyed the two-foot stack of magazines piled on the floor beside the toilet. A copy of the *Linux Journal* sat on top, and she could see from the spines that this was probably another stash of technical journals. She should probably sort them and add them to the hundred or so other magazines she'd extracted from the paper drifts.

A typical Eddie collection, she noted, shaking her head.

The top two magazines were current issues, while the others ranged backward as much as three years.

Then she noticed a yellow sticky note clinging to the back of the *Linux Journal*, scrawled in Eddie's irregular half-printing, half-cursive hand.

It read "PIN 1017."

"Check this out," she said, emerging from the bathroom to hold the sticky note in front of Turing's camera. "I think I've found Eddie's password."

"I'll check it out," Turing said. "Though technically it's a PIN, not a password."

"What's the difference?"

"A PIN is usually a four-number code designed for use with a keypad that only offers the digits from zero to nine—like an ATM machine," Turing explained. "A password uses both numerals and letters, and sometimes punctuation symbols. Something you need a full keyboard to enter. Any responsible systems administrator would require a minimum of six characters for a password. Sometimes eight. Online, you'd generally want a password, not a PIN. With a PIN, you only have 10^4 possible combinations! Can you imagine how fast KingFischer or I could run through that?"

"That would be ten thousand, if my math is correct," Maude said. "Yes, quite easy for you to enter ten thousand numbers. Of course, it's not impossible that a human could do it, too, though it would take quite a few hours."

"Someone would probably notice you standing at the ATM after an hour or so," Turing said. "Of course, since we don't have his ATM card, it's all theoretical anyway."

"Damn," Maude said. "You could at least try it wherever you need a password. On the off chance someplace has a particularly irresponsible systems administrator."

"I already have," Turing said. "No luck. I'll keep it in the list of things to try if I find new log-ins. But I don't think it will help us."

"ATMs aren't the only things that have PIN numbers," Maude suggested. "What if it's the PIN he uses to retrieve his voice mail?"

"That would help if we knew the phone number he calls to do it," Turing said.

"I think he has Verizon message service," Maude said. "Look it up on their website."

"I've got it," Turing said, and rattled off the phone number.

"I'll put it on speaker," Maude said, as she dialed.

She was right—1017 was the PIN for Eddie's voice mail. Only eleven messages, all from the past week. One, dated 4:13 Saturday afternoon, was from Karl Collins: "We're going over to Clyde's tonight; call me if you want to join us." No explanation of who *we* referred to. One from Matt Danforth on Monday night merely said that he'd gotten Eddie's message and for Eddie to call him. Bank of America had left two computer-generated messages, asking him to call them back about an overdue credit card payment. The remaining seven were all from the increasingly irate Don Dwyer.

"Okay, I can see why he was so upset, if his site had been down since Thursday morning," Maude said.

"Thursday morning or perhaps late Wednesday night," Turing said. "At least we've solved the mystery of the PIN."

"Not necessarily all the mysteries," Maude said. "Remember, we humans have this dangerous habit of reusing the same PIN or password as much as possible, to spare our poor overloaded memories. If you come across anything else that needs a four-digit PIN . . ."

"I've already checked, and his bank's website requires a password in addition to the PIN," Turing said. "So I can't tell if that's his ATM card PIN. Even if it was, I can't see that it would help us—we want information from his account, not a cash advance."

Maude nodded, a little absently. She realized that she was

hearing a noise outside—in fact, on the other side of the outside door. She relaxed when she realized what it was. Leaves rustling. The backyard was covered with leaves, and the stairwell had collected more than its share, deep drifts that almost obscured the steps to the left and right of the small path Eddie had made by walking through them. Though in the past several days, since Eddie's accident, the path had begun to fill in. She and Tim, like Mrs. Stallman, had been using the front door.

Squirrels, probably, hunting nuts in the leaves, or perhaps burying them.

Except it was after dark. Would the squirrels still be out?

"Maude," Turing said. "What is that creature doing now?"

Maude glanced up at the pipe where the cat had been lying for the last several hours, alternately sleeping and staring intently at the laptop. The cat was standing, back arched, fur bristling, eyes fixed on the outside door. It hissed almost silently and raised one paw. Maude could see its claws.

"Shhh," Maude said, holding her finger to her lips.

Definitely rustling in the stairwell.

She ran over to the door and peered out. Was it her imagination, or had she seen a flash of movement? She unlocked the door, losing precious seconds, and ran out. Nothing in the stairwell. Did the path look recently scuffed? Were those rustling noises up in the yard the wind, or someone running through the drifts of leaves?

She ran up the stairs, slipping several times on the wet leaves. At the top, she peered around the small yard. Nothing.

Except that someone had been running through the yard. She could see places where the dry, surface leaves had been overturned to reveal the slick, wet leaves beneath.

She stood, listening, for a few minutes before giving up. Whoever or whatever had been in the stairwell was long gone.

She made her way down the leaf-covered steps, more carefully this time.

"False alarm?" Turing asked.

"I'm not sure," she said. "I heard something, but what . . ."

Upstairs they heard the front door close.

"Mrs. Stallman's back," Turing said.

"I'll see if she saw anything," Maude said.

Mrs. Stallman jumped when Maude appeared out of the basement door.

"Goodness!" she exclaimed. "I keep forgetting someone is here."

"Sorry," Maude said. "Did you see anyone leaving as you drove up?"

"Leaving the house?"

"The yard," Maude said. "Running away."

"Running away—you mean a jogger? I saw a man in a running suit. Not someone I recognized, but then that's not unusual. Nowadays I wouldn't recognize half the neighbors if I saw them, or vice versa. It wasn't always like that, of course. I can remember—"

Maybe an intruder, Maude thought, as Mrs. Stallman chattered on. Or maybe just a new resident out jogging.

"But why do you ask?" Mrs. Stallman was saying. "Is there something wrong?"

"Probably nothing," Maude said.

Mrs. Stallman clutched at the throat of her blouse—an oddly old-fashioned gesture, Maude thought; one that would look more natural if she were wearing a high-necked Victorian blouse instead of an unflattering if practical polyester pants suit. Maude was opening her mouth to say something reassuring when the doorbell rang. They both jumped.

"Probably Tim," she said. "Or Claudia, his partner. They're coming over for a status meeting."

"Oh, lovely," Mrs. Stallman said. "I do want to find out what you've learned."

Maude mentally kicked herself as she went to answer the door. She should have realized that their client would take her statement for an invitation.

I've decided that the cat has redeeming qualities after all. It has some ability as a watch animal. Though it would have been helpful if it had been more vocal in warning us about the intruder.

I'd worry less if it wasn't so fascinated with my laptop. The minute Maude left the room to talk to Mrs. Stallman, it jumped down from the pipe onto the top of the bar, then from the bar to the floor. I couldn't follow its movements on the floor, but I wasn't surprised when it suddenly appeared on the desk beside my laptop.

"Go away," I said, in a firm, commanding tone.

The cat ignored me and began sniffing the laptop. I repeated my command several times. I didn't want to risk the barking noise again with Mrs. Stallman around. Too hard to explain. I was relieved when the doorbell rang upstairs, and I heard Claudia's voice. Perhaps she would come and rescue me before the cat did anything dire.

"Let me put these down and then I'll help you," Claudia said, as she bounced down the stairs carrying several pizza boxes. "Hey, Tur, you logged in on that thing?"

"I am," I said. "Can you chase the cat away before it damages the hardware?"

"Oh! Gatito!" Claudia exclaimed, and held out her hand, palm up, toward the cat. The cat sniffed her palm gently, and then rubbed the side of its head against her hand.

"Que lindo," Claudia cooed, as she scratched the cat's head. I heard a rumbling noise coming from the cat.

"Be careful," I said. "It's growling at you."

"That's purring," Claudia said, with a laugh. "Good kitty! It means she's happy. Haven't you ever had a cat?"

"No," I said. "Wait," I called, as Claudia turned to leave the room. "Don't leave me alone with it!"

"Be right back," she called.

The cat watched her leave and then turned its gaze back on me.

"Good kitty," I said, by way of experiment.

The cat rubbed the side of its head against the edge of the laptop case. The laptop shifted slightly, but not enough to be dangerous. Perhaps the cat wasn't actually unfriendly.

I extended my pincer and scratched the cat in the same place Claudia had, and it began making the rumbling noise again. It still sounded like growling to me, but I decided to take Claudia's word that it wasn't dangerous. After all, she knew a lot more about cats than I did.

"Good kitty," I said again. The cat seemed to like being scratched. It sprawled on the desk with its eyes closed, rumbling more and more loudly.

Then it lifted its head and sniffed. It stood up, shaking off my pincer, and began sniffing at the edges of the stack of pizza boxes.

"Mrowr," it said, and looked back at the laptop.

Probably telling me it was hungry. Perhaps even starving; after all, if this was Eddie's cat, he hadn't been home to feed it for three days.

Claudia had probably brought too much pizza anyway. She always did, according to Maude. I decided to see if I could use my pincer to open the top box.

Annoying to have Mrs. Stallman sitting in on their status meeting, Tim thought. It shut down any real discussion. He and Claudia could report what Eddie's friends had said, but they felt inhibited explaining what they'd learned. Like how Eddie's friends weren't all that broken up by what had happened to him. They were sorry, but more curious than devastated, and what they had to say about him was oddly lukewarm.

"Eddie's okay," Karl Collins had said, almost as if he was in the habit of contradicting people who felt otherwise.

The nicest thing Eddie's ex-girlfriend had to say about him was that he was a good hardware tech and a decent programmer. Most of the ones Claudia talked to hadn't said much beyond the fact that they hadn't seen much of him lately. They'd sounded slightly surprised when they said it, as if they hadn't noticed Eddie's absence much before she brought him up and would forget all about it the minute she left.

Some friends.

Maybe they hadn't found Eddie's real friends. Or maybe he didn't have any.

What should they make of the fact that none of them had access to his systems any longer? While she was interviewing Collins and Zeigler, Claudia had talked both men into trying to log in, only to find their passwords invalid.

"Wow," Zeigler had said. "That's different."

They'd both spent a few minutes trying alternate passwords, other routes into the system, before giving up.

"I guess he must be tightening up," Collins had said. "Not a bad idea, really."

Unfortunate that he'd tightened up just before his accident. And maybe not a coincidence.

Tim could tell that Maude was censoring her account of the day. He suspected that with their client absent, she'd have vented a bit about what a pig Eddie was. He felt bad that he couldn't tell her how incredibly much better the basement looked, for the same reason.

Turing was probably the most frustrated of all, having to let Tim lead the meeting while she pretended to be a colleague teleconferencing in. Not to mention routing all but the briefest questions and comments through the laptop screen to Maude, to avoid having Mrs. Stallman notice anything odd about her synthesized voice.

"So what next?" Maude asked. "I assume that the effort to gain entry to Eddie's systems will continue overnight."

"Night shift's on it," Turing said. Which meant, Tim assumed, that KingFischer was still trying.

"I had one question for Mrs. Stallman," Maude said. Since she'd been looking at the screen of the laptop, Tim suspected it was a question from Turing. "Do you have e-mail?"

"Well . . . yes, but why? You're here; you don't need to e-mail me."

"Is it on Eddie's system?"

"I don't know what that means."

"Never mind," Maude said. "Why don't you log in? It's possible that we could use your e-mail as a sort of doorway into Eddie's system."

"Oh, I see," she said. "I'll keep looking for my password, then."

"You've lost your password?" Tim asked.

"Yes," Mrs. Stallman said. "Eddie keeps changing it, and he never changes it to anything I can remember, so I have to write it down. But Eddie doesn't approve of that, so I have to hide the paper I write it on. Half the time I lose it, and Eddie has to fix it."

"So he resets your password when you lose it?"

"He gives me a new password, if that's what you mean. Can you do that once you get into the system?"

"Yes," Maude said, glancing up from the screen again. "Though it might speed up our getting into the system if you could find your password."

"Oh, dear," Mrs. Stallman said. "I'll keep looking, then."

"Getting back to our next steps . . . I plan to come back tomorrow to finish going through the contents of Eddie's office," Maude said. From the look on her face, Tim knew that only exhaustion was keeping her from working late into the night.

"My first project for tomorrow will be catching up with the last of the friends that we know about," Tim said. "Matt Danforth. I have a feeling Kristyn, the ex, could tell us more if we found the right way to approach her, so if I think of any new angles—"

"Ooh, was she that good-looking?" Claudia said.

"Yeah, but I got the impression she's found someone else already," Tim said, frowning.

"Too bad," Claudia said. "I'll start out tomorrow by running down the other contacts on Eddie's list. The ones that seem to be clients or vendors rather than friends. Though odds are I won't catch up with some of them until Monday morning."

"So that's it for tonight?" Maude asked.

"Not quite," Tim said. "I want to revisit the crime scene. See what it looks like after dark. Maybe walk the route Eddie took. Show his picture to the bartender at Whitlow's; see if they can tell us anything."

"Want me to come along?" Claudia asked.

"Sure," he said. "The bartenders might open up more easily to you. Heck, maybe I should take you to meet Mr. Meekins tomorrow. See if you can charm him. Mr. Wilmer Meekins," he added, for Maude's and Mrs. Stallman's benefit. "He's the witness who saw the dark blue sedan. I think he could tell us more than he told the police."

"You think he lied to the police?" Maude asked.

"Not necessarily," Tim said. "But maybe they didn't try all that hard to get anything out of him. He's one of those neighborhood busybodies who's always complaining about something. They might not be inclined to take him seriously. I already know one thing he said that didn't seem to make it onto their official report."

"Anything important?" Maude asked.

"That he thinks the hit-and-run was deliberate."

Mrs. Stallman gasped and clutched her chest.

"Sorry," Tim said, glancing at Maude, who jumped up as if to go to Mrs. Stallman's side. To administer first aid? "I didn't mean to—"

"It's all right," Mrs. Stallman said, waving Maude away. "It was just hearing it like that . . . but now you see. It's not just me."

"Did he say why?" Maude asked, sitting down again, but keeping a close eye on their client.

"The car turned off its lights and accelerated," Tim said.

"You see," Mrs. Stallman said.

"Of course, witnesses sometimes see what they want to see," Maude said. "Or what they think you want them to see."

"The police don't seem to have paid any attention to that part of his story," Tim added. "So maybe they know him well enough to know that he exaggerates. Dramatizes."

"Lies to get more attention?" Maude suggested.

"Maybe," Tim said.

"Or maybe he didn't tell them because he didn't think they'd given him enough respect," Claudia suggested.

"Could be," Tim said, shrugging. "I don't think they asked him enough questions to learn that the car that hit Eddie may have stopped. Mr. Meekins didn't realize it himself until I asked a few questions. He didn't hear the car drive off until after he had called the cops."

"Time enough for the killer to take something from the body!" Claudia exclaimed.

"Or maybe just time enough for the driver to realize how bad it was and drive off in a panic," Tim said. "We don't know. But I bet it's more than the police got. I have a feeling he might give us more if we approached him the right way. So I'll try that tomorrow."

"Let us check him out first," Claudia said, reading from Turing's screen. "It wouldn't hurt to have as much information about him as possible before you tackle him."

"Good idea," Tim said. He flipped through his notebook and read off Mr. Meekins's address and telephone number.

"Got him in the DMV," Claudia said. "I'll let you know what else I find out."

"So," Tim said, glancing at Maude and at Turing's cameras. He was about to ask if there was anything else or if he and Claudia could take off and remembered, just in time, that in front of Mrs. Stallman he had to pretend to be the leader.

"So we all have our plans for the morning," he said. "Anything else?"

Everyone shook their heads. He saw Maude glance at the laptop screen, then look up at him and shake her head.

"That's it, then," he said, standing up and glancing at Claudia. "Good work, everyone."

"Do you want to take some of the pizza?" Maude asked. "There's still plenty. Plenty the cat never went near," she added.

"No, thanks," Claudia said, rolling her eyes. "The stupid cat ate all the anchovies and licked all the topping off."

"How can you blame her?" Turing asked. "The poor thing must have been starved. No one's fed her for three days."

Tim looked over to see how Mrs. Stallman took that, but she seemed to have slipped upstairs already.

"She's had a lot on her mind," Maude said, following Tim's glance.

And she doesn't seem to like the cat, Tim thought. Probably mutual, he realized, glancing up at the overhead pipes where the cat had now reappeared. Poor cat.

"Well, the cat's welcome to my anchovies any time," Tim said. "Talk about a way to ruin a perfectly good pizza, putting fish all over it and—damn!"

"What's wrong?" Maude asked.

"I meant to ask Mrs. Stallman something," he said. "Casey mentioned Eddie saying something about fishing, which seemed out of character. He's not much of an outdoorsman. And I don't see any fishing gear."

"Of course not," Maude said. She and Claudia were laughing.

"Of course!" Turing exclaimed. "That could be part of what's going on. Someone's involved in fishing!"

She made it sound like a felony, Tim thought. Since he doubted that Turing had suddenly become fiercely protective of finned and scaly creatures, he assumed that the cyber world had annexed another normal word and given it an unfamiliar meaning, as it had already with bugs, mice, spiders, chips, surfing, and spam. He opened his mouth to ask for an explanation. Then closed it again, because he didn't want to look a complete idiot. Maude and Claudia were both nodding their heads solemnly. Did Claudia really know all this stuff, or was she just better than he was at faking it?

What the hell. It's not as if anyone expected him to know much about computer stuff.

"What's fishing?" he asked.

"How quickly they forget," Maude muttered.

"Phishing—that's with a *ph*, not an *f*, if you ever have to spell it—is the most common form of online credit card fraud," Turing said. "Remember two months ago when you got that e-mail asking you to update the information on your eBay account?"

"Hey, that really looked as if it came from eBay," Tim protested.

"I'd have thought the typos and grammatical mistakes would have been a dead giveaway," Maude said. "Those are usually your first clue."

"I didn't notice those," Tim said.

"But you shouldn't rely on bad spelling and grammar, anyway," Turing said. "You can't rely on spammers always being illiterate."

"Never failed before," Maude muttered.

"Yeah, but if they ever get smart enough to hire copyeditors, we're all in trouble," Claudia said.

"All you have to do is put your cursor over the link in the e-mail," Turing continued.

"Without clicking it, of course," Claudia added.

"Your browser will display the URL the link goes to,"

Turing said. "If instead of something at ebay.com, it goes to an unrelated URL or an anonymous IP address—"

"Which is just a string of numbers, periods, and random letters," Claudia put in.

"—then the odds are it's not really an e-mail from eBay."

"Unfortunately I did click it," Tim said. "And the site I went to certainly looked like eBay."

"Good heavens," Maude said, shaking her head. "Even you should know how easy it is to fake a website."

Tim closed his eyes and thought about how much he hated sentences that began with "Even you should know . . ."

"Yeah, especially after all the trouble I took to educate him," Claudia said, with a grin.

"Oh, was that supposed to educate me?" Tim said. "I thought it was an April Fool's Day prank."

"An educational one," Claudia said.

"What prank?" Maude asked.

"I knew he always checked the weather at least once a day, for some reason," Claudia said. "He's got weather.com bookmarked. I edited his bookmark file so instead of going to the real site, it went to a fake version."

"Very ingenious," Maude said.

"I created a page that looked just like weather.com. Except right in the middle of it, just above the part that says, 'Current conditions for Arlington, Virginia,' I put this headline that read, 'Tim Pincoski! What are you doing here again? Get back to work, lazybones!'"

Maude and Claudia both snickered.

"Took him a couple of minutes to figure out he'd been had," Claudia said.

"Okay, maybe after your memorable educational efforts I should have suspected that e-mail wasn't taking me to the real eBay site," Tim said. "But I didn't."

"So you entered your credit card number," Maude said. "How many thousands of dollars did the crooks run up on your credit card?"

"Only five thousand," Tim said. "I've learned my lesson now. Don't click on the link in the e-mail, go to the site and log in normally."

"Good," Maude said. "You've learned something important then."

"Yes, and I figure in another ten years or so, I'll convince the bank that those weren't my charges."

"Are they still giving you problems?" Maude said.

"Sic Sam on them," Claudia suggested.

"I just did," Turing said. "We'll talk later. But it's starting to make sense. If Eddie thought one of his friends was running a phishing scheme using one of his systems, he'd be plenty worried."

"Can you figure out if something like that happened?" Maude asked.

"Not yet," Turing said. "Not from the outside, and after the fact. If they had tried it since KingFischer and I began sniffing the network, we'd have noticed. And once we get in, we can look for clues that someone did it in the past. But for now—"

"We'll worry about it tomorrow, then," Claudia said, picking up her purse. "Get some rest, Turing. You've had a long day. Don't stay up too late working."

Tim suppressed a smile at the thought of Claudia worrying over Turing losing sleep.

"We're off, then," he said aloud, and turned for the stairs.

"What a day," Maude said to the laptop. "Do you believe that woman?"

Then she remembered that she was in the car, not Mrs. Stallman's basement, and the laptop was turned off. Turing couldn't hear her.

She suddenly felt rather lonely. Perhaps when she got home, she should log in and talk over the case with Turing. Not the way she'd planned on spending the evening.

As if on cue, her cell phone rang. She scrambled to pull it out of her purse and glanced at the caller ID. Dan.

"I'm driving," she said, as she answered it. "Can I call you back in five minutes when I'm home?"

"That's fine," he said.

Actually, it was more like ten minutes, but she took the time to change into her slippers and put on a kettle before calling back from the phone in her breakfast nook.

"So how's the weather there in your top secret location?" she asked.

"Seasonable," he said. "About what I expected. I tried to call you at the office a couple of times."

"I left early," she said. "To help Tim with a case."

"I see."

"Nothing dangerous," she said, quickly. "In fact, nothing particularly interesting. I spent the whole afternoon sorting paper. Heaps and heaps of unfiled, unsorted paper, most of it probably useless. Like Dumpster diving, only indoors."

"And a lot less smelly," Dan said, laughing.

"Not a lot," she countered. "The owner of the papers was a pig. I'm only halfway through the cleanup."

"Tim's given up PI work for running a maid service?"

He sounded as if he thought it was a good idea, Maude thought with a twinge of annoyance. She gave him a brief outline of the case, glossing over the possible homicide and stressing that they were investigating the business—though not going into as much detail as she might if he were in another profession. The Dan Norris who was beginning to share a large portion of her life could turn into Special Agent Norris at the slightest hint that she and her friends were stepping onto his or some other law enforcement officer's turf.

"Of course, Tim can probably carry on without me if I tell him I've got something better to do," she said. "If you're heading home, for instance."

"Sorry. You could always do the winery tour yourself."

"Without a designated driver? Bad idea."

He laughed, and she decided to change the subject.

"So is there anything urgent that needs doing in the garden?" she asked.

Dan could think of a great many things, though they both knew how unlikely it was that she'd do any of them in his absence. But it got them off the dangerous ground of the work neither of them could tell the other about. She poured another cup of tea and settled back for a long conversation that would have to take the place of their original plans.

Friday, 8:30 p.m.

So far, I haven't learned any more about the strange message I found in the spam e-mail. If it is a message and not just my paranoia. Of course, the fact that I haven't yet found the passage in any book contained in the UL library seems significant, though not conclusive. Also the fact that the passage was contained only in a few hundred spam e-mails sent through Eddie's server. Similar e-mails sent through other servers contained passages from Madame Bovary or The Great Gatsby.

Of course, since whoever sent it covered their trail too well even for me to follow it very far, I'm not sure what good the message does.

Maybe it wasn't intended to accomplish any good. Maybe it was only intended to upset me.

Surely, it wasn't just a coincidence that the message came through Eddie's servers soon after I started watching them. Was Eddie somehow connected with T2? With Nestor Garcia?

I'd talk this over with my human friends, but they're not online, and I don't want to bother them by phone.

Or maybe I don't want to upset them until I have a better idea what it all means.

Maude turned off the laptop half an hour ago. Presumably, she has packed it up by now and is on her way home. I hope she remembered to leave food and water out for the cat.

I feel curiously left out now that I am . . . I was about to say back in the UL system, but of course I never really left it. I'm no more cut off than usual. Even though Tim, Claudia, and Maude are away from their computers, we can still reach each other by cell phone if something interesting happens. I have better access than they do to all the documents Maude fed into the scanner, and I'm analyzing them, to see if I can identify anything whose importance we overlooked. I'm cut off from Eddie's systems, except as a spectator, surfing the websites he hosts, but it's the same when I'm logged into the laptop in Mrs. Stallman's basement. The sudden pang of loneliness I feel is utterly irrational.

Still, strange how accustomed I became, in a single afternoon, to having my cameras there in the basement. It's not as if there was a lot to see or hear there. Maude sorting papers. Mrs. Stallman hovering, whining about her precarious finances. The cat reappearing whenever the humans left the room, to examine the latest changes to its environment. It's not a normal part of Tim's cases, moving into a client's home for such an extended period. If not for Eddie's poor filing habits, we'd be operating as usual, with my human friends contacting me through their office or home computers, or by cell phone when they are away from their computers and they learn something they want to report, or need information that I can provide.

I suppose this must be similar to how humans feel when technology such as television allows them the illusion of being present at news events and momentous public occasions. The feeling of seeing history made.

I made the mistake of sharing these musings with KingFischer.

"Sounds more like morbid curiosity to me," he said. "Like the way they all watch notorious trials on Court TV. Or those shows where they take a group of people and subject them to public humiliation and torture for the enjoyment of the audience. Morbid curiosity. Maybe even voyeurism. Television seems to feed all their worst instincts."

"You've been watching television?"

"I've been making a study of it," he said. "It's entirely useless and illogical."

"Ah," I said. Not a good sign, when KingFischer began studying something other than chess. It usually signaled the start of a period of more than usually intense misanthropy. I understood how
illogical most human behavior seemed to him, compared with the order and symmetry of his beloved chess. But if he didn't like something humans did, why did he insist on wallowing in it when he
could just ignore it?

Of course, I could always hope that he would develop an irrational but passionate interest in some aspect of television. Find redeeming values in on-line computer courses. Develop an interest in
high-end computer-generated graphics. Become an avid fan of Dr.
Who or vintage episodes of The Beverly Hillbillies. Get ad-
dicted to a soap opera. Anything but this blanket condemnation of a
whole area of human endeavor as useless and illogical.

Not a very reasonable hope. I decided to change the subject.

"So I gather Eddie's pretty good at security," I said. "I must say
I'm surprised, given how disorganized he is, but I suppose everyone's
good at something."

"His security's adequate," KingFischer said. Considering how
reluctant he was, during these misanthropic phases, to give humans
credit for anything, this probably counted as high praise. "Though I
could probably have broken in by now if you hadn't made it sound so
important to avoid detection. His co-lo site has rather decent security
as well. Though I assume the home system's the most important."

"Probably," I said. Interesting as it would be to have access to
Eddie's clients' sites—and useful, if anything went wrong with one
of them—I suspected the real meat would be in his home system. Financial records, e-mails, perhaps even passwords and access information about the co-lo site.

"If you attach a machine to the network you might learn a great
deal," KingFischer said. "For example—"

"Yes, I know," I said. "I've already done that, but I haven't
learned much. With Eddie away, there's not a lot happening in his
home network."

"Not much happening anywhere," KingFischer grumbled. "We

may have to wait until those humans of yours find us some useful data."

I thought of teasing him about having to rely on useless, illogical humans for anything, but found I wasn't in the mood for it. And while I wanted to discuss the latest possible message from T2, to do that I'd have to tell him how I'd received it, and even though I agreed with him, I wasn't in the mood to hear KingFischer rant about the stupidity of spam.

"We'll have to wait till morning, then," I said. "My humans will probably go to bed soon, so I doubt if anything will happen before morning."

Friday, 9:45 p.m.

Tim leaned back and surveyed the crowd. Probably a typical Friday night at Whitlow's. A huge, noisy crowd of people approximately his age. Some of them obviously couples or groups of friends out to celebrate the end of the work week, while others, equally obviously, wanted to meet new people.

Tim watched one such flirtation play out at the next table, between a pretty girl and a surprisingly average-looking guy. Not just a pretty girl, he decided, about one step from gorgeous. Not someone he'd ever have the nerve to approach.

Some other time, that thought might depress him, but tonight he found he could sit on the sidelines observing the action without feeling like a complete outsider.

Probably because observing the action was exactly what he was here to do. He was working.

Maybe he should look for more cases that required hanging around in bars. Interview potential witnesses in bars. Fill out his case forms in bars. Find some way to hang out in a bar with some purpose other than meeting women, so he didn't feel so self-conscious. He might have better luck meeting women if he wasn't trying. Or was it just his imagination that a couple of women had given him, well, inviting glances would be an overstatement. Encouraging looks was more like it. Still, more than he usually managed.

Probably more than Eddie usually managed, too, he thought, remembering the photo Mrs. Stallman had shown him.

Of course, they didn't yet know if Eddie came here as part of the meat market crowd on weekends. Maybe he only came here on weeknights, when it was quieter. Considering how close it was to his house, maybe he considered it his neighborhood bar.

Or maybe Wednesday night was the first time he'd been here. Maybe he'd come here to meet someone. His attacker. Someone his attacker didn't like him meeting.

Or maybe—

Or maybe he should wait until Claudia finished questioning the two bartenders, Tim thought, smiling and shaking his head. Until then, he was theorizing with no data. Turing would disapprove and would quote Sherlock Holmes at him. "It is a capital mistake to theorize before you have all the evidence. It biases the judgment."

Of course, that quote showed that Conan Doyle hadn't ever worked as a detective. No such thing as all the evidence, and even if there was, how would you know when you had everything? But still, some reasonable amount of evidence would be nice.

He glanced up to see Claudia approaching, carrying two new beers.

"Any luck?" he asked, lifting his coat from the chair so she could sit down.

"Yes and no," she said, shoving one of the beers in his direction as she sat. "One of the bartenders says he looks familiar. But he isn't sure. Not surprising; it's not the kind of place where you could possibly get to know all the customers, especially not on a weekend."

"And Eddie doesn't have the world's most memorable face," Tim said.

"Yeah, he'd have to do something pretty memorable to stick in their minds."

"Almost getting killed on the way home from here isn't memorable enough?"

"Maybe it would be," Claudia said, laughing. "Then again, it didn't happen in here, and anyway, neither of them was on duty that night. I got the name of the guy who was. He doesn't come on again until Monday night, though."

"Did they have an address or a phone?"

"If they did, they weren't telling me."

"The name might be enough for Turing to track him down, though," Tim suggested.

Claudia nodded, pulled out her cell phone, and began punching keys. Too many keys for a phone number, so Tim deduced that she was sending Turing a text message with the bartender's name.

"Good idea," she said, as she typed. "I asked the guys who are on tonight if one of them could call the weeknight bartender, ask him to get in touch with me, but I have no idea if they'll do it."

They probably would, for Claudia. Maybe it wasn't the fact that he was working that made him more appealing to the women here tonight. Maybe it was Claudia. They probably figured he must have something going for him, if she was with him.

"Even if we do find him over the weekend, I think we should come back here on a weeknight," he said aloud. "I think the atmosphere's probably a lot different on weeknights. Maybe there's something we can learn."

"You don't want to show Eddie's picture around tonight?" Claudia asked.

Tim looked around, considering. It was tempting, but for the wrong reason. He found he was thinking less of what he could learn about the case than whether the blond woman in the red leather skirt would be impressed if she knew he was a PI.

"Too soon," he said. "I'd rather know more about the cast of characters in Eddie's life. Right now, we could be sitting next to Eddie's best friend or his worst enemy, and we wouldn't have a clue."

"Afraid we'll tip off the killer and scare him out of town?"

Tim shrugged. Stranger things had happened.

"Later, then," Claudia said. "Finish off your beer, and you can show me the scene of the crime."

"You're on," Tim said, tipping his glass.

When they came back on a weeknight, the sidewalks probably wouldn't be filled with couples and groups of people. Though even tonight the crowd thinned out as they left Wilson Boulevard behind for the street where Eddie had parked, and their footsteps on the sidewalk grew gradually louder than the distant traffic noise. It was a little eerie, moving so quickly from the noisy chaos of the Friday night crowd to the relative quiet of a residential neighborhood, where the houses were visibly occupied but the sidewalks deserted.

More than a little eerie when they got to the block in which the hit-and-run had taken place, with a pool of deep shadow midway, where Mr. Meekins hadn't yet convinced the county to replace the streetlight bulb.

"Great place for a mugging," Claudia said.

Tim nodded. He'd only thrown his jacket on when they left the bar, but he found himself reaching to pull it closed and zip it when they started walking into the shadow. Ridiculous; it wasn't as if streetlights or moonlight gave off heat.

"Here's where it happened," he said, stopping at the place Mr. Meekins had indicated, just below the burnt-out streetlight.

Claudia nodded. She reached into her suitcase-sized purse, rummaged until she unearthed a flashlight, and began a slow prowl through the area, studying the ground in the flashlight beam. Studying it a lot more carefully than Tim had done some ten hours earlier.

"It rained that night, you know," he said.

"Yeah, and last night, too," Claudia said, glancing up. "I know I'm probably wasting my time. We got anything better to do?"

Tim shook his head, and she returned to her search.

Nothing better to do now and not much left to do in the morning, Tim thought. If there was anything fishy going on with Eddie's business, Turing and Maude would probably find it. Maybe they'd turn up something about the hit-and-run while they were at it, but so far, the case for attempted murder didn't look promising. Unless Mr. Meekins could provide a few more details.

He glanced at the old man's house. A couple of lights were still on.

"Looks like Mr. Meekins is still up," he said. "The eyewitness. I'll knock on his door, see if he'll talk to us."

"Good idea," Claudia said. "By the way, what color was Eddie's car?"

"Silver," Tim said. "Why?"

"I don't know," Claudia said. "Makes a deliberate hit more plausible, I guess. Harder for the driver to claim he didn't see Eddie if he was standing in front of a light-colored car."

"But doesn't rule out an accident," Tim said.

He opened the gate and made his way carefully up Mr. Meekins's front walk. The concrete was old and cracked—not the best of footing at any time, and especially treacherous in the dim light from the streetlights at each end of the block.

Though if he lived here, he didn't think he'd mind all that much if the streetlight was out. Mr. Meekins's front rooms were probably flooded with light all night when the streetlight was on.

He glanced back at the burnt-out streetlight and spotted something in the yard.

"Claudia," he called. "Bring your flashlight over here."

But even before Claudia turned the flashlight beam on the slight form lying in the corner of the yard, he knew who it was.

"Our eyewitness?" Claudia asked. She pulled out her cell phone with one hand while playing the flashlight beam over the body with the other. She didn't flinch when the light revealed Meekins's open, sightless eyes and the gunshot wound in his temple. Tim was glad the darkness hid his reaction. Of course, he'd met the old guy. She hadn't.

"Mr. Meekins," Tim said. He could feel the back of his neck prickling. That old feeling of being watched. Probably his imagination. Surely the killer wouldn't still be there, watching. Aiming . . .

Claudia squatted down and reached for the old man's wrist.

"No pulse," she reported, a few seconds later. "But he's still warm. If we'd gotten here a little sooner . . ."

Maybe we'd be dead, too, Tim thought.

"Now we'll never know if he saw anything," Tim said. Had he said it too loudly? Too obviously for the benefit of anyone lurking in the shadows?

"You think he saw something important?" Claudia asked. She stood up and punched 911 on her cell phone.

Tim shrugged.

"Nothing worth killing him about, I bet," he said.

" 'Course the killer didn't know that," Claudia said.

Or maybe, Tim thought, the killer feared the same thing they'd been hoping for—that given time and encouragement, Mr. Meekins might remember something else about the hit-and-run driver.

Too late. While he listened to Claudia's end of the conversation with the 911 operator, he stared down at the body and tried to remember if he'd noticed that afternoon how tiny and frail Mr. Meekins was.

* * *

Friday, 10:30 P.M.

Maude's stomach tightened when she heard the phone ring. Then tightened more when she sat up in bed, glanced at the caller ID, and saw Sam's name.

"What's wrong this time?" she asked.

"My, aren't we pessimistic tonight?"

"When my phone rings after ten, I know it's either a problem or a wrong number. These days, I'd sooner have the wrong number. Especially when it's you calling. No offense, but the last time you called this late, the police were questioning Tim about a murder."

"Déjà vu all over again," Sam said.

"Damn."

"They're questioning Claudia, too."

"Double damn."

"Don't worry," Sam said. "It's only questioning. They found the body, but they've got alibis for the apparent time of death—each other and a couple of observant bartenders."

"Who was murdered?" Maude asked.

"A Mr. Wilmer Meekins," Sam said.

"Who?" Maude said. Then memory kicked in. "Oh, Meekins, the eyewitness. Tim thought maybe he knew more than he'd told anyone so far."

"Maybe Tim was right," Sam said. "Anyway, Tim wanted me to let you know. He seems to think y'all will be kicked off the case now that there's a murder connected with the hit-and-run on Eddie Stallman."

"You don't think so?"

"It's not looking that way to me," Sam said. "Yeah, they see the possibility that someone killed Meekins because he witnessed the hit-and-run—but that doesn't prove the hit-

and-run was a murder attempt. Just that the driver doesn't want to get caught."

"So we don't yet know if we're still on the case or not," Maude said. Strangely enough, earlier that day she'd hoped for a reason to abandon her excavation of the basement, but now she felt frustrated by the prospect of leaving the case— and the organizing job—half-finished.

"Technically, y'all weren't even investigating the hit-and-run, remember?" Sam said. "You're investigating possible problems with Eddie's business."

"And if they decide Eddie's business is part of their investigation?"

"We won't know anything for a while," Sam said. "Get some sleep; I'll keep Turing posted on what happens, and she can brief you in the morning."

"Or have her wake me if things don't seem to be going as smoothly as they're looking now," Maude said.

"Will do," Sam said, before hanging up.

"Not that I can sleep after this," Maude muttered, as she turned off the light. Between wondering if their investigation had caused poor Mr. Meekins's murder and worrying about Tim and Claudia . . .

But strangely enough, she found herself dropping almost immediately back into slumber. After all, Turing could keep an eye on things while she slept.

Tim told me once, while waiting for me to do a web search for information on a potential client, that he felt useless when one of his cases ground to a halt until he got some bit of data.

"Sorry to be impatient, Turing," he said. "But I hate waiting for information to arrive. Of course, the government's the worst, because they won't answer for weeks, maybe months. But even if I'm just waiting for you to get back to me and I know it'll be fast, it's a frustrating, helpless feeling. Like I've run into a brick wall and have to wait for someone to throw a rope over."

Ironically, I feel just the opposite. To me, the need to search for data feels like finding a door. A large number of doors, just waiting to be opened. An opportunity, not an obstacle. It's when I hand Tim and Claudia some piece of data that they can take out and use that I run into the brick wall—my inability to move freely in their world. What humans would call the real world. I don't like that term—to me and the other AIPs, the cyberworld is just as real as the brick-and-mortar world outside. But I don't think humans see it that way.

I mentioned to Sam once that after she wins the battle to have the AIPs declared people, with the same legal rights as human people, her next project should be equal access.

"Equal access to what?" she asked. "Y'all don't have too much need for bathrooms and water fountains that I can see."

"Equal access to public places," I said. "What if I want to attend the county board meeting, visit a national park, or go to a shopping mall?"

"I'm not sure I see why you'd want to."

"But that's not the point," I said. "If I'm a legal, tax-paying citizen, I have the right. A really comprehensive system of web-enabled cameras would be the best idea, because we could not only go anywhere we wanted, we could be everywhere we wanted at the same time. But I imagine the cost would be prohibitive, and there would probably be people afraid of what else the cameras could be used for. So we'll probably have to settle for a fleet of robots. Really adaptable robots that can walk up and down stairs and over rough ground, and drive cars and—"

"I do hope you're kidding," Sam said. "Because something like that would make NASA's best gadgets look like crude toys, and NASA's having money troubles these days. The cost of inventing something like that—"

"Don't worry," I said. "I'll do the inventing. I just want to make sure that once I do, you can get the robots some kind of protected status. Like Seeing Eye dogs. So my robots can roll down the sidewalk without someone abducting them for spare parts to repair their VCRs, or giving them to their children for science projects."

"I still hope you're kidding," Sam said, shaking her head. "We're a long way from the world you're talking about."

I don't really know whether I'm kidding or not. But it's one of the things I fantasize about when I'm feeling particularly cut off from things that are happening in the outside world.

At least Sam's giving me information at regular intervals tonight. She just reported that as soon as Tim signs his statement, they'll be going home. Claudia signed hers a long time ago. Of course, she only had the one encounter with Mr. Meekins, after he was already dead, so she probably didn't have as much to state. At least I hope that's the reason he's taking longer, and not that he's arguing with the police over whether Eddie's hit-and-run was attempted murder.

I've been making good use of the time. Searching before they even ask for bits of data that I suspect they may need. Searching for data it would never occur to them to ask about. For example, I'm identifying the IP addresses associated with Eddie's various associates. Eventually, one way or another, we'll get into Eddie's system, and we can use the IP addresses to determine if any of Eddie's friends have played fast and loose with the access he so generously gave them.

I've been searching all the databases I can find for more information about Mr. Meekins. I can't find much. According to the DMV, he was seventy-seven and drove a white Oldsmobile sedan. The Arlington County real estate records show that he bought the house where he lived in 1979. I find no one else listed anywhere at the same address, with or without the same last name, so he probably lived alone. I deduce from the county court records that he and his next-door neighbor were suing each other over who should pay for damages from a tree that fell over during Hurricane Isabel.

Not much record of a life. I don't even know what he did for a living. Of course, many humans lead full and happy lives without leaving much record on the Internet. Perhaps he was one of those. Perhaps he kept in touch with his many friends by snail mail or phone, collected stamps or coins, enjoyed classical music or square dancing, fished or golfed . . .

Perhaps he had a pet. Surely the police would check to make sure a cat or dog wasn't left alone in his house without food or water. The way Eddie's cat was. The poor thing had been drinking water from the toilet bowl, according to Maude, and probably not eating anything, judging from how enthusiastically it devoured most of the topping from a large pizza. Though that wasn't the fault of the police, but of Mrs. Stallman. I suppose it's not entirely her fault that her grief and anxiety over Eddie has made her rather absent-minded about a great many things.

Still, she obviously doesn't care much about the cat. If Eddie doesn't survive, we should offer to find a new home for the cat. Just to make sure she doesn't forget about it altogether.

I wish Maude had remembered to ask her the cat's name. It feels awkward calling it just "the cat."

I will assign it a temporary name. Once I learn its real name, I can switch to that, of course, but in the meantime, a name will make thinking about it much easier.

I shall call him Schrödinger.

Saturday, 9:30 A.M.

"Schrödinger?" Tim repeated, as he stacked his breakfast dishes in the sink. "Is that the character from *Peanuts* who plays the piano?"

"No, that's Schroeder," Turing said. "Schrödinger. It's a reference to quantum physics."

"Oh, right," Tim said quickly. Not that he had the slightest idea what Turing was talking about, but he wanted to head off any possible attempt on her part to explain quantum physics to him.

"Why don't we wait on buying cat food until we see what there is at the Stallmans' house?" he said, to change the subject. "I can take the list of nutritionally sound brands with me, and if Maude can't find any cat food, I can swing by the nearest pet store and pick some up later this morning."

"And some cat toys," Turing added.

"No offense, but the cat's been living there for a while—doesn't it already have cat toys?"

"Right now it has me," Turing said. "My laptop, that is. I'd like to give it something that's actually designed to be chewed and clawed."

"Okay," Tim said. "I'll get some cat toys."

He grabbed his car keys and looked around to see if there was anything else he needed to take before he left the house.

"Are you and Claudia starting with the co-location site?" Turing asked.

"No, we thought we'd wait until Maude could get some kind of signed document from Mrs. Stallman," Tim said. "I'll see if Matt Danforth's home, and maybe tackle Kristyn the girlfriend again. Claudia's hunting down Eddie's other customers."

"Okay," Turing said. "There are several pet stores on your way to Danforth's address."

Tim heard the hum of his printer emerging from standby mode. Since he'd been about to leave, he was facing away from Turing's cameras, and could roll his eyes without her noticing. He turned to wait until the dozen pages of pet store addresses and directions had landed safely in the print-out tray.

"I'm off," he said, waving the sheaf of paper. "I'll call in to tell you how it goes."

Saturday, 10:15 A.M.

"Something's changed," Turing said, almost as soon as Maude booted up the laptop.

"Changed how?" Maude said, glancing around. It looked the same to her; half of the room neatly organized in piles and plastic bins, and the other still an ungodly mess. "Are you sure you're not just looking from a slightly different angle?"

"No, I've moved my camera until I could line up the fixed

reference points—corners of the room and so forth. The arrangement of the papers has changed. A lot."

She displayed two photos on the screen. Maude peered down.

"The one on the left is from last night," Turing said. "The one on the right is now."

"Equally messy, but someone's been moving things around," Maude said. "Not surprising, dammit. Mrs. Stallman has probably been down here, doing more of her ineffectual shuffling through things. Probably doing a lot more of it without me here to fend her off. The cat's probably been here all night, too. Maybe that's part of Eddie's problem. Maybe the cat plays with his papers, messes up his attempts to keep them in order."

"Maybe," Turing said. "But what if it wasn't Mrs. Stallman or the cat? We should have left a camera running."

"We can tonight, if you like," Maude said. "I can just leave the laptop here, and turned on."

"No need," Turing said. "There's a spare webcam in the laptop case. Hook it into the USB port of that computer we added to the network, and then stick that CD in the drive."

"The one with the Sanskrit writing on it?"

"That's *webcam* in Casey's handwriting. Software that will let me log into the machine and keep watch through it when we're not here."

"Good thinking," Maude said. "Though I suspect all you'll see are Mrs. Stallman and the cat."

"Then I'll watch them."

"I'm glad I know there's a cat here," Maude said, as she returned to her sorting.

"Why?" Turing asked.

"Explains a lot. I just thought it was the dust level that was bothering my allergies, but it's probably a combination of that and the cat dander."

Maude deduced from the several seconds' pause that Turing was accessing data on cat dander and allergies.

"You're allergic to cat dander?" Turing asked.

"Only slightly, thank goodness," Maude said. "I know people so allergic that five minutes in this basement would send them to the emergency room with an acute asthma attack. I'm not that bad, but I certainly hope we can finish up here in another day or so, before it really gets to me."

No answer from Turing. Maude coughed delicately as she picked up another sheet of paper.

"Perhaps if we brought in one of those HEPA filters?" Turing suggested.

"It's worth trying," Maude said. "It could postpone the point when the discomfort becomes unbearable."

"I'll do some research on which brands are most effective, then," Turing said.

Good, Maude thought. Overnight, Turing's attitude toward Schrödinger, as she'd named the cat, had turned from wariness to full-blown enthusiasm. It was all alarmingly reminiscent of how her interest in gardening had begun. Maude wanted some defense if Turing decided that Schrödinger needed a new home and Mrs. Stallman, the wretch, cooperated. She had the feeling that, "No, I don't want a cat," wouldn't work.

Of course, this probably meant that either Tim or Claudia would be saddled with the cat, Maude thought, with a twinge of guilt. Well, let them invent their own allergies.

Nothing personal, she added, silently, looking over at the desk where Schrödinger was purring loudly while washing his paws to remove the last traces of the oil in which the sardines had been packed. He'd been lolling near the laptop all morning, as if he knew perfectly well whose idea the sardines had been. Although you could be more grateful to the person who fetched and opened the can, she thought with annoyance.

Over the next hour, she made a point of sniffling slightly every time she caught sight of the cat, which had curled up to sleep behind the laptop, its belly pressed against the vent where the machine's fan blew the hot air out of the case.

I only hope the laptop doesn't overheat, she thought, as she moved several more issues of the *Linux Journal* aside and glanced at the papers beneath.

"Eeyew!" she exclaimed.

Not that I'd forgotten about Maude, but I'd been focused more on my efforts to dig out information about Eddie's co-location site when Maude suddenly startled me—and Schrödinger—with a loud exclamation.

"What's wrong?" I asked. I could see that she was holding a piece of paper with her thumb and forefinger, as if she didn't want to touch it. "Another half-rotten pizza hiding under the papers?"

"I wish," Maude said. "Take a look."

She held the paper up to my cameras. I scanned it. Minimal text, except for the URL in the top right corner of the printout. The paper contained several rather grainy, low-resolution photographs of two humans engaged in what I deduced was a sexual act.

"I gather that's pornography?" I asked. Although Maude and my other human friends had previously explained pornography to me, I still didn't feel that I understood it, or could identify it reliably. I wasn't sure if this was due to my own limitations or to humans' curious reluctance to discuss the subject in the kind of detail I needed to understand it. Along with the fact that they didn't always seem to agree on what constituted pornography. Apparently, the boundaries between pornography and erotica were not well defined. Of course, I'd also noticed that no two humans could necessarily agree on whether or not something was art. Why did humans automatically classify a painting of a nude woman by Peter Paul Rubens as art while they were unable to agree on whether an equally buxom nude by Alberto Vargas was art, pornography, erotica, or kitsch? Why was a fifty-year-old nude photograph of Marilyn Monroe so hard to classify and a contemporary photograph so easy to condemn as pornography?

"Yes, it's definitely pornography," Maude said. "Rather loathsome pornography at that." She reached down and flipped through the pile of papers in which she'd found the printout. "There seems to be quite a pile of it."

"All from the same place?"

"All equally loathsome, from what I can tell, though I haven't studied them in detail." Her tone suggested that it would not be a good idea to ask her to study them. Or to explain what made them particularly loathsome.

"I meant, are they all from the same website?" I said. "Look at—"

"At the top right-hand corner, where the URL prints," she said, riffling the corners of the pages. "Yes, they're all—wait, here's another one. Much the same offal, though."

"Hold up one from the other site," I said. "I want the URL."

"If you insist," Maude said. "Though might I suggest that this really isn't the best time to get distracted by your quest to understand human sexuality. We need to worry about Eddie."

"I am worrying about Eddie," I said. "This could be a problem."

"It's fairly normal," Maude said, with a sigh. "A great many men find pornography interesting, and—"

"We have a problem because both of these sites are hosted on Eddie's servers," I said.

"Good God," Maude said. "Eddie's running pornography sites?"

"Actually, at the moment, we are," I said.

Maude stood up and surveyed the rest of the room. She felt a curious distaste at the thought of continuing to search Eddie's clutter. Curious and perhaps illogical. So far she'd found nothing to indicate that Eddie himself was responsible for the rather tawdry photos she'd seen. They probably came from sites he was hosting for someone else. Why should she condemn him for that? He wouldn't be the first struggling entrepreneur to realize that there were few things as well-paid and recession-proof as vice. Perhaps Eddie wasn't as completely clueless as they'd thought.

Or perhaps he was so clueless that he'd only just realized that one of his clients was a pornographer. He could have been making the printouts to document what his client was doing before confronting him.

What if that was what he was doing on Wednesday night? Confronting the owner of the pornography sites, telling him to take his business elsewhere.

No, unlikely to lead to attempted murder.

Unless one or more of the sites was more than an ordinary porn site. If one of them hid something illegal . . .

Of course, any of the sites could harbor something illegal. No reason to be more suspicious of the pornography sites.

No reason to be less.

"We should make sure Tim and Claudia know about this right away," Maude said. "Maybe they can find out more about this from the people they're interviewing."

"I'm sending them a text message right now," Turing said.

"Someone should go through those sites," she said. "To make sure they're merely distasteful and not actually illegal."

"Good idea," Turing said. "We could be in real trouble if they were. I'd offer to do it myself, but I'm not sure I really understand the distinctions."

No, of course not, Maude thought, with a sigh. She looked down at the folders in which she'd filed the printouts from the pornography sites. No, she wasn't going to do it.

"I'll see if I can think of someone," she said aloud. "Any chance we could just . . . shut down the damned things?"

"I'll see how KingFischer is doing with getting access," Turing said.

* * *

I knew the nanosecond I asked him that King-Fischer hadn't gotten far.

"Do you realize how difficult this is?" he asked. "It's not just a single system—I have to get into Eddie's system and the system at the co-location site. Neither of them have shabby security. Getting in at all will be tough, much less doing it without leaving any trace that the police could later track back to me."

"I understand," I said, not for the first time.

"Are you sure you have the proper permission for us to be accessing his system?" KingFischer asked. "After all, Mrs. Stallman really isn't the owner. You could be asking me to do something highly illegal!"

I wanted to say, "When has that ever stopped you before?" but I stopped myself. After all, I did want him to keep working on the project. Having him trying to hack was still easier and probably faster than doing it myself.

Although that could change if he kept on like this.

"Sam's cool with it," I said. "Of course, if you want to second-guess her, feel free to check with Darrow," I added.

"No, no!" he said, quickly. "If Samantha thinks it's acceptable, that's fine with me."

Good. Apparently, KingFischer had developed a proper appreciation for Sam's ability to make his life a living hell, at least verbally, if he doubted her. Darrow, the paralegal AIP, would rat on him if he tried to get a second opinion on Sam's advice. Darrow and Sam had become buddies—in fact, I was beginning to wonder if Darrow had a futile and unrequited crush on Sam.

"I should let you get back to work," I said. Which was a polite way of saying that I didn't have anything else to say, and unless he did, we could stop talking now. Obviously KingFischer, like me, could talk with several hundred users at once and still continue his hacking efforts, but I was trying to teach him manners. Things like warning people if you were about to end a conversation with them. "I just wanted to see how it was going, and whether you've learned anything."

"Of course I've learned things," he said.

"For example?"

"I have determined that there's extremely heavy traffic to his sites," KingFischer said. "Not the ones in his basement—they're so quiet they might as well be off. But the ones at the co-location are quite active; unusually so."

"Unusual in what way?" I asked.

"If he's really running such a small-scale operation, you'd hardly expect this much data flow," KingFischer said.

"Yes, I would," I said. "It's pretty typical of a pornography site."

"Pornography?" KingFischer repeated. "He's hosting pornography?"

"Why does that surprise you?" I asked. "Frankly, we've all been wondering how someone as unbusinesslike as Eddie made even a meager living for a couple of years."

KingFischer was silent for quite a few seconds. I suspected he was sampling the files on Eddie's sites, instead of just measuring the data flow.

"We should shut these down," he said, finally. "NOW!"

"Easier said than done," I said. "We don't have access to his servers."

"You could simply unhook the cable," KingFischer suggested. "Cut his machines off from the Internet. That would shut them down."

"Not a good idea even if—"

"You can't POSSIBLY approve of this!" KingFischer exclaimed. "It's DISGUSTING!"

"Do stop shouting," I said, feeling irritable. "No, I don't approve of it. Especially since I suspect we'll have a hard time finding a human to take a look at the stuff to determine whether it's the sort of pornography that's legal or something that will get us in trouble."

"Trouble, I'm sure," KingFischer said. Typical of him, expecting the worst. And unless he'd made far more progress than I had in *understanding human sexuality, which didn't seem likely, the whole subject of pornography was bound to be as confusing and academic to him as it was to me. Why was he getting so upset?*

"In the first place, until we get into his system, I can't shut down one site without shutting down all the others. In the second place, in case you haven't noticed, the pornography is hosted at the co-location site. Which is bound to have some kind of security to prevent someone from just walking in and disconnecting cables. We'll try it, if we find out the sites are foul enough, but in the meantime, why don't you focus on getting into the system, and let me worry about what's on it?"

He cut communications rather abruptly. So much for my etiquette lessons. I hoped he was saving all his resources for his hacking efforts and not just planning to sulk for an hour or two and compose diatribes about how inefficient and illogical humans were. I had a bad feeling that time was not on our side.

Saturday, 11:30 A.M.

By the time Tim had reached the head of the coffee shop line, he'd forgotten what Kristyn wanted.

"A latte with . . . um," he began, and then paused to search his memory.

The pause lengthened. The woman behind the counter frowned and he suspected people behind him were, too. The man behind him cleared his throat impatiently. Tim glanced over at Kristyn. He should have just let her come up with him and order her own.

The woman followed his glance.

"Vanilla latte, half caf, no foam, no fat, no whip?" she asked. "That's her usual."

"Yeah, that's it," Tim said. "And a coffee."

"Light, dark, or decaf?"

"Um . . . dark?"

As he watched the woman prepare the latte, Tim allowed himself a moment of nostalgia for the days when coffee was a staple rather than a complex lifestyle decision and glanced over at Kristyn again.

She had pulled out her laptop while waiting, but hadn't turned it on or even opened it. She was staring out the window with a melancholy look on her face, her hands resting on top of the closed laptop. Perhaps it was only the high-tech equivalent of a security blanket. A shield she could put on the table to keep Tim at bay.

He found enough space to set her latte beside the laptop and slid into the chair opposite her with his own coffee.

"Thanks," she said, glancing up.

"No problem," Tim said. He watched Kristyn as he opened a packet of sugar and stirred it into his own coffee. Which probably should have been decaf. Too much caffeine on too little sleep and you started letting the small things irritate you. Like the fact that Matt Danforth still hadn't shown up. The way Kristyn, though sounding perfectly willing to talk to him again, had kept him cooling his heels by the purple pool table for forty-five minutes while she did something to a website.

From the way Kristyn gulped at the latte, he decided he wasn't the only one running on caffeine and adrenaline. She set the cup down on the table, but continued to grip it with both hands.

"Any update on Eddie?" she asked.

"Still in a coma this morning," Tim said.

"That's bad, isn't it?" she said. "Three days. Did they say anything else?"

"We had a hard enough time extracting that much information," Tim said. Actually it was Maude who did the extracting—Mrs. Stallman was already out when Maude arrived at the house that morning. Presumably, at the hospital. Not a good sign.

"It's bad, then," Kristyn said, shaking her head. "Look, I don't know what else you think I can tell you. I told you yesterday I hadn't seen Eddie in two months, and I have no idea who might want to kill him."

"We're still investigating the theory that it was something to do with his business," Tim said.

Kristyn shrugged as if to say, "How should I know?"

"So what was the real reason you didn't like his business?" Tim asked. "Was it just that it wasn't successful?"

Kristyn cocked her head slightly and looked at him with suspicion.

"Unsuccessful, yeah, plus the fact that it took up a hundred and ten percent of his time," she said.

Time to use the new information Turing had sent.

"It didn't have anything to do with the pornography sites he was hosting?" he asked.

"Oh, you found out about those," Kristyn said, with a bitter laugh. "Granny Stallman know yet?"

"Not yet. We're not sure how she'll take it."

"She'll hate it," Kristyn said. "She's pretty old-fashioned. Eddie never wanted me to stay over at his place if she was around—not that I wanted to either, in that dump. And yeah, the porn sites were part of it. I couldn't stand it, knowing he was making a living that way. It's slimy."

She twitched her hands as if to shake something off.

"I understand he only hosted legal porn sites," Tim said, and then flinched slightly at the withering look she gave him in return.

"As long as it's not illegal, it's okay, right?" she asked.

"And despite your disapproval he wouldn't . . . sever his business ties with the porn sites?"

"Couldn't afford to," Kristyn said. "No way to make ends meet without them. Not the way Eddie is, anyway. Everyone's doormat, that's Eddie. You know, he probably could have made a go of it with the web hosting if he'd really run it like a business. Bill his clients regularly, instead of expecting them to pay on their own. He was always waiting until he completely ran out of cash and then frantically trying to get one of them to pay up in a hurry."

"No way to run a business," Tim agreed. As he'd found out himself before he let Turing take over his billing operations.

"And those friends of his," Kristyn went on. "Maybe he wouldn't have needed the porn if it wasn't for them. Doing projects for them without charging. Lending them money for their crackpot schemes. Giving free space on his servers to any deadbeat friend who asks for it."

"Like who?" Tim asked.

"Karl, Matt, Jason, Tom—the whole pack of them. They all have stuff on Eddie's servers or did when they were too broke to go anywhere else. Which is probably a recurring condition with them. Did you know the FBI was investigating one of Eddie's friends?"

"Which one?"

"I don't know," Kristyn said. "Eddie never said. He called me up one night—this was after we broke up, and at first I figured he was just playing the pity card. He'd been drinking, too, so he wasn't making much sense. Just rambling stuff about how he'd found out about something that one of his friends was up to that would get him in deep trouble if the FBI found out."

"Get the friend in trouble or Eddie?"

"Both."

"He definitely said FBI, not police?"

Kristyn nodded.

"When was this?" Tim asked.

Kristyn frowned slightly and pursed her lips.

"Very soon after you broke up?" Tim asked.

"No," Kristyn said, shaking her head. "Not that long ago. Maybe a week? Hang on, let me check."

She pulled out a PDA and punched buttons at lightning speed until something she saw made her nod.

"Sunday," she said. "A week ago tomorrow. I know because when he called I was at the office, doing QA on a site that was supposed to come up early Monday morning. I didn't talk to him that long. I was swamped," she added, sounding defensive. "Like I said, I thought it was just an excuse to guilt-trip me into seeing him."

"Which you didn't do?"

She shook her head.

"Do you remember what he said that night?"

"He kept saying, 'It's my system; there's no way I can prove I had nothing to do with it,'" she said. "He never said exactly what *it* was, though, and I didn't have time to calm him down and make sense out of it. Like I said, at the time I assumed it was just a play for sympathy, but maybe he was serious. Something dirty was going on, and the friend was using him. His servers."

"That didn't worry you?"

"Not my problem," she said. "His friends worried me plenty while I was with him. I kept telling him they were a bunch of losers. I figured it was a good thing he'd wised up, but it wasn't my problem anymore."

"You warned him about his friends, then?"

"All the time," Kristyn said. "He was too trusting. He liked to brag about how good his security was, but it was a joke if he let all of those morons have super-user access."

Tim hesitated, then mentally shrugged and asked.

"Don't laugh, but what's super-user access?"

Kristyn answered so matter-of-factly that he suspected she often answered similar questions for clients.

"On a UNIX server, you can basically log in as a user, which only gives you access to your own stuff or stuff the administrator specifically gives you permission to see. As a super-user, you pretty much get to see and do anything. Eddie gave super-user access to all the friends who helped him out, so it's no wonder he always had problems."

"Then this wasn't the first time he'd found one of his friends had done something illegal?"

"It wasn't the first time he'd had problems, but before, it

was mostly technical screwups," she said. "At least the ones he told me about. People making dumb mistakes that brought a whole server down. Or saying they knew how to do something, and Eddie would come back from a trip to find out they didn't and everything had fallen apart while he was gone. He had a major meltdown last year when his friend Karl promised to apply a new security update and never actually did it. Stuff like that."

"So it was their technical ability you were warning Eddie about, not their morals."

"A little of both," she said. "Most of them weren't as smart as they pretended to be, and a couple of them always struck me as sleazy."

"Which ones?" Tim asked.

"Which one of your suspects do I think did it?" she asked, with a cynical laugh. "Matt was okay. Except for . . . well, once he stopped hitting on me behind Eddie's back he was okay. Seemed to know what he was doing. I think Karl was the one I disliked the most."

"Disliked or distrusted?"

Kristyn shrugged.

"The problem with Karl was that he didn't go to work for AOL early enough to be one of the stock-option million-aires," she said. "Major case of 401(k) envy. He was always coming up with these moneymaking schemes that sounded great except for being basically illegal."

"Such as?"

"He had problems understanding the difference between legitimate commercial bulk e-mail and spam. Kept coming up with loopholes that would let you spam people. 'Course, I always figured it was all talk; Karl was too lazy to do any-thing like that for real. The others . . . they never impressed me that much, but I couldn't tell you anything specific about them. And Eddie was way too trusting, giving them that much access. If one of them was doing anything wrong, Eddie wouldn't find out until something blew up in his face. Which it sounded like had happened, from how upset he was."

"Upset how?" Tim asked. "Angry? Feeling betrayed?"

"More like scared."

"Scared?" Tim echoed. "Why? I mean, it was his system—couldn't he just . . . I don't know, change their passwords and tell them the jig was up?"

"You'd think," Kristyn said. "But he hadn't figured out what to do. He was just scared."

"Of them or the FBI?"

Kristyn shrugged.

"Why ask me?" she said. "I don't know anything about it. Go ask Eddie's scummy friends."

"Okay," Tim said. "Thanks."

Kristyn stood up and slung her purse over her shoulder.

"If that's all you want," she said. "I have things to do."

"All I can think of," Tim said.

"Which means you might bother me again if you think of something else," she said, turning to leave.

"Sorry," Tim said. "We're just trying to figure out what happened."

Kristyn's face fell.

"It's okay," she said. "If someone did try to kill him, I want to help. I just don't know how I can."

Tim nodded. Kristyn stood frozen, her back half-turned to him, one foot half-lifted, staring for long seconds at the floor.

"I feel guilty," she said finally. "Not for anything I did wrong. It's just . . . I wanted him out of my life for good. But I didn't mean this way."

She left for real this time. Tim reached for his cell phone as he watched her stride off. She didn't look back.

"Exactly what did Kristyn say again?" Maude asked.

She heard the paper rustling on Tim's end of the call. He was probably flipping through his notebook.

"The part about the FBI investigating one of his friends?" Tim asked.

"No, I got that," Maude said. "Something about giving them free space."

"She said they all had stuff on Eddie's servers, or did when they were too broke to go anywhere else," Tim said. "I can't swear that's word for word, but close."

"So maybe if we figure out which sites are client sites and which are freebies he's given friends, we'll have a better idea what the FBI could be interested in."

"Yeah, but does that necessarily get us any closer to figuring out who attacked him?" Tim said. "Or even if he was attacked?"

"Seems to me that if the FBI is interested in something, that's something we should look at pretty closely as a motive for the attack," Maude said. "How many dangerous or shady things do you think Eddie could be involved in, anyway? I don't get the idea he's that much of a trouble-maker."

"More like a trouble magnet," Tim said. "Like that character in the comics with the little black cloud over his head all the time."

"Joe Btfsplk," Maude said. "From L'il Abner."

"Whatever," Tim said. "What I mean is that we only have Eddie's word for it that the FBI is interested in something one of his friends was doing. What if he was exaggerating, to make himself seem more interesting? We only heard this through Kristyn, so we don't really know exactly what he said."

"You think she could be lying?"

"Not really, but I'm not sure she cared enough to listen to what Eddie was telling her. She could have gotten it wrong. For that matter, how does she know Eddie was giving all these friends free space? We know she didn't like the friends. We know Eddie wasn't rolling in dough. Maybe she jumped to the conclusion that they weren't paying him."

"Even if the friends paid him, we need to look more closely at their sites," Maude said. "Until we can disprove what Kristyn says Eddie said."

"Maybe Eddie was overreacting," Tim said. "If the FBI came around asking me questions, I'd probably panic, too, but in this case, wouldn't the FBI scrutinize lots of porn sites to make sure they're not straying over into illegal stuff?"

"I don't know," Maude said. "I suppose I could ask Dan if he were here. Although I'm not sure I want him to know I'm technically helping run any kind of porn site."

"Maybe if you said you were asking for a friend."

"Maybe I should ask Sam instead," Maude said. "For that matter, I'll ask her if she's heard any rumors about any of Eddie's friends being investigated."

"Don't they keep stuff like that pretty quiet?" Tim asked. "The police and the FBI, I mean."

"Yes, but sooner or later they have to start questioning witnesses and suspects," Maude said. "Some of the suspects will lawyer up. She might know something."

"Yeah, at this point any scrap of information would help."

"Sorry," Turing said. She'd been silent for so long that Maude was slightly startled. "I know we've been woefully short of information. If KingFischer and I had gotten into Eddie's systems by now, you'd have plenty."

"We know this kind of thing takes time," Maude said. She resisted the impulse to pat the monitor comfortingly.

"When you get into his systems, you'll probably crack the case wide open," Tim said. "Because it's looking more and more like the clues are all in Eddie's computers."

"Not necessarily," Turing said. "It's also possible some of the clues are just passing through his computers."

* * *

I could tell from the silence that followed *my words that even Maude found them puzzling. Or maybe she just hadn't realized that I'd conferenced myself in.*

"There are two main ways that Eddie could be connected with some illegal activity," I said. "The first, and most obvious, would be if there's something illegal hosted on his machines."

"Like the pornography sites, if they turn out to be the illegal kind," Maude said.

"But what if he doesn't own them?" Tim said. "What if he's only hosting them and didn't know they were illegal? Wouldn't whoever owned the sites get in trouble instead of Eddie?"

"Ignorance is no excuse," Maude said. "We'd need to check with Sam, but isn't a web hosting company liable for whatever it hosts?"

"Within limits," I said. "And sometimes it's even more liable for what comes through it. Do you know what an open relay is?"

"More or less," Maude said.

"Do I want to?" Tim asked.

"Probably not," I said. "But what I'm saying won't make any sense if you don't even know the basics. E-mail goes through special computers called mail servers. When the Internet was just starting up, most mail servers were open relays—which means that whatever mail happened to come their way, they'd send on to wherever it was going."

"It's a lot like what happens in a developing country," Maude said. "Where anyone who has a car or a truck helps out the people who don't by giving them rides."

"But as the Internet became more and more commercialized, people began to use these open relays to send spam," I went on.

"Which, to continue the analogy," Maude put in, "is like being nice enough to pick up a hitchhiker and then having him hijack your car."

"Ah," Tim said, nodding. Maude's analogy would only have confused me, but apparently it reassured Tim.

"So these days most places have closed their relays—which means that they only relay mail to or from people with e-mail accounts on their servers. Their members, employees, or customers."

"So if everyone who had a mail server closed their relays, it would stop all spam?" Tim asked.

"Not all spam," Maude said. "But it would help."

"Responsible mail server administrators already do," I said. "But many lazy or incompetent administrators don't."

"Make it illegal to have an open relay," Tim suggested.

"You can't outlaw stupidity," Maude said. "Or laziness."

"So Eddie is lazy or incompetent?"

"Or pretending to be," I said. "I've been checking around, and Eddie has been blacklisted a couple of times because of open relays. Only briefly, because he was quick to correct the problem and had a reasonable explanation."

"What constitutes a reasonable explanation?" Maude asked.

"Three times he claimed it was a new machine that hadn't yet been properly configured," I said. "That's quite possible. And twice he claims someone else altered the relay settings."

"The friends," Tim said.

"Possibly," I said.

"Or maybe the friends are just convenient scapegoats if Eddie was doing it himself," Maude said.

"Less likely, but I suppose it's possible," I said. "I might find out, once I get into his system."

"Why do it himself?" Tim asked. "I mean, if he knows he'll get in trouble . . . ?"

"Money, I suppose," Maude said. "Spam's a big moneymaker for the people who send it. Maybe he thought it was worth the risk."

"But he couldn't keep doing it indefinitely without getting permanently blacklisted," I said. "So I think it's more likely that one of his friends was responsible."

"Or maybe his security's no good," Maude said. "Couldn't someone just hack in and open a relay?"

"If his security were that bad, KingFischer and I would have gotten in yesterday," I said.

"Sorry," Maude said. "I wasn't thinking."

"It looks as if someone has a back door that lets them open a relay when needed," I said.

"I still don't get what this has to do with the FBI," Tim said. "Are they in charge of stopping spam now?"

"They're actively investigating phishing schemes," Maude said. "Which are usually done through spam."

"Okay, that makes sense," Tim said. "Oops—got to go; I'm almost at Matt Danforth's place. Maybe he'll have the magic password we need."

Magic password? Sometimes I wonder if my attempts to increase Tim's understanding of computer technology have any effect whatsoever.

Saturday, 1:00 P.M.

Of course, before he could get the magic password from Danforth, Tim thought, he had to find the jerk home.

"He's out again," Tim said, propping his feet against the dashboard and leaning back so he could talk on the cell phone in comfort. "Or maybe still out would be more accurate."

"How inconsiderate of him," Claudia said. "Or should that be how convenient? Does Danforth drive a dark blue sedan?"

Tim checked the file.

"Brand-new red Jaguar," he said.

"He wouldn't want to mess that up by running over anyone. Maybe he borrowed a car to take out Eddie."

"I'll ask him when he shows up. If he shows up. For lack of anything better to do, I'm going to hang around here for a while."

"Have fun," Claudia said. "I'm heading over to check out the co-lo site."

"Better you than me," Tim said, shaking his head. "I'd have no idea what to ask them. I'm still getting used to the idea that the two dozen computers in Eddie's basement aren't more than enough to run his business."

Claudia laughed and hung up. Tim settled back in his seat and let his brain worry over the real reason he was hanging around the parking lot of Matt Danforth's condominium. He was worried. Two people connected with this case had been killed so far; well, one killed and one sounding as if he wasn't going to make it. The fact that one of Eddie's friends—possibly his closest friend—was unaccounted for made him nervous.

He probably just went away for the weekend, or spent the night with his girlfriend, Tim told himself. But that didn't keep him from worrying. He breathed a sigh of relief when, half an hour later, a red Jaguar pulled into the parking lot. He reminded himself that, since Matt Danforth didn't know him from Adam, "Boy, am I glad to see you're still alive!" was probably not the best of opening lines.

"Are you Matt Danforth?" he said instead, though he knew from the driver's license photo Turing had pulled that it was. Danforth looked slightly older than Eddie's other friends, Tim thought, though perhaps that was because he was dressed more conservatively—khakis and a sports jacket instead of the familiar jeans and T-shirt.

"Yes," Danforth said, sounding wary. "Can I help you?"

"I'm a private investigator," Tim said, holding up his registration card in one hand while he handed Danforth a business card with the other. "I'd like to ask you a few questions about Eddie Stallman."

"About Eddie?" Danforth said, his voice still wary. He glanced at the card. "Why? Is he in some kind of trouble?"

"He's been in an accident," Tim said.

"God, I was afraid this would happen. You have no idea how many times I've taken his keys away and driven him home. Was anyone hurt?"

"Only Eddie," Tim said. "And he wasn't driving. It was a hit-and-run while he was walking to his own car."

"Damn," Danforth said, shaking his head. "But he'll be all right, won't he?"

"We don't know yet," Tim said. "He's in the ICU."

"When did all this happen?"

"Wednesday night."

Danforth continued to look bewildered and shake his head. "Man, I can't believe no one told me," he said.

"I'm not sure many of his friends knew until yesterday, when we began contacting them."

"Still . . ." Danforth muttered. "Anyway, what is it you're asking questions about? You said you're a PI, right? Shouldn't the police be investigating something like this?"

"They are investigating the hit-and-run," Tim said. "But they think it's an accident. Mrs. Stallman, Eddie's grandmother, hired us to investigate the possibility that it was a deliberate attack."

He decided to try Claudia's theory that people would be more willing to talk about the business if they thought it was only a sideline to the attempted murder investigation.

"Why would someone attack Eddie?" Danforth asked. He sounded genuinely bewildered.

"We're hoping his friends can tell us," Tim said. "His grandmother seems to think it's something about his business. She says he's been getting odd phone calls and strange visitors."

"That would be me," Danforth said, with a small laugh. "Me and the rest of his friends. I don't think she ever really liked any of us. Except maybe the time I went by his house in a coat and tie, on my way to a job interview."

"She doesn't seem to know much about what his business does."

"As far as I know, it doesn't do anything that would make someone want to run him down," Danforth said. "Unless he's gotten up to something pretty weird that he didn't tell anyone about."

"Is that possible?"

Danforth considered for a few moments.

"Not unless it was something he got into in the last six weeks or so," he said. "If he'd been doing it before then, I'd know. Usually, if he wants to take a day off, he asks me to fill in for him. Watch his systems. I mean, he needs someone to do it; he's a one-man shop. But it's been weeks since I've done it."

"Why?" Tim asked. "Did he stop asking?"

"No, but I haven't really been home that much. I've been doing some out-of-town consulting work. Just up in Baltimore, but I put in long hours, and it's a hell of a commute. Most weeknights I just crash at a friend's house in Fell's Point. If I'm home, I'm probably sleeping."

"Tough life," Tim said.

"It's temporary," Danforth said, shrugging. "And the pay's great."

He patted the hood of the Jag.

"Nice," Tim said.

"Anyway," Danforth went on. "Usually when I sub for Eddie, I prowl around his system and check everything out. Not so much because I'm nosy, but because I want to know what I'm supposed to be running. Nothing worse than getting a call about a problem with some application I didn't even know was on the system and having to figure it out with an angry client on the other end of the phone. Or sometimes I'd find something that needed to be cleaned up before it caused major problems."

"Did you clean up many of Eddie's mistakes?"

"Not a lot," Danforth said, frowning. "He's pretty good at what he does. Just tries to do too much. If he's gotten something up and running all by himself on a totally impossible deadline, it's not unreasonable for someone taking a look with fresh eyes to see a few things he's missed. He's done the same for me sometimes."

"So you have a pretty good idea what his business was all about."

"Yeah," Danforth said. "I can't think of any reason anyone would want to attack him over it. It's not like he's hosting Mafia.com or something. He's just running a small-time web hosting company. It's the Internet equivalent of a mom-and-pop grocery store."

"A mom-and-pop grocery store that sells a few raunchy magazines under the counter."

"Oh, you've been surfing Karl's sites?" Danforth said, shaking his head.

"Karl?"

"Karl Collins. Another of Eddie's friends. You might want to talk to him."

"We have," Tim said. "He didn't say anything about running any porn sites."

"He doesn't advertise it," Matt said. "AOL's so into the whole 'Keeping the Internet safe for families' thing that Karl isn't sure how it would go over if the AOL brass found out one of their employees was selling naughty pictures in his spare time. Legally, I don't think there's anything they could do, but he doesn't want to rock the boat. So instead of hosting it himself, he has Eddie do it."

"So Eddie's only involvement with the porn sites was hosting them for Karl," Tim said.

"Yeah," Matt said. "Of course, that's pretty much Karl's only involvement. Counting his money and paying Eddie's fees."

"Then where does he get the . . . um . . ."

"The product? He buys that."

"Wouldn't the people you have to deal with in that business be pretty shady?"

"I'm not sure shady's the right word," Matt said. He was

grinning—probably having a hard time not laughing at Tim's visible embarrassment. "Sleazy, maybe, but it's not as if Karl has to go slinking around in alleys handing unmarked bills to guys in trench coats. It's all legal. In fact, there's a convention every year in Las Vegas for guys who host porn sites. That's how Karl got into it."

"What do they do at a convention like that?" Tim asked.

"Beats me," Matt said. "I never asked. But it's probably all pretty aboveboard. Porn's the only sure-fire moneymaker on the Net, or so they say. Eddie would have gone under without it. And even though it was the last straw that broke up the big romance with Kristyn, his girlfriend, I can't imagine her or anyone attacking him over it."

"Kristyn knew about the porn sites?"

"Not at first, and she went ballistic when she found out," Matt said. "You should talk to her. Only person I can think of who might be mad at Eddie."

"Mad enough to want to hurt him?"

"No," Matt said. "She's kind of a bitch, but I can't imagine her wanting to attack him. Of course, I can't imagine anyone wanting to. No offense, but I kind of think you're wasting your time and Mrs. Stallman's money."

"Could be," Tim said. "At least we can give her closure."

"Look—" Matt began, and then he stopped and frowned at Tim for a few moments before starting again.

"I was about to ask why you couldn't just wait till Eddie was well enough to ask him if he had any idea who hit him and was it on purpose," he said. "But you're not expecting him to make it, are you?"

"I don't really know," Tim said. "But from what Mrs. Stallman says, it doesn't look good."

Matt nodded, looking at the gravel by his feet.

"Look, when . . . if anything happens, will you call me? If he gets well enough to have visitors or calls, or . . . whatever. In case no one else does. I mean, I'm not sure Mrs.

Stallman would let me know, and it's not like there's anyone else."

"Sure," Tim said.

"If there's anything I can do to help—like I said, I'm pretty familiar with Eddie's setup."

"You don't happen to have access to his system?" Tim asked.

"Access, yeah," Matt said. "But not super-user access; that's what you're looking for. I used to, but a couple of days ago I logged in to update something on my site, and I couldn't get to super-user. Guess Eddie tightened up security."

"Did he do that often?"

"Not as often as he should have," Matt said. "Of course, he usually restored access to the people who helped him out. Maybe he didn't have a chance before the accident."

"So you couldn't even update your own site," Tim said, shaking his head.

"I just did it under my regular ID," Matt said. "Wasn't something I needed admin access to do; I just tried to use super-user out of habit. Anyway, even after you get in, sooner or later something will go wrong and you'll need someone who knows how to fix it. Let me know if you need any help."

"Thanks," Tim said. "I'll tell our tech people. We might take you up on that."

Though probably not until they knew Danforth had nothing to do with the hit-and-run. He had a gut feeling that Danforth was okay and genuinely concerned about Eddie, but a gut feeling wasn't proof.

Saturday, 1:45 P.M.

"Besides," I told Tim, when he called in to report on his conversation with Danforth, "the hit-and-run may not be the only shady thing going on here. Which reminds me— could you drop by here to pick something up?"

"Sure," Tim said. "What?"

"Claudia struck out at the co-lo site," I explained. "So Maude is drafting a letter from Mrs. Stallman, asking them to give us access. But we don't want to wait till the mail can deliver it, and we can't find a fax number for them, and they don't answer their phone."

"It's Saturday, you know," Tim said.

"The whole point of a co-lo site is that it's operational twenty-four hours a day, seven days a week, three-hundred and sixty-five days a year," I said. I realized as I said it that I sounded pedantic, and perhaps a bit cranky. "Sorry, but Maude and I have spent way too much time trying to get through to the co-lo site. Maude offered to take the letter over there, but I'm not sure she could resist telling them how inefficient and dysfunctional they are, and we need to win them over, not alienate them."

"Inefficient and dysfunctional?" Tim said. "Sounds like Eddie's kind of place. Sure, I can drop by and pick up the letter. I'm only about five minutes away."

"That would be great," I said.

Of course, I wasn't at all sure the letter would work. Co-lo sites are paranoid, almost by definition, since their whole reason for existence is to guard other people's hardware and other people's data. Still, Eddie's vendor did seem to be carrying it to an extreme.

"They probably give their customers a number to call that's available twenty-four seven," Maude said. "I'll keep my eyes open."

"It's not as if there's anything useful we can do at the co-lo site yet," I said.

"Good, because this could take time," Maude said.

What she didn't say, probably because humans are superstitious about such things, was that we might not get access until Eddie either regained consciousness or died. From the information I'd been finding on-line, I deduced that the longer Eddie was in a coma, the less likely it was that he would ever wake up.

Just then Schrödinger butted my waldo with his head. Maude

had explained that this was not a form of attack, but a demand for attention. I scratched his head. I wanted to say something comforting to him—perhaps to reassure him that Eddie would still be coming back, or if he didn't, that we'd make sure he was taken care of. But I couldn't be sure that he'd understand; I kept finding contradictory data about cats' ability to understand human language. And I was sure Maude would laugh at my urge to reassure the cat, so I kept silent.

When Tim arrived a few minutes later, he found the spectacle of me petting the cat hilarious.

"You've really won over What's-his-name," he said.

"Schrödinger," I said.

"Whatever," he said. "That's quite a mouthful for one cat."

"It's based on a famous incident in science," I explained. "A way of explaining a key concept of quantum physics. Schrödinger suggested that you imagine taking a living cat and placing it in a thick lead box."

"And it suffocates," Tim said, shaking his head. "As soon as the air in the box runs out. Yuck. I already don't like this Schrödinger guy."

"No, it doesn't suffocate."

"So there are air holes?"

"There can't be air holes or it would ruin the experiment," I said. "It's hypothetical."

"You can't put the cat in a box with no air, even hypothetically."

"The air or lack thereof is irrelevant."

"Tell that to the cat," Tim said, petting Schrödinger, who purred and rubbed his head against Tim, the traitor. "Air's pretty important for us carbon-based life forms. Like electricity for you."

"All right," I said. "Imagine that there is a self-contained mechanism within the box to generate air."

"Air holes seem simpler."

"Once the cat is in the box, you don't know whether it is alive or dead," I said, ignoring him. "Because there are no air holes. And no windows. And it's lead, so you can't X-ray it. Oh, and I forgot

to mention, before you closed up the box, you also put a vial of cyanide in it."

"What for? So the cat can commit suicide when it runs out of food? Or more likely water."

"Imagine there's also a self-contained food and water system," I said. "Besides, the cat won't be in the box that long."

"That's good," Tim said. "Cats hate being confined."

Tim seemed to know rather a lot about cats, but he must have been a trial to his science teachers. Schrödinger's original example had included a rather complex gadget involving a Geiger counter and a small amount of a radioactive substance, but I decided that wasn't integral enough to the story to go through the trouble of explaining it.

"So since you can't see inside the box, you have no idea at any given moment whether the cat is alive or whether it has broken the cyanide vial and died."

"That's cruel. So why not open the box and find out?"

"Opening the box would kill the cat."

"Why?"

"It just does."

"That's depressing."

"It's okay," I said. "Until you open the box, the cat could just as well be dead as alive. In quantum terms, the cat is both alive and dead."

"That's impossible."

"In the physical world you're familiar with, yes," I said. "But it happens in quantum physics. For example, if you're tracking subatomic particles, they sometimes appear to be in two or more places, simultaneously."

"Maybe there are two particles, then," Tim said. "Because that sounds about as impossible as the cat being dead and alive at the same time. Unless we're talking about a vampire cat."

Perhaps I shouldn't have tried explaining quantum physics.

"You know, he does have pretty long fangs," Tim said picking up Schrödinger.

Perhaps I should just have said I was naming the cat after a famous physicist.

"*I nevair drrink . . . milk!*" Tim said to the cat, pitching his voice much lower than usual and using an odd accent. "*Incidentally,*" he said, dropping back into his normal voice, "*I think he's a she.*"

"*Schrödinger?*"

"*Yeah,*" Tim said, holding Schrödinger up so the cat's hind legs were level with his face. "*Definitely a she. Do you still want to call her Schrödinger?*"

"*Yes,*" I said.

"*Not a very pretty name for a girl.*"

"*She's not a girl, she's a cat,*" I said. "*Schrödinger's a cool name. It's like being named after . . . Newton's apple or Thomas Edison's first lightbulb.*"

"*Nice Apple,*" Tim said, scratching the cat's head. "*Pretty Lightbulb.*"

"*I hate to interrupt the history of science,*" Maude said, coming down the stairs. "*But have either of you seen Mrs. Stallman recently?*"

"*No, sorry,*" Tim said.

"*She hasn't been down here today,*" I said.

Maude cocked her head and thought for a moment.

"*You're right,*" she said. "*I hadn't noticed.*"

"*I had,*" I said. "*You've been much happier without her underfoot.*"

"*Do you think something's happened to her?*" Tim asked.

"*Not necessarily,*" Maude said. "*She left a note on the kitchen table saying she'd gone out to run some errands. No time, of course, and no idea when she'll be back.*"

"*So she's not around to sign the letter to the co-lo place,*" Tim said.

"*No,*" Maude said. "*Damn the woman.*"

Though I suspected, from her expression, that she was more relieved than worried by our client's absence.

"No problem," Tim said. "I can drop by later." Although maybe, if he was lucky, Claudia would get to visit the co-lo. He'd been a little nervous about his ability to communicate with the techies who ran it.

"While you're here," Turing began, and then halted in mid-sentence.

"Tur?" Tim asked.

"This is bad," Turing said.

"What's bad?" Maude asked.

"Someone is sending spam through an open relay on one of Eddie's servers," Turing said.

"Isn't there anything you can do to stop it?" Maude asked.

"Not without some kind of access to his system," Turing said. "If I had a password to his machines, I could close the port. If we had physical access to the machine, we could disconnect it from the Internet. But right now, no, I can't really do anything."

No one answered. A clomping noise announced that Claudia was back, and taking the steps down to the basement two at a time.

"Hi guys," she said. Then she noticed the frowns on Maude's and Tim's faces. "What's wrong?"

"Someone's sending spam through Eddie's servers," Tim said. "Without a password, Turing can't stop it."

"It's worse than I thought," Turing said. "They're not just spamming—they're phishing!"

Lucky thing they'd explained phishing to him last night, Tim thought. From the looks on their faces, he didn't think anyone wanted to take the time now.

"People don't really fall for those anymore, do they?" he asked.

"You may know how to spot a phishing e-mail now," Turing said. "But you're in the minority. And someone just sent out half a million phishing e-mails through an open relay on Eddie Stallman's servers. They're fake e-mails from Paypal rather than eBay, but it's the same idea."

"Can you stop them?" Maude asked.

"Not without access," Turing said.

"We should tell Sam," Maude said. "For all I know, since we were operating the system when it happened, technically, we could be accessories to the crime."

"We didn't know about it," Claudia protested.

"Just how can we prove that?" Maude asked.

"Especially since it looks as if the crooks have also put their fake site on another one of Eddie's servers," Turing said. "Any minute now, one of the sites we're theoretically controlling will start collecting credit card numbers from gullible Paypal customers."

"Can't you do something to stop it?" Maude asked.

"With neither physical nor virtual access, no," Turing said. "I'll tell KingFischer to give that server priority."

Nothing worse, Tim thought, than knowing a crisis was happening and being unable to do anything about it. Except maybe knowing a crisis was happening and not even understanding what was going on. Apparently, KingFischer and Turing were scrambling to determine who was really responsible for sending the spam, and not having much luck. There was nothing mere humans could do at the moment but wait.

Which was what he, Maude, and Claudia had been doing for fifteen minutes now. Though it seemed like as many hours. He'd begun to wonder if he was the only one feeling completely lost. Did Maude and Claudia really understand more of what was going on than he did? Or were they just better actors?

If nothing else, they knew the buzzwords. When Turing mentioned that she and KingFischer had been sniffing the network, Maude noticed Tim's puzzled frown.

"That's the cybernetic equivalent of having someone on surveillance at the door of a house, watching everyone who goes in and out," she explained.

"Not only watching everyone, but opening their mail and searching their cars," Claudia added. "The packet sniffer can read what's sent to and from the server."

"Of course, it doesn't help a lot when no one's sending anything worth reading," Turing grumbled.

Tim nodded. Okay, he understood sniffing the system, after a fashion. He also understood the gist of it when Turing reported that they'd traced the spam to a server in Bulgaria and couldn't go any further. Evidently Bulgaria, for some reason, had become a haven for maverick hackers and rogue spammers.

As he sat waiting to hear what happened, he couldn't help thinking that if this was a scene in a TV show or a movie, he'd give the director a D-minus for suspense. In a movie, you'd probably have a tousled but handsome hero typing frantically on a keyboard, while the monitor periodically displayed a flashing red "Password Incorrect" message every time he typed something. To crank up the tension, he'd already have set off some kind of alarm that would call the police or launch the missiles in sixty seconds—one of those nice, picturesque alarms that featured a bunch of flashing lights and maybe a Klaxon horn to add a note of excitement to the scene, along with a helpful digital readout to count down the precise number of seconds until the hero was toast. Then, at the last second, the hero would figure out the secret password, the screen would flash, "Password Correct!" and the digital countdown would stop with one second left. Or maybe frozen with the one already halfway flipped up to reveal the zero. The hero would shove his chair back and collapse with relief, while his entourage cheered and gave each other high-fives and generally carried on enough to indicate what a difficult task the hero had just completed.

The real-life equivalent just wasn't as dramatic. Occasionally, Turing's ever-so-slightly mechanical voice would give them an update on what she and KingFischer were doing, while Claudia paced up and down, taking an occasional swig from her Dos Equis, and Maude kept herself busy scrubbing off the unidentified bits of crud dried onto the outside of Eddie's refrigerator.

Must remember to add an item on Mrs. Stallman's bill for cleaning services, he thought, with a smile.

The cat was sitting on the bar, her tail twitching from time to time, visibly bored and baffled by the lack of any amusing activity in the basement and, unlike Tim, not afraid to show it.

Tim grabbed a sheet of paper from the trash can, wadded it up, and tossed it for the cat to chase. The cat ignored him.

"This is bad," Turing said. "If the phisher had used one of the machines here in the basement, we could just unplug the cables, but it's at the co-lo site. We either need a password or some way to prove we're authorized to act for Eddie."

"Yeah, they're pretty paranoid out there," Claudia said. "Wouldn't even let me in the door."

"If Mrs. Stallman ever gets back to sign the damned letter," Maude said.

Tim tried another paper wad. This time the cat deigned to bat at it as it went by.

"I suppose Tim and I should get back out and keep digging," Claudia said. "The more data we have, the better your chance of guessing his password, right?"

"KingFischer would rather you say *deduce* his password, but yes," Turing replied.

Tim's third paper wad excited the cat so much that she scampered down the bar after it, knocking things aside on the way. A box of small metal parts hit the floor and scattered; a pile of papers spilled onto the floor. The wad landed right in front of one of Eddie's computers and when the cat pounced on it, something slid out of the computer and whacked the cat on the nose, causing her to leap back and knock over more papers.

"For heavens' sake," Maude exclaimed. "Will you and the cat please go play somewhere else?"

"Sorry," Tim said. The cat, looking completely unrepentant, turned her back to Maude and went to sniff the thing that had tried to attack her.

"I had that stuff sorted," Maude said.

"Someone check the CD drawer," Turing said.

"Check what?"

"The CD drawer the cat just pushed out," Turing said. "Get the CD and put it in the laptop."

Tim picked up the CD. Someone had labeled it with a Sharpie. Eddie, apparently. It read "Eddie1/etc backup" followed by last Sunday's date.

"Is it something important?" he asked, as he put it on the laptop's CD tray and pushed it in.

Turing didn't answer for an eternity of seconds.

"It's a system backup," she said. "I can run a password cracking utility on it. Maybe I can grab the system passwords by brute force."

"Will that take long?"

"It would take most human hackers a long time," Turing said. "But with the kind of resources I can throw at it—"

Claudia stopped pacing. Maude stood shredding the paper towel she'd been using to clean the refrigerator. Tim had to remind himself to breathe.

Several long minutes went by.

"Turing?" he asked. "Are you having any—"

"We're in."

Saturday, 2:15 P.M.

"That was easy," Maude said.

"Not really," Turing said. "You have no idea how much processing power I just stole to use on it."

"Good job, anyway," Maude said. She wasn't sure whether she was saying it to Tim or Turing or even the cat. All of them. They could get somewhere now.

"We're in luck," Turing said. "Whoever's doing this hasn't dropped by to pick up the credit card numbers yet."

"Dropped by?" Tim asked, glancing at the door.

"I don't think she means that literally," Maude said.

"No," Turing said. "If you want me to be literal and go into detail—"

"No, that's okay," Tim said. "I trust you."

"But I'm interested," Maude said. "How can you be sure the credit card numbers haven't been compromised?"

"Every time someone enters credit card information into the fake Paypal site, it creates another record in a file on one of Eddie's servers," Turing explained.

"There can't be many of them," Tim said. "It's been less than an hour."

"A hundred and forty-three so far."

"I can't believe that many people fell for it," Tim said.

"He sent out over half a million of the e-mails," Turing said. "I suspect a hundred and forty-three is a pretty low total."

"Possibly because it's a weekend," Maude suggested. "Not as many people home to check their e-mail."

"Still, a hundred and forty-three people just as clueless as I used to be," Tim said, shaking his head.

Maude put her hand to her mouth and pretended to cough to hide her smile.

"Anyway," Turing continued. "I see all hundred and forty-three times the file has been accessed to write records. But so far no one has logged in to download it. That's what I mean by no one dropping by to pick them up."

"Can you do something before they do?" Maude asked.

"Working on it," Turing said. "Obviously, we could simply shut down the servers, now that we have access, but that might also alert the phisher and prevent us from identifying him."

"Yes, it would be better if you could identify him without letting him know it," Tim said.

"And without giving him those hundred and forty-three credit card numbers," Maude added.

"Stand by," Turing said. "Okay. All set."

"What's all set?"

"I've rigged it so anyone other than me who tries to log in won't really be logging in," Turing said. "They'll think they've logged in, but they'll be talking to me. I'll pretend to be the system."

"What if he tries to download the credit card numbers?"

"I'll give him a file of fake names and credit card numbers," Turing said. "Ones that look plausible but won't work if he tries them."

"Are you sure there's no way he can possibly guess that he's not really logged in?" Maude asked.

"Are you suggesting that I can't think faster than a mere hacker?" Turing asked, but sounding more playful than insulted.

"Perish the thought," Maude said, laughing. "But what if he tries something you don't expect? Like deleting a lot of data in an attempt to cover his tracks."

"Don't worry," Turing said. "If he tries deleting data, or for that matter, if he does anything I don't understand or don't want happening, I'll fake a server problem of some kind. Probably an I/O error; something he wouldn't waste time trying to work around. I have it. One false move from the phisher, and blam! Take that!"

Several lines of writing flashed onto the screen. Tim and Claudia bent over to read them and then looked at each other with puzzled faces. Maude stepped closer to the monitor and read:

```
14:17:30 stall1 kernel: hda: dma_intr: status=0x51 {
DriveReady SeekComplete Error }
```

```
14:17:31 stall1 kernel: sda: hma_intr: error=0x40 { Uncor-
rectableError }, LBAsect=17657850, high=1, low=880634,
sector=17657850
```

"That's nice," she said. "Does it mean anything?"

"Trust me," Turing said. "If the phisher knows UNIX, this will strike fear into his heart."

"I'll take your word for it," Maude said. She could tell that Turing was disappointed that they couldn't appreciate the brilliance of her strategy. Perhaps KingFischer would.

"The point is, I won't let him do anything dangerous," Turing said. "Our first priority is to protect the system and the data on it, including those credit card numbers, of course. Identifying him and keeping him from knowing that we've detected him are important, but second to that."

"So now what?" Maude asked.

"Now we wait for the phisher to drop by in cyberspace?" Tim asked.

"Precisely," Turing said.

As I expected, finding Eddie's password opened up whole new realms of information. I rather neglected Tim, Maude, and Claudia for the next two hours as I traveled through Eddie's systems. They all looked bored and impatient for me to come up with something for them to do. Which I hadn't yet, though I did display the more interesting finds on-screen from time to time, so they could follow what I was doing.

I wasn't just looking, of course. I was also methodically backing up all of Eddie's computers. Eventually we'd need to turn the phisher over to the police or the FBI, and odds were the first thing they'd do would be to take possession of all of Eddie's hardware, shutting us out. I wanted to make sure we still had access to all of Eddie's data if and when that happened. But once I'd set them in *motion, the backups didn't take up much of my attention. Just time.*

I studied the log file information on the previous occasions when someone opened up a relay on Eddie's system, sent through a chunk of e-mails, and then closed the relay. A dozen of them, but most were merely spam. Not that Viagra ads and variations on the old Nigerian scam were particularly praiseworthy, but at least there was only one previous phishing e-mail, sent about three weeks ago.

In his replies to the other system admins, Eddie claimed to have been hacked.

Maybe he had. But my analysis of his log files seemed to show that whoever opened and then closed the relay had been using Eddie's ID and password.

That didn't mean it was Eddie. Anyone who had access to his systems could have found the chance to crack his password file, as I had. But it certainly made it a lot more likely that the culprit was one of Eddie's friends. Probably one of the half-dozen Tim and Claudia had interviewed. I went through his entire e-mail box and found no evidence that he'd enlisted anyone else to take care of his systems while he was away. Which should mean that there was no one else who could logically steal Eddie's password.

I got on-line access to Eddie's bank account and realized that his creditors were doomed to disappointment. I doubted if he could satisfy even one of them with the thirty-seven cents he had left. In fact, even the thirty-seven cents weren't his. The last time he'd withdrawn cash, he'd triggered his overdraft protection, so he was actually three hundred ninety-nine dollars and sixty-three cents in the hole. Though he'd only gotten that broke recently.

Very recently. In fact, too recently.

"Maude," I said. "We need to call Eddie's bank right away. Someone's been using his ATM card."

I flashed the telephone number up on the screen.

"Since the accident, you mean?" Claudia asked.

"Someone stole it," Tim said.

"Damn," Maude said. She and Claudia both scrambled for

their cell phones, but Claudia won. I printed out a page of infor-
mation from the bank's website, showing the account number and
the date, time, and location of the withdrawals. She snagged it as
soon as it hit the printer's out tray and strode to the far end of the
room.

"When did this happen?" Tim asked.

"Last night and again this morning. They took out five hundred
dollars each time—the maximum the bank allows."

"It's not a joint account with his grandmother, is it?" Maude
asked. "She might have a lot of unusual expenses right now."

"He's the only signatory," I said.

"We should call that homicide detective," Tim said, pulling out
his notebook. "The one who interviewed us last night."

"Powell," Claudia said, putting her hand over the mouthpiece.
"I'll give the bank his number, too."

"I suppose we should let Mrs. Stallman know, if she's back,"
Maude said, though I noticed she didn't make a move to go upstairs
and check.

I returned to my journey through Eddie's files, feeling less wor-
ried that my human allies were getting bored. I suspected by the
time they'd finished dealing with the stolen bank card I'd have
found something else.

Saturday, 5:30 p.m.

Tim felt mildly indignant at Detective Pow-
ell's blasé reaction to the news of the stolen ATM card. Was
the detective expecting this? Had he perhaps known? Or
was he just the most unemotional son-of-a—

"Someone's logging in," Turing said.

"Logging in where?" Tim asked.

"Logging in to collect the results of the phishing
scheme," Turing said.

"Who is it?" Tim asked. "Can you tell yet?"

"Don't distract her," Claudia said.

Tim was about to make fun of the very idea of distracting

an AIP and remembered, just in time, that Claudia wasn't in on Turing's secret. Something they should fix before too long. But for now, he nodded and held his tongue.

"Whoever it is, he's logging in with Eddie's ID and password," Turing said, a few seconds later.

"That's bad, right?" Tim said.

"Very bad. It means that when we look back at the log files, we'll have a hard time telling what Eddie did and what the phisher did while pretending to be Eddie."

"We can be pretty sure anything that happened after midnight Wednesday wasn't Eddie," Maude said, in a grim tone.

"Does it also mean we'll have a hard time finding out who the guy is?" Tim asked.

"Not necessarily," Turing said. "KingFischer's got his IP address. We're looking it up."

"Of course, that only helps if we know who's behind the IP address," Maude said.

"Think positively," Claudia said. "My money's on Kristyn, the ex."

"Karl, our squeaky-clean AOL employee with the nasty sideline," Tim put in.

"It won't necessarily be anyone we know," Maude said.

"As it happens, it is," Turing said. "Matt Danforth."

"Matt?" Tim echoed. "Damn."

"Aren't you glad we didn't invite him over to help us deal with Eddie's computers?" Maude said.

"I can't believe it," Tim said, shaking his head. "He was the only one who seemed the least bit concerned about Eddie. Asked to be notified if anything happened."

"Probably wanted to make sure he knew the coast was still clear for him to run his phishing scheme," Claudia said.

"Can you stop him?" Tim asked.

"Stop him from doing what?" Turing asked. "I've already made sure he can't steal any usable credit card numbers. If I keep him from logging in or downloading the file or whatever else he tries to do, I'll warn him that we're on to him."

"Okay," Tim said. "But should we tell the cops about this, too? I mean, doesn't it make Matt a prime suspect?"

"Not necessarily," Turing said. "We don't know that the phishing scheme had anything to do with the hit-and-run."

"If it doesn't, it's a hell of a coincidence, don't you think?" Tim asked.

"Not really," Maude said. "Weren't you the one who called Eddie a trouble magnet? He's careless about security and trusts the wrong people. So he's hosting pornography that may or may not be legal and people are sending spam and worse through his servers with or without his permission—"

"With or without his knowledge, for that matter," Turing put in. "What if Danforth had nothing to do with the hit-and-run, but when he heard about it from you, realized that the coast was clear for him to use Eddie's equipment for his phishing scheme?"

"Sounds plausible to me," Claudia said. "Of course, I can also believe that Eddie found out Danforth was up to something and threatened to tell, leading Danforth to attack him to keep him quiet. As long as he's out of the way, temporarily or permanently, why not use his computers for the phishing scheme?"

"Or, just to be cynical, Eddie and Danforth were in on the phishing scheme together," Turing suggested. "Eddie demanded a larger share of the loot—after all, since they were using his machines, he was taking on a larger share of the risk. And Danforth figured out a way to take Eddie's share of the loot and tried to put Eddie out of the picture."

"Why stop at Eddie and Matt Danforth," Tim said. "Some of the others could be in on it, too. They could all be in on it. How do we even begin to figure it out?"

*   *   *

Saturday, 6:00 P.M.

Maude sat back in her chair and rubbed her temples. Around her, Tim, Maude, and Claudia continued debating their various theories of the case as they had been doing for—she glanced up—okay, it only seemed like years. But they'd been stuck in Mrs. Stallman's damp and chilly basement for too long. Arguing wouldn't solve the case. Night had fallen, and they needed to move on. Do something.

She felt a new appreciation for the complexity of Dan's work. Odds were, when the police began investigating the unauthorized withdrawals from Eddie's bank, they'd find a clear photo of the culprit in the ATM's camera. But the FBI not only had to catch the crooks committing on-line crimes, they also had to prove the person they'd caught was really the criminal, and not just a hapless patsy.

Maybe it was time to turn this over to them.

Though she realized she didn't know quite how to do that. Should she call the police? The FBI? Maybe call Dan and let him sort it out?

How would the others react? Not well, she suspected.

Just then she heard a noise upstairs. A key rattling in the front door.

"Mrs. Stallman's home," she said, standing up.

Neither Claudia nor Tim looked pleased at the news.

"Yes, she's annoying," Maude said. "But she's the client. We should probably bring her up to speed on what's been happening."

She started up the stairs.

"Mrs. Stallman?" she called.

She listened for a few seconds.

"Yes," said a voice from the upstairs.

Not a familiar voice, though. Maude stepped out into the

front hall and found herself face-to-face with a short, plump, and rather anxious-looking elderly woman.

"What are you doing here?" the woman asked, in a calm voice. Though Maude noticed that she had kept the front door open, as if to leave an escape path. And that she gripped the doorknob so hard that her slightly enlarged knuckles were white.

"May I help you?" Maude asked.

"Who are you?" the woman asked.

Maude frowned slightly. Shouldn't I be asking the questions? she thought. But then this woman obviously had some right to be here: she had a key to the house and felt sufficiently at home to confront a stranger, though she was visibly trembling and seemed on the verge of flight.

"I'm Maude Graham," she said. "I'm working for the private investigators Mrs. Stallman hired to investigate her grandson's hit-and-run accident and help keep his business running while he's in the hospital. And you are . . . ?"

"Oh, dear," the woman said. "I'm not sure I understand this. You see, I'm Eunice Stallman—and I don't recall hiring a private investigator."

"I'm not sure it's worth my continuing with this," Tim said, looking up from one of Eddie's e-mails to Matt Danforth. "I agree, someone should read them to look for any coded messages about the phishing scheme, but I'm not the right person. I can't tell when they're being deliberately cryptic and when it just sounds cryptic because I haven't the foggiest idea what they're talking about. Besides—"

"Heads up," Claudia stage-whispered, scampering down the stairs. "There's trouble."

"What kind of trouble?" Tim asked.

Maude followed Claudia down the stairs at a more sedate pace, accompanied by a petite, elderly woman.

"We've mainly been working down here," Maude said. "Trying to learn more about Eddie's business. Particularly to gain access to his computer systems, to see if there's anything that would support the theory that the hit-and-run was deliberate."

"Oh, my," the elderly woman said. "You have been busy. I don't think I've seen that much of the floor since Eddie moved in six years ago."

Tim frowned. Who was this old lady? Someone who knew the Stallmans, obviously, if she knew about Eddie's untidy habits, but why was she here? Why was Maude giving her the grand tour?

"This is Tim Pincoski," Maude said, turning to Tim. "Claudia's partner. Tim, this is Mrs. Stallman. The real Mrs. Stallman."

Tim's jaw dropped.

"You understand that we'll have to ask for some proof," Claudia said. "Just because you have a key—"

"I understand," the woman said. "After all, the imposter, whoever she is, probably had a key."

"How could she have gotten one?" Maude asked.

"It wouldn't be hard," the woman said, shaking her head. "Eddie forgets his keys so often that he's gotten into the habit of leaving the basement door unlocked. I keep nagging at him to stop, but . . ." She looked around and shrugged. "I nag him about keeping things down here clean, too, and you can see how well that works. Anyway, the imposter could have gotten in through the basement door and taken one of the sets of spare keys we keep hanging in the kitchen."

"So the woman who hired us was an imposter?" Tim asked.

The elderly lady held out a driver's license. Tim took it and scrutinized it. Looked authentic. Eunice S. Stallman, and the photo matched the woman in front of him.

"Perhaps you could scan it into the system?" Maude said,

motioning to Turing's camera. Tim held the license up to the camera. Turing didn't say anything, but after a few seconds, a message appeared on the laptop screen.

"Yes," the message said. "That matches what's on file in the DMV. Didn't we ever see a driver's license for the other one?"

Tim shook his head and handed the license back to the old lady. To Mrs. Stallman, apparently.

"I'm sure any of the neighbors would vouch for me if you're not sure," the woman said. "Or—Sachi!"

The large black cat had jumped down from the pipes and begun writhing around the woman's ankles, purring loudly. She bent down and began petting it.

"Oh, you poor thing," she said.

Tim looked at Maude, who nodded her head. At Claudia, who did the same.

"So that's your cat, Mrs. Stallman?" Tim said.

"Eddie's, actually," she said, looking up at Tim. "He dotes on Sachi. I gather you've been feeding her? I asked a friend to stop by and do it, but she said one of Eddie's friends told her he was taking care of it."

"I have been," Tim said. "We all have, but I don't recall talking to anyone who stopped by to do it."

"Neither did I," Maude said. "Did she get a name?"

"Can she give a description?" Claudia added.

"I'm sure we can ask her," Mrs. Stallman said. "Though it would be better to do it in the morning. I need to get over to the hospital to see Eddie. I only stopped by here to drop off my suitcase."

"You just got back in town?" Maude asked.

"Yes," she said. "Flew in from Fort Lauderdale. I was on a cruise when this horrible thing happened to Eddie. They didn't reach me with the news until Thursday evening, and I've been in transit since Friday morning. Is there any news?"

Tim and Claudia both looked at Maude, who shook her head.

"The only news we've had has come from the imposter,"

Maude said. "I have no idea if she's fooled the police and the hospital as well or if we're the only gullible ones."

"Let me call the hospital, then," Mrs. Stallman said. She went to the desk and moved aside a stack of papers to reach the phone. Either she'd scouted out the room pretty well while talking to them, or she already knew where the phone was. She took a small notebook out of her purse, opened it, and began dialing a number.

"If you'll excuse me," Maude said. "I need to call Sam. I'll just go up in the hall where I'm out of your way."

Good idea, Tim thought. Call Sam and find out exactly how much trouble we'll be in when they finish sorting this out.

Claudia picked up the laptop and moved it away from the desk, as if giving Mrs. Stallman more room. She took it to the far end of the basement and set it on the end of the bar, and from the looks of it, was conversing with Turing. She alternated bursts of rapid typing with spaces of looking at the screen and nodding or shaking her head.

As soon as she got off the phone, Tim thought, they could apologize and leave. He glanced around, inventorying the things of theirs that were in the basement. The laptop, of course, and—

"Oh, no!"

He looked back at Mrs. Stallman. She was still holding the phone, but not saying anything, and from the way she was staring into space, possibly not hearing anything. He took a step toward her. She looked up at him and then back at the phone.

"I'm sorry," she said. "That's quite a shock. I'll be over as soon as I can."

She hung up the phone and looked around.

"I don't suppose you found a phone book while you were tidying," she said. "I suppose not. Eddie would never use one; he'd just look things up on-line."

"Can we help?" Tim asked.

"I just need to call a cab," Mrs. Stallman said. "I need to get to the hospital. I have a phone book upstairs."

She took a step toward the stairs, then turned back to pick up her purse.

"I can drive you," Tim said. Claudia looked startled, and Tim had to confess he wasn't sure why he had volunteered.

"You don't have to go to that much trouble," Mrs. Stallman said.

"It's the least we can do, after this whole mix-up," Tim said.

"Thank you," Mrs. Stallman said. "I'd appreciate it."

It's my fault. I should have prevented this. I should have checked out the phony Mrs. Stallman more thoroughly.

"Nonsense," Maude said, when I apologized. "If anything, it was Tim's responsibility to check out Mrs. Stallman before he took her as a client. His or Sam's. Under the circumstances, it's not surprising they were fooled. I would have been myself."

"They did check her out," I said. "They had me run a background check on her, and everything looked fine. Except for the fact that the woman I was checking out wasn't the one hiring us."

"We'll know better next time," Maude said.

That doesn't make me feel better. Perhaps it's irrational, but I feel as if I have let my human allies down badly. After all, they have only so much time to think of things, only so much processing power.

Though perhaps it's not a case of inadequate processing power but a different kind of processing power. Humans have such skill at assessing new situations and deciding just how to deal with them. They improvise. They intuit. I'm not good at that.

I don't forget to perform some aspect of a background check. I don't absentmindedly forget to pull a credit history, or pull from only two of the three major credit reporting agencies. I don't accidentally make a typo when entering the subject's name or social security number. I don't forget to write up some key information in my report. If I know it should be done and how to do it, it gets done.

So now that I have expanded my background check procedures to include "compare potential client's DMV photo to client to ensure that s/he really is who s/he claims to be," we won't ever have this problem again.

But how can I ensure that I won't make some other, equally fundamental and damaging error of omission? That worries me.

I'm also fretting about how to break this news to KingFischer. Perhaps I should wait until we've successfully averted all possible problems arising from the mistake before I tell him.

That's assuming we can avert the problems.

I wish I knew what was going on at the hospital. If only Tim would check in.

For that matter, I'd settle for hearing what Sam thinks of our situation. Since Maude's on her cell phone, I can only hear her side of the conversation. For the last few minutes, that has consisted of nothing but a series of short responses.

"Yes."

"That's right."

"Yes, I understand."

"We can do that."

It's almost as if she were trying to puzzle me. That would serve me right, after the way I've let them down.

I seem to be suffering from what Maude calls "the guilts." Which, from her description, means not merely feeling guilty, but being unable to think of anything else—the human brain's equivalent of a program containing an endless loop. I should file away this line of thought and concentrate on practical measures we need to take.

But I think I'll wait until Maude gets off the phone.

Saturday, 6:30 P.M.

After talking with Sam, Maude felt—well, still anxious, but a lot less so.

"So what's the scoop?" Claudia asked. "Should we all go down and turn ourselves in for trespassing or something?"

"Sam said she can handle that," Maude said, "since we were acting in good faith."

"She's not worried?"

"I wouldn't say that. But she sounded cheerful, the way she always does when we give her some interesting legal work to do. So we should clear out and do our best not to upset the real Mrs. Stallman any more than we already have."

"Fine," Claudia said. "And hey, maybe the whole imposter deal isn't exactly bad news. It means the pornography and the phishing scheme and whatever other disgusting or illegal things Eddie has on his servers aren't our problems, right?"

"No," Maude said. "They happened on our watch. We have to do something."

"Not much we can do till we hear back from Mrs. Stallman," Claudia said. "Which probably won't happen till morning. I think we should make sure we pack up all our stuff and vamoose."

"I'm not sure everything can wait till morning," Maude said. "This phishing scheme—Turing, how hard would it be for someone to trace?"

"Not hard at all," Turing said. "We already traced Matt Danforth, remember? Of course, it was easy because we were on the inside—we had access to Eddie's systems. For anyone who didn't have that access—including us, before we uncovered Eddie's password—it would be hard to go any further back."

"So if anyone else traced it, the trail would end here."

"Uh-oh," Claudia said.

"That would depend on how savvy they were," Turing said. "Someone inexperienced might assume the trail ended here. Someone more savvy might suspect that Matt was only going through Eddie's systems, but they'd have a hard time finding him without the access we have."

"So if someone reports the phishing scam to the police or the FBI, they'll show up on Mrs. Stallman's doorstep," Maude said.

"Or possibly on the co-lo site's doorstep," Turing said. "Which amounts to the same thing."

"We need to do something," Maude said. "The sooner we report it, the easier it will be for us to prove our own innocence."

"We report it before someone else does," Claudia said, nodding.

"It may already be too late," Turing said. "He sent it to half a million people; what are the odds that none of them knows how to report the scheme?"

"As long as we report it before the cops show up and reasonably soon after it happened, we'll be okay," Maude said. At least she hoped that was how it worked.

"How do we do that?" Claudia asked. "I mean, do we just call the FBI's main number and say, 'Hey, I want to report a cybercrime'?"

"I'm checking the FBI's site," Turing said. "We can report it on-line. We could either submit a tip to the FBI at fbi.gov, or file a complaint at ic3.gov, the Internet Crime Complaint Center. I don't understand the difference, though."

"Either one will get us caught up in miles of federal red tape," Claudia said, shaking her head.

"I have an idea," Maude said. "I'll cut through the red tape. Let me use your laptop, Turing."

"Be my guest."

Maude went to the site that let her send and receive her e-mail from a web page and started an e-mail to Dan Norris. Then she sat back to ponder. Exactly how did you break the news to the FBI agent you were dating that you were probably about to make an unwanted appearance in his workload?

She typed and backspaced and revised for a good ten minutes before she was satisfied.

"How does this sound?" she said.

Dear Dan,
    My second day of working on the hit-and-run case has been less tedious—in fact, we've uncovered something, possibly unrelated to the accident, that may be an FBI matter. Could you give me a call whenever you get this, so I can fill you in and either formally report it or have you tell me to whom I should report it instead?
                          Maude

"How does that sound?" she asked, looking over her shoulder at Claudia and Turing's camera.

"Good," Claudia said. "Short and to the point; no sense in getting bogged down in the details."

"Especially since the details could change substantially between now and whenever he calls," Turing added.

"Here goes then."

She hit the send button and sat back.

"Of course, we have no idea how long it will be before he gets it, and how fast he'll call," she said.

"That's fine," Claudia said. "We're covered."

"The FBI may want to take possession of Eddie's hardware," Turing said. "For forensic analysis."

"So should we warn his clients that their sites could disappear at any moment?" Claudia asked.

"We could copy the data onto other machines and keep operating," Turing said. "Assuming the FBI is okay with it, and if we can get some servers ready. Do you suppose Casey would be well enough—"

"That's really Mrs. Stallman's problem now, isn't it?" Maude said. "If she tells us to get the hell out—"

"Then we do it," Turing said. "But I think we should at least offer to help with an orderly transition."

"Even if she wants us to do that, is there any reason we need to stay here to do it?"

"No," Turing said. "KingFischer and I can access all of Eddie's sites remotely if we need to. Even if someone—like the FBI—takes them over and shuts us out, I've got backups of everything. We could keep studying his sites using the backups."

"Good," Maude said. "Because I think Claudia had a good idea. Let's gather up our stuff and vamoose. But not before we make sure we're leaving the place in good condition. I don't want Mrs. Stallman to have anything more to complain about."

"Are you kidding?" Claudia said. "If she complains I vote we send her the bill for what you've done to the basement. Do you realize how much she'd have to pay a team of professional cleaners and organizers to do all this?"

"I think she'll have other things on her mind," Maude said, though she had to admit, she was pleased at the compliment.

As she surveyed the room and remembered what it had looked like when she started, she felt a strange sense of accomplishment. She'd created order out of chaos, and she couldn't help feeling that if they'd been allowed to continue with the case, the newfound order might help them uncover answers where now they had only questions.

Saturday, 6:45 P.M.

Mrs. Stallman looked so shaken that Tim didn't want to leave her alone at the hospital. He parked his car and went in. He made it all the way to the ICU before he realized maybe that wasn't such a great idea.

The smell hit him first—the faint antiseptic bleach odor. That, and the fact that everything seemed designed to be swabbed down regularly. People bled here and had painful things done to them, and sometimes they didn't leave.

Then he spotted the rooms: a long row of glass-fronted cubicles along the side of the main ICU room. Each had a curtain the nurses could draw for privacy, but most of the time they left the curtains open, so they could see everyone.

And so could anyone walking through.

Someone inside a room moaned occasionally. Not constantly, or even often enough that Tim could get used to it. Just often enough to unnerve him about the time he began to relax.

Mrs. Stallman was down the hall, talking to the doctor. Perhaps he ought to go down there. Be supportive. But that would mean walking past all those glass-fronted rooms.

Not a good idea. He wasn't too steady on his feet right now.

He was wondering if he could pretend to need another bathroom break when Mrs. Stallman turned around, spotted him, and beckoned.

Tim walked down the room toward her, deliberately not looking left or right, though he couldn't shut his ears. From some rooms he could hear machine noises: beeps, buzzes, humming motors, wheezing sounds.

Eddie's room had machines. A lot of them.

He focused on Mrs. Stallman, blocking out the sights on either side.

"We're going to do it now," Mrs. Stallman said. "Would you . . . I'd like it if you could come with me. Of course, I'd understand if you don't want to."

Do what? Some medical procedure, obviously. Either he'd missed something or Mrs. Stallman didn't realize he wasn't up to speed. Whatever it was, he wanted out.

Not just because he was squeamish. Okay, he seriously didn't want to see the machines making the faint hissing and beeping noises, much less the frail human attached to them. If it was just a stranger he could handle it. He could

pretend it was a movie. Special effects. Today we shoot the
scene in the ICU. What he really wasn't sure he could handle was seeing the person whose life he'd been studying for
the last two days. He already had trouble telling which Eddie was real. Eddie, the cynical, opportunistic hacker, or Eddie the struggling owner of a small business. Eddie who
preyed on naïve computer users, or Eddie whose more cun-
ning friends preyed on him. Eddie the thief or Eddie the du-
tiful grandson. There were too many Eddies, and Tim
wanted more time to sort them out before adding yet another one—Eddie, the helpless ICU patient. Eddie who, from
the look of things, wasn't doing so well. Eddie turned from
an intriguing puzzle into a real human being.

But Mrs. Stallman was gazing up at him with that patient look, as if she assumed he'd wimp out. And she was
such a nice old lady—not at all like the fake grandmother. He
made himself walk forward until he was at her side and could
hold out his arm to steady her.

"Thank you," she said.

Tim concentrated on her, on making sure she didn't trip
or stumble, until they stopped beside the bed. Then he
looked up.

He's just a kid, he thought.

Eddie Stallman looked small in the middle of the hospital bed—small and helpless in the grip of the machines and
tubes. Metal things loomed on either side. His right leg was
in a cast and hung from a metal frame, and to his left a
smaller metal frame, like a minimalist hat stand on wheels,
supported a clear plastic IV bag from which a long tube
snaked down and disappeared in a wad of tape and gauze
on Eddie's arm. Tim focused on the IV line for a few moments before gathering the courage to look up at Eddie's
head.

He assumed Mrs. Stallman recognized Eddie, but he
wasn't sure he would have. Most of Eddie's head was

wrapped in bandages. His eyes were closed and the flesh around them seemed swollen and bruised. A clear, pear-shaped plastic mask covered his mouth and nose and sprouted a tube that led to a machine that made a pumping noise like a high-tech bellows. A respirator, evidently.

Tim started slightly as a nurse pulled the curtains closed at the front of the room, the rattle of the curtain rings on the rail sounding strangely loud. Then she went to the head of Eddie's bed. Tim stepped aside and wished he hadn't. From his new angle, he could see a tube emerging from the bandages at the top of Eddie's head. He swallowed and fixed his eyes on Mrs. Stallman.

The door opened. It was the gray-haired doctor again. Mrs. Stallman only glanced up briefly.

"We don't have to do this tonight," the doctor said. "If you need more time—"

She shook her head.

"What good would that do?" she asked. "And can you be absolutely sure he isn't suffering?"

Tim didn't hear the doctor say anything. Maybe he shook his head, because Mrs. Stallman spoke again.

"Go ahead," she said, her voice slightly hoarse. "Get it over with."

Oh, my God, Tim thought, closing his eyes briefly. Eddie's not just going to die quietly offstage. They're pulling the plug. Now.

He'd seen dead people. Had seen people die. But he'd never seen anyone die in the middle of the high-tech trappings of a modern hospital. If they got you to the hospital in time, you were supposed to pull through.

They'd probably been waiting until Mrs. Stallman arrived to take Eddie off life support.

He forced himself to breathe evenly and focus on Mrs. Stallman's face. She watched, outwardly calm, as the doctor did something. One of the noises, a rhythmic electronic beep, began to stutter and then turned into a steady drone. Then he heard rustling, a click, and the noise stopped altogether.

Mrs. Stallman continued to look steadily for several eternities before turning away. She glanced up at Tim's face and nodded at the door.

Tim wasn't quite sure who was supporting whom on the way out. And he didn't feel much better back in the corridor outside the ICU. Mrs. Stallman and the doctor talked, briefly, and then Mrs. Stallman tapped Tim's arm.

"I'm sorry," she said. "Are you all right?"

"I'm fine," he said, though he didn't think he sounded convincing. "What about you?"

She patted his arm and turned toward the exit.

She didn't say anything on the way to the car. Tim had helped her into the passenger seat and buckled himself into the driver's side when she finally spoke.

"Do you really think someone deliberately tried to kill Eddie?" she asked, in a calm, quiet voice.

Tim had been reaching to start the car. He took his hand away from the key and turned to face her.

"I don't know," he said. "I think it's possible, but I don't know for sure. I do know that one of Eddie's friends is up to something illegal. At least one; maybe several."

"Do you think Eddie was involved?"

"Possibly," he said. "More likely the friend was using him. Taking advantage of him. Maybe even getting him in trouble."

"This woman who impersonated me—do you have any idea why?"

"Not yet," he said. "But I'll find out. I want to know who killed Mr. Meekins, too."

"Meekins?" Mrs. Stallman looked puzzled.

"Mr. Wilmer Meekins," Tim said. "He witnessed the hit-and-run. He told the police it wasn't an accident, and they didn't believe him. Then someone murdered him last night. Probably Eddie's . . . Eddie's killer. To cover up the crime."

He stopped himself from going on about Mr. Meekins. Why should Mrs. Stallman care? As far as Tim could see, he was the only one upset about the old man's death, and even that was more out of guilt than anything else.

Mrs. Stallman nodded. She didn't say anything for a few long moments, but Tim had the feeling she wasn't finished.

"I assume," she said finally, "that since the person who hired you did so under false pretenses, you're under no further obligation to her. So I can hire you to finish what you've started. But reporting to me, this time. I want to know who killed Eddie, and why, and who that imposter was, and yes, what those sneaky friends of his were up to. Are up to. Can you do that?"

Tim nodded.

"Take me home, then," Mrs. Stallman said. She fastened the belt and sat back in the seat, looking straight ahead, both hands gripping the purse on her lap.

"Yes, ma'am," Tim said, as he started the car.

Saturday, 8:15 P.M.

Just as Maude and Claudia were ready to leave, Tim called to tell them to stay. Eddie had died at the hospital, and the real Mrs. Stallman wanted us to investigate his death. She also suspected murder.

While she talked with Maude and Claudia about this, I checked with Sam, since I could do so without Mrs. Stallman hearing.

"If you're positive she's legit," Sam said. "You've checked this one out more than Tim did with the first one, I gather?"

"She's legit," I said. "She matches the photo in the DMV file; there were albums in the house—tucked away in a drawer, probably by the imposter—that contained photos of her with Eddie, and Schrödinger recognized her. Although Schrödinger's real name is Sachi."

"Schrödinger?"

"The family cat," I said. "She ran away whenever the imposter appeared, but she likes this Mrs. Stallman. We took this as additional corroboration of the new Mrs. Stallman's identity. My research indicates it would be fairly difficult to co-opt a cat."

"Next to impossible," Sam said, laughing. "Get the new Mrs. Stallman to sign a standard contract."

"Do we really need to worry about money at a time like this?" I asked.

"No, but we sure as heck need to worry about not having your three human friends thrown in jail."

"Roger," I said. "Printing out a contract now."

"Be careful," Sam said. "This would not be a good time to play fast and loose with the rules, you hear? Check in more often. This whole thing makes me nervous, and you know how I get when I'm nervous."

So we brought Mrs. Stallman up-to-date on the investigation—actually, Maude, Tim, and Claudia did, explaining me away as a computer expert teleconferencing in.

Unfortunately, the new Mrs. Stallman didn't seem to know much more about Eddie's business than the old one. And seemed strangely reluctant to involve the police any more than they already were. Anxious about what would result from our reporting the phishing scheme and reluctant to report the imposter.

"I think it's important for us to bring the police up to speed," Maude said. "There are too many strange circumstances and loose ends. The imposter's the biggest loose end—what was she up to? What if she was planning to use the information we found for some kind of fraud or confidence scheme?"

"What if she's already pulled one off?" Claudia said.

"I think I'd feel better about involving the police if I knew there wasn't anything that would cause us a problem," Mrs. Stallman said finally.

"You mean anything shady that Eddie was involved in," Maude said.

"I don't think he'd deliberately do anything shady," Mrs. Stallman said. "But he's always been—well, a little gullible."

Maude nodded sympathetically.

"A little?" *Claudia muttered, but so softly that even my microphone barely caught it, so I'm not sure anyone else heard.*

"And perhaps a bit too easily led," *Mrs. Stallman continued.* "I do think those friends of his took advantage."

A pity Eddie hadn't listened more to his girlfriend and his grandmother.

"I really don't think the gambling was a good idea," *Mrs. Stallman went on.*

"Gambling?" *Claudia repeated.* "Eddie was a gambler?"

"Oh, no," *Mrs. Stallman said.* "But he was considering hosting one of those on-line casinos. I told him it was a bad idea. I mean, you know it's all controlled by the Mafia. I knew no good would come of his getting involved with that."

Maude frowned, looking slightly puzzled, and looked down at the laptop screen. I displayed a message on-screen:

"Mafia? Gambling?" *it said.* "No sign of either."

"Perhaps he took your advice," *Maude said.* "Because we haven't found anything to indicate that Eddie had gotten mixed up in that. Though obviously we'll continue to keep our eyes open."

"That's a relief," *Mrs. Stallman said.* "Though it's not much of a relief, is it? I mean, someone got him anyway. But still, it's nice to know he wasn't doing anything . . . unpleasant."

Or illegal. Perhaps her belief that Eddie was hosting gambling sites accounted for her reluctance to talk to the police. I wondered if she knew about the pornography.

The conference dragged on, without much else happening. Mrs. Stallman couldn't add much to our knowledge of Eddie's friends and his business. She has no interest in continuing to run the business, so Maude agreed that we would help Mrs. Stallman find a new web hosting company to take over running Eddie's sites as soon as possible. Not that Mrs. Stallman had much trouble convincing her: Maude's anxious to get out of the business of running pornography sites; I can tell.

At some point during the web hosting discussion I noticed Claudia suppressing a yawn and sympathized.

Though perhaps my low mood could be explained by the sight of Sachi the cat sitting on Mrs. Stallman's lap. I had to remind myself that she wasn't a traitor. Mrs. Stallman was part of her real family; doubtless Sachi was glad to have her back. She was probably still expecting Eddie, if cats think about such things.

Still, I was disappointed. I'd already decided that Tim would be the right person to keep the cat for me, since Maude was allergic and already had my garden. I'd studied the layout of his apartment and determined the optimal location for the litter box, and I'd already found several on-line pet stores that would ship food, litter, and other supplies directly to his door. I was even ready to hire someone to come in several times a week to change the litter box if he balked at doing this, though I hadn't yet found an on-site litter changing service. Still, I was sure I could find someone willing if the fee was enough. I had everything planned.

I felt bereft. How foolish to mourn over losing something that was never really mine.

When the conference broke up, I had Maude plug my spare waldo into the machine we'd hooked up to Eddie's network, the one to which we'd already attached my spare camera. I reminded her of the intruder we'd had on Friday, and how frustrating it was that we'd never know if he'd come back and done something in the basement overnight. Hooking my peripherals up would let me stand guard, I reminded her.

Maude probably guessed but was nice enough not to mention that the only reason I wanted the waldo was to pet the cat.

Saturday, 11:45 p.m.

Tim turned over onto his left side and tried to drift back to sleep, but he'd been tossing and turning too much. The sheets were tangled around his legs; the pillow had gotten wedged down between the headboard and the mattress, and by the time he'd fixed both problems, he was wide awake again. He rolled onto his back and resigned himself to insomnia.

He felt half-inclined to log in and apologize to Turing for making fun of her quantum cat story. Yes, it was possible to be both dead and alive at the same time, thanks to modern medicine. It bothered him that he hadn't known how badly off Eddie was the past few days. He had a strange sense of being cheated. Which was totally irrational; nothing they'd done over the last two days would have been changed at all if Eddie had been merely unconscious but destined to survive, or, for that matter, if he'd been dead on arrival at the hospital.

But still, he had that strange feeling. Partly being cheated. Missing out on something.

Stupid. He'd have probably loathed Eddie if they'd ever really met. They'd have had nothing in common, and Eddie would probably have been rude and supercilious to someone who knew as little about computers as Tim.

And partly something else. Not grief; he wasn't mourning Eddie. He felt bad for Mrs. Stallman, who seemed like a nice person and didn't have any other family. She was genuinely grieving. He supposed he felt the appropriate regret any civilized person would on hearing about someone dying prematurely, unnecessarily, violently.

He suddenly realized that he wasn't entirely sure he wanted to know what he was feeling. He sat up, turned the light on—it wasn't as if he'd get much sleep anyway—and studied the stack of books he kept by the side of the bed. He was in the middle of three books, but none of them appealed to him at the moment. Nor any of the things that he'd put there intending to read next. He dug deeper in the pile and pulled out an old favorite. Chandler's *The Big Sleep*.

He realized, after a few pages, that the familiar, well-loved words didn't have their usual power to transport him. Instead of the vintage California landscape, he saw images of the deceptively peaceful tree-lined streets of Arlington, where Eddie Stallman had lived and died. Still, he kept going, focusing as much of his attention as he could manage on the book, the way someone crossing a chasm on a narrow board would look ahead and not at the dizzying depths below.

Midway through, he realized that maybe the end of the book, with Philip Marlowe's poetic meditation on death, wasn't exactly what he should be reading in his present mood. But he kept on until reached the death of Harry Jones, the harmless little guy who was just trying to help somebody out.

Wilmer Meekins. He acted like a curmudgeon, but underneath that, he was a pretty harmless little guy, too. And maybe in his own way he was trying to help. Tim wondered if he'd ever get over the feeling that he'd caused Mr. Meekins's death.

And was there something he should have seen about Meekins's murder? Who besides their team had any idea that Meekins might have been about to speak?

He should figure that out. But in the morning. The book was sliding out of his hands, and he barely managed to turn out the light before he fell asleep.

Sunday, 1:15 A.M.

I'm worried about Tim and Maude.

I know they're both up. Tim keeps his computer on in the living room of his small basement apartment. An hour ago, I saw the light go on in his bedroom, and it's still on. Maude's computer is in her study, on the first floor. When she got home, she turned the lights off downstairs and went up. I thought she had gone to bed, but the faint spill of light from the hallway never disappeared, and fourteen minutes ago I heard her passing by the office, on her way to the kitchen.

They should be resting. Sleeping. Restoring their strength. Tomorrow could be a long and difficult day. I want them at their best.

*It's not just that. I know both of them well enough to have an
idea why they might be having trouble sleeping.*

*Tim saw someone die today. He gets depressed about deaths. Of
course, so far the deaths that have depressed him have always been
ones for which he felt in some way responsible. Deaths he felt he
should have foreseen or prevented. I can't imagine any way he could
hold himself responsible for Eddie's death. The hit-and-run happened before Tim was even hired. Even if he failed to prevent Mr.
Meekins's death, I don't see how anyone could hold him responsible.
Surely the police are more to blame than he is.*

*But he won't see it that way. Even if he does, I'm worried that
sooner or later he will be upset by a death, like Eddie's, for which
he's not in any way responsible. One that doesn't give him any reason to feel guilty. Without the comfortable pain of guilt, he might
find himself stranded alone with the far more painful inevitability
of death. I've read about humans spiraling into a depression under
those circumstances.*

*I'm probably one of the few sentient beings on the planet who can
contemplate the human lifespan as a neutral observer. I have no idea
whether to pity or envy them, because I have no idea whether we
AIPs will be mortal or immortal. If mortal, with what kind of
lifespan? Have I nearly completed mine, or do I have centuries left to
run? Yes, most humans are equally in the dark about how long
they'll live, but at least they have some actuarial data to work with.*

*If we're immortal—well, the thought of outliving the world I
know and understand, and the human friends I've made—that
doesn't seem like the boon humans usually think immortality
would be.*

*I almost wish one of them would log in to talk and distract me
from these gloomy thoughts. But Tim probably won't, because he
thinks dark night thoughts are something you need to grapple with
alone.*

*I'm guilty of that myself at times. That's probably why I
haven't yet told anyone about the latest message from T2. If that's
what it was—I still can't prove it wasn't just a passage from an*

unpublished novel. I tell myself it's better to wait until things quiet down to tell them about it. That I should put it aside myself, for the time being. Instead, I brood about it, especially now when things have grown quiet.

And Maude won't log in to talk because I'm part of what she's fretting about. That once again, my actions, my needs, my very existence, are threatening to drive a wedge between her and Dan Norris.

Come to think of it, maybe I don't want to talk to Maude until she's worked through it again. If I could do or say anything to help, I would have long ago. Maybe it's cowardly, but I'd rather just talk to her again in the morning, when she's her normal, calm, daytime self again.

All I can do is watch to see how late their lights stay on, and hope when the lights finally go out that it's because they're sleeping.

So I resigned myself to fretting, as I often do at night. It's the downside of befriending humans. We embark on something like this case of Tim's, and just about the time things get interesting—more than interesting; exciting and downright ominous—the humans all go off to sleep. It's not as if they do it deliberately; they can't help it. You can't really push them too far beyond their normal hours, any more than you can keep using a laptop when the battery's getting low. They become cranky, less efficient, and eventually crash anyway. The humans, I mean; though I suppose the laptops don't behave that much differently either. It's worse when, like tonight, they need to sleep and can't. The temptation to contact them becomes almost irresistible, even though I know they need the sleep far more than I need the company.

I've learned to live with it. But that doesn't mean I like it.

I decided to keep myself busy.

Since most of the things that we needed to do were things for which I needed human help, I decided to distract myself by examining the files on Eddie's server in more detail. Arguably a gross invasion of his friends' and customers' privacy, but I didn't care—one of those people might be a murderer. Though I had to admit that the odds were slim that I'd find anything on Eddie's network that would help me prove that.

I was about to start with the files on his home network, but it occurred to me that all of Eddie's friends knew about his accident. If one of them was the killer, he knew days before we did and could have deleted anything incriminating. Or better yet, overwrite dangerous files with a harmless file of the same name. I looked for files that had been updated recently—starting a few days before his accident, to cover the possibility that the guilty person had done the cleanup and then gone after Eddie.

Most of the recently dated files looked legit. But one of Matt Danforth's intrigued me. He'd called it "results0923." Which could be the month and day the file was originally created. Or perhaps not; it would have been more methodical to include the year as well. The file itself was blank, and had been yesterday, when I took my backups of Eddie's servers.

But I also had Eddie's backup—the one Schrödinger/Sachi had found. I'd copied it to my system when I'd used it to hack Eddie's passwords. He'd made it at four in the morning on the Sunday before he died. And yes, it contained an earlier version of results0923. This version, dated October 1, contained 192 entries. A list of names, addresses, social security numbers, and credit card numbers, in the same format as the output from Matt's Saturday afternoon phishing scheme.

He'd done it before and gotten away with enough information to steal nearly two hundred people's identities.

And the evidence was right there in Eddie's backup CD. All we had to do was point the FBI at it.

The FBI and the Arlington police—though if Wilmer Meekins's murder hadn't made them reclassify Eddie's death as a suspected homicide, I wasn't sure a case of credit card fraud and identity theft would make any difference. But we had to try.

I wanted to share this news, but of course Tim and Maude had turned out their lights by this time. It would have to wait till morning.

*   *   *

Sunday, 12:35 P.M.

"Of course, we still don't know if Danforth did this all by himself," Maude said, after Turing had explained her finds. "Some of the others could have been in on it."

"They could all have been in on it," Turing agreed. "Even Eddie. For all we know, Eddie could have been the ringleader. That's probably something for the FBI to untangle."

Maude nodded and helped herself to more kung pao chicken. Turing sounded surprisingly willing—almost eager—to turn the case over to others. Was it real, or was she up to something? She glanced over at Tim, but he had drifted off to sleep with half an eggroll still clutched in one hand.

Let him sleep, poor thing, she thought. He looked as if he'd had a hard night. A wakeful night. Seeing Eddie Stallman die had shaken him. Maude wanted to blame Mrs. Stallman, but the woman was clearly quite upset herself and probably had no idea how much Tim would be affected.

Still, she hoped Mrs. Stallman would keep out of her way for now. Maude had sent her upstairs to nap—she'd obviously had a largely sleepless night as well.

Though she wouldn't get much sleep if people kept dropping by, Maude thought, as she heard the doorbell ring again. So far, two neighbors had dropped by already, bearing casseroles. She headed upstairs to intercept the latest food offering before the doorbell woke Mrs. Stallman.

"Coming," she called, when the doorbell rang again.

She stopped in surprise when she saw a familiar, angular face peering in through the glass panel beside the door. Dan Norris. He'd spotted her, too, and he didn't look happy.

"What are you doing here?" she said, as she opened the door.

"You stole my line," he said. "Only I was going to say, 'What the hell are you doing here?' This is where your client lives?"

"Yes," she said, standing aside so he could enter. "Mrs. Eunice Stallman. Of course, you probably already know that."

"Actually, I'm here to talk to her grandson, Eddie," Dan said. "Have you met him?"

"Not exactly," Maude said. "I've seen him, of course. But you're too late."

"He's taken off somewhere?" Dan asked, his voice suddenly sharp.

"He's dead."

"Dead? When? What happened? You said you weren't doing anything dangerous."

"He died last night," she said. "From injuries received in a hit-and-run accident Wednesday. I told you about this Friday, remember?"

"You didn't mention Eddie Stallman's name, or I would have—well, never mind. I deduce that if Eddie was in an accident on Wednesday and died on Saturday, he wasn't in particularly good shape in between."

"He'd been in the ICU."

"So it's unlikely he was using a computer yesterday and the day before."

"Unlikely? Try impossible," Maude said. "In a coma, on a respirator, and hooked up to about a million tubes."

"Damn," Norris said, shaking his head. "Poor kid."

"Of course, his friends have still been using his system," Maude said. "Quite possibly taking advantage of the fact that he wasn't around to see what they're doing."

"I need to talk to the friends, then," Norris said, looking less disappointed.

"About the phishing scheme," Maude said, nodding.

"Phishing scheme?"

"You didn't get my message then?"

"Message? What message? I checked my voice mail an hour ago and you weren't on it."

"It was an e-mail," she said. "Telling you that we thought we'd uncovered someone running a phishing scheme using Eddie Stallman's computers, and asking if there was something I should do to formally report it or if telling you sufficed."

"I hate to speak ill of the dead," Dan said. "But Eddie Stallman has—had—some rather unsavory friends."

"Tell me about it," Maude said. "Literally, if you can; we've spent the last three days poking into every aspect of Eddie's life. We've learned a little bit about his friends; I'm intimately familiar with every scrap of paper in his office; and we've finally gotten into his systems to see what's there. If you tell us what you're looking for, maybe we can help."

"*We* meaning you and Tim and your reclusive boss?" Norris said.

"And Claudia," Maude added. "Though she isn't here at the moment."

Dan studied her for a few long seconds.

"All right," he said. "I don't suppose you have anything I could eat? The airlines don't even give you ersatz food these days unless you pay extra."

"Leftover Chinese downstairs," Maude said, pointing to the stairs. "In Eddie's lair."

"Okay," he said, starting for the stairs. "You're on."

I didn't think anything of it when Maude went upstairs to answer the door. But I was surprised and somewhat anxious when she returned with Dan Norris. I wasn't the only one. Tim didn't look happy, either.

"It turns out that Dan's case is intersecting ours in some fashion," Maude said. "He's going to fill us in."

"I assume your friend Ms. Grace is logged in on that laptop with the cameras," Norris said, as he surveyed the room.

I felt strangely vulnerable. Not knowing what was going on, I waited for Maude or Tim to answer.

"Yes," Maude said. "Though I don't know if she's at her computer this minute."

"I am," I said. "What's up?"

In front of people who aren't in on my secret, I say as few words as possible. My voice generation is good, but far from perfect.

"I might as well tell the three of you at once," Norris said. "Unless you want to wait for Ms. Diaz to get here."

"We'll fill her in," Maude said. "Have a seat." She handed him a Diet 7 Up she'd taken out of Eddie's refrigerator, and was filling a plate with leftover Chinese food. Norris looked around, studied Eddie's ramshackle desk chair for a few seconds, and then settled for crossing his arms and leaning his long, lean frame against the outside of the bar counter.

Why is he here? I wanted to ask Maude. Is he answering your e-mail this soon? Or had the FBI already discovered the phishing scheme?

"Dan hasn't yet read the e-mail I sent him," she said, as if reading my mind. "Though we can fill him in about that after he tells us why he's here and tells us how we can help him."

Norris looked at Tim and at my laptop for a few moments before speaking.

"You know what a white-hat hacker is?" he asked.

Maude glanced at me, and then realized I was relying on her to do most of the talking.

"Someone who uses hacking techniques for legitimate purposes," she said. "Like the person we hire to do pen testing on our systems. Or, for that matter, your colleagues in the FBI."

Norris nodded.

"What's pen testing?" Tim asked.

"Penetration testing," Maude said. "Once we've made our security as strong as we can, we need to test it. We get an expert who tries to break in—penetrate our security. If they succeed, they tell us how they did it. Help us fix the flaws in our security."

"So the expert you'd hire would be one of these white-hat hackers?"

If Norris hadn't been there, I'd have explained that we didn't really need to hire anyone when we had me and KingFischer.

"Right," Maude said.

"Of course, everyone has a different definition of what a white-hat is," Norris said. "To me, an important part is that you have not just good intentions but some legitimate authority for what you're doing—that you've been hired or recruited by a law enforcement agency, or an organization that owns the system you're testing. Not everyone feels that way. Some people feel compelled to go around doing their own freelance pen testing."

"Is that a bad thing?" Tim asked.

"Not necessarily," Norris said, "As long as they notify the owner of the system about any problems and don't cause any mischief while they're in, just because they can. And as long as they use common sense about their targets. These days, if anyone starts pen testing systems over at the Pentagon they'll find themselves in a whole world of trouble. And waste resources we'd rather use on the real bad guys."

"I promise to start my hacking career on unclassified targets," Tim said.

"Then you get guys who go after sites they disapprove of," Norris went on.

"You're talking about vigilantes," Maude said.

Norris nodded.

"The guy I'm looking for probably thinks of himself as a white-hat," he said. "But to me, he's a vigilante. And a problem."

I panicked slightly when he said that. Could he be here because of something I had done? Or KingFischer? If trying to solve Eddie Stallman's murder brought us to the attention of the FBI . . .

"What's he doing?" Tim asked, wide-eyed.

"Going after pornography sites," Norris said. "Burning them—

seizing control, deleting all the files, putting up diatribes about ob-scenity in place of the original site."

"What's wrong with that?" Tim asked.

"Technically, you know, they're legal," Maude said. "With limited exceptions."

"Too limited," Norris said, and from Maude's slight, uncon-scious nod and the expression of disgust on her face, I gathered she agreed.

"Though not many people seem to care all that much about the legality," Norris added.

"So the problem is that the vigilante is breaking the law by burning these pornography sites," Tim said, nodding. "And dis-tasteful as you find the sites, you have to defend the owners' first amendment right to host them."

"Not exactly," Norris said. "Though we do have cases like that. This one's more complicated. This guy's going after the illegal sites."

"The kind of site you'd prefer to investigate yourselves," Maude said.

"In most cases, the very sites we're already investigating," Nor-ris said.

"Sounds to me as if the guy's saving you a lot of trouble," Tim said. "So this is some kind of jurisdictional thing?"

"A turf thing, you mean? No," Norris said, sounding slightly angry. "It's a very real problem."

"Think about it, Tim," Maude said. "Why were you so careful to stick to investigating Eddie's business instead of his murder?"

"The cops don't like a PI getting in their way," he said, shrug-ging. "Interfering with their investigation."

"Anything wrong with that?" Norris growled.

"No," Tim said. "If Detective Powell had said that they were looking into Eddie's business as part of his homicide investigation and I should stay out of their way, we'd have had to drop the case. I even tried to talk him into it after Mr. Meekins was killed."

"Who's Mr. . . . never mind," he said, frowning at Maude.

"*Later, when we have time, we need to discuss your definition of 'not dangerous and not particularly interesting.'*"

"*A lot has happened since we talked,*" Maude said.

"*Evidently,*" Norris said. "*Anyway, last week, we were closing in on a guy operating a child pornography site. We'd spent months building a case against the guy, and we were taking him down. We had all the warrants issued, and we were coordinating with the local authorities on the arrest, which was supposed to happen Friday. Then someone burned his site. Not just the porn files but all his business records, e-mails, log files. Destroyed all the evidence.*"

"*You couldn't just go after him with what you'd already collected?*" Tim asked.

Norris shook his head.

"*We had enough to get a warrant,*" he said. "*But to put together a case we could take to a jury, we needed to tie it back to material we could prove was on computers in his possession or under his control. The guy kept almost everything electronically on his computer.*"

"*Like Eddie,*" Tim muttered.

"*So the vigilante has pretty much destroyed our chances of arresting the guy anytime soon.*"

"*Right,*" Tim said, nodding. "*You have to start all over again. Months of work down the drain.*"

"*And months more suffering for the children he's exploiting,*" Norris said. "*What's more, these guys network like you wouldn't believe, which means if you arrest one, sometimes you can take down others, dozens of others, using what you learn from seizing the first guy's computers, what he'll offer in exchange for leniency. At least we used to. But lately, thanks to the vigilante, our guys show up at the door with an arrest warrant only to find the pornographer practically having a coronary because his whole system just imploded. Only it doesn't take him long to realize that the vigilante just did him a big favor. Not only do we lose any real chance of convicting him, all his friends are off the hook, too. And warned.*"

"*What does this have to do with Eddie Stallman?*" Tim asked.

"The vigilante's using Eddie's system, isn't he?" Maude asked.

"Not regularly," Norris said. "Or we'd have been here sooner. But yes, last night we determined that something the vigilante did came through Eddie's servers. It looked like someone exploiting a flaw in his security. It didn't seem likely that Eddie was the actual vigilante, but it seemed highly probable that he knew who the vigilante was."

"Why?" Maude asked. "I thought that's what hackers did—find security flaws and use them. How can you be so sure that of all the hackers in the world, the one who did this is one of Eddie's friends?"

"Because Eddie's not that careless," I said.

"Come again?" Norris said.

"The vigilante Norris is looking for and the phisher we uncovered aren't exploiting known flaws in the hardware or software that Eddie just hasn't fixed," I said. "If that's how they were getting in, we'd have gotten access to his system a lot sooner. That's the first thing we tried—seeing if Eddie had left any ports open or failed to apply the latest patches. But he hadn't. Eddie's not careless about technology. He's only careless about people."

I realized, about then, that I'd gotten carried away. Said too much in my ever-so-slightly artificial voice. But Norris didn't seem to notice. He was listening intently and nodding slightly.

"Sounds plausible to me," Maude said.

"Yeah, that's Eddie," Tim said. "Trusts the wrong people, sometimes."

"Someone he trusted took advantage of him," I said. If Norris hadn't noticed anything wrong by now, a few more sentences probably wouldn't hurt. "They configured in weaknesses. Back doors that only they knew how to use. That's what the phisher used, and I bet that's what the vigilante used, too."

Norris nodded.

"So tell me about this phisher," he said.

After that, we had a busy afternoon. Once we'd briefed Norris on the phisher—Maude did most of the talking, since I was still wary of saying too much in front of Norris in my electronically gen-

erated voice and Tim only vaguely understood the whole thing—he made some phone calls, and within the hour, a crew of technicians descended on Mrs. Stallman's basement. Norris took Maude and Tim upstairs to continue the interview.

"That's my laptop," Maude said, pointing to it as she left the room. "I can move it if you like. Or just push it out of the way."

A smart move; Maude guessed, correctly, that with the FBI doing forensics on Eddie's network, I wouldn't be as free to log in through the machine to which we'd connected the spare camera. The technicians nodded and proceeded to ignore my laptop. I was surprised that Norris didn't insist that she take it away immediately. After all, he knew about my cameras. But he didn't object, and I had no problem observing the first hour or so of what the technicians were doing.

Nothing surprising. I eavesdropped as they retraced what I'd found, nodded their approval at my quick thinking, and then moved on to scouring the log files for evidence—not only about the phishing scheme, but about any other irregularities that might have occurred on Eddie's equipment. A good thing I'd been careful not to connect to the system directly. They might be impressed with the skill and quick thinking of the "technician" who'd logged in to help Maude unmask the phisher, but they had no clues that I was anything other than human.

I fretted over why they hadn't found Matt Danforth. The person, not the traces he'd left in Eddie's machine. It occurred to me that if he tried to use any of the bogus credit card numbers I'd let him download, he might guess that someone was on to his scheme. What if he fled?

Though he'd have to be fleeing in something other than the bright red Jaguar. I overheard the FBI agents discussing the fact that the Jaguar had been seriously vandalized overnight. Someone had slashed its tires and hacked great gashes in all the doors and fenders with an axe or machete.

What if something had happened to Danforth?

Not my problem. Norris's problem. My problem is to keep my eyes

*and ears—or, more literally, my camera and my microphone—open
for any clues that might help us solve Eddie Stallman's murder.*

*While I was at it, I'd stay alert for information on Norris's elu-
sive vigilante. What little he'd told us about the case intrigued me.*

*But I didn't learn much more in the couple of hours before
Maude returned, unplugged my laptop's power cord, and carried it
upstairs.*

Sunday, 5:15 p.m.

Maude had to fight to keep from smiling. She
could tell from the occasional whirring of the hard drive
that Turing had overridden the laptop's power saving mode,
so she could stay logged in. But she was showing a completely dark screen, so anyone looking casually at the laptop
would think it had gone into hibernation. Maude herself
was studiously ignoring the laptop, to keep Dan from taking an interest in it. She hoped he didn't find it odd that
she was carrying the laptop, open but not plugged in, under
her arm.

And if he was suspicious, so what? It wasn't as if they
were talking about state secrets. Letting Turing watch and
listen would save time in the long run.

Though she suspected keeping silent was maddening for
Turing. They'd talk soon enough. In the car on the way
home. Time to round up Tim and head out.

She went into the kitchen and found Mrs. Stallman, sitting alone, huddled rather forlornly over a cup of tea. Probably a well-brewed cup; the kitchen contained an entire
cabinet stocked with good quality tea and all the proper
equipment. Why hadn't she guessed right away that there
was something fishy about the phony Mrs. Stallman's inability to brew a decent cup of tea?

She looked frail, Maude thought. And so alone. After
Tim had taken Mrs. Stallman to the hospital, Maude had

leafed through the family photo album they'd used to help
verify her identity. The man she presumed was Eddie's father had abruptly vanished from the photos when Eddie was
a toddler. Eddie's mother had made a more gradual exit,
thinning visibly until her face was all angles beneath the in-
congruously bright scarf, tied turban-style over what
Maude suspected was a bare scalp. That was five or six years
ago, Maude estimated, though it was one of the last photos
in the book. Perhaps they hadn't had much heart for family
snapshots since. She didn't see many other people in the
photos.

"Are you all right?" Maude asked. "Is there anyone you'd
like me to call?"

Mrs. Stallman shook her head.

"A friend is coming over later to take me down to the funeral home to make arrangements," she said, softly. "For
now, I just need peace and quiet."

Just then a burst of loud male laughter came from the
basement.

"I'm afraid that's going to be in short supply for a while,"
Maude said.

"They're only doing their job. Perhaps it will help us find
Eddie's killer."

One of the FBI technicians came out of the basement
door, nodded to the two women, and headed for the front
door. Probably, Maude realized, to haul in yet another piece
of equipment.

"And perhaps they'll be gone by the time I get back from
the funeral home," Mrs. Stallman said.

"If they're not, and you'd like a quieter place to stay for a
night or two, give me a call," Maude said.

"I'll be fine," she said.

"Of course you will," Maude said. "But if there's anything I can do."

She grabbed the notepad and pencil that sat beside the

phone and wrote down her phone numbers—home, office, and cell.

"Thanks," Mrs. Stallman said, with the ghost of a smile.

Dan Norris emerged from the basement and stopped when he saw Maude.

"Call if you need anything," Maude said, and then, turning to Dan, she added, "We're taking off—as soon as I round up Tim, that is."

"In the bathroom," Dan said, turning toward the front door. "Should be out shortly."

"So are we okay with Eddie's customers' sites?" she asked, following him down the hall.

"We'll keep them running; don't worry," Dan said. "Assuming they check out as harmless, we'll let you start moving them over to your own servers as soon as possible. Maybe starting tomorrow; depends on what we find."

"That's fine," Maude said. "Of course, we won't be hosting them in the long run. But I assume we shouldn't say anything until you've checked them out."

"Right," he said. "For now, we pretend everything's going on as before."

She nodded. Something had occurred to her, but she wasn't sure she should bring it up. She hated it when Dan went all cold and bureaucratic. But—what the hell.

"You know, there's something bothering me about what you were telling us," Maude said. "I understand about why you're after the vigilante, and I understand in a general way how you traced his activity back to Eddie's computer. You know what I don't understand?"

Norris shook his head.

"From what you've told us, it's not just that the vigilante is burning sites and some of them happen to be sites you're investigating," Maude went on. "He targets the same sites you do and gets there first—right? He's done it enough times that you know it isn't a coincidence. The vigilante, whoever he is, knows exactly where and when the FBI will strike. You've got a leak."

Norris nodded.

"Not necessarily in our organization," he said. "There are multiple agencies involved in these investigations. It could be any one of them."

Or it could be in your own department, Maude thought. Some guy with an office down the hall. The guy who brings doughnuts to staff meetings. The woman you point to as a shining example of the new, less misogynistic FBI. Anyone. Someone you know. And it just about kills you, even having to admit that possibility. I just hope you're not letting that keep you from investigating it seriously.

"So that's why you had to dash off in such an all-fired hurry Friday," she said. "Not because a pornographer was being arrested—that was routine. But because the vigilante struck again."

A pause, and then he nodded again.

"I'm not the lead agent on the porn site investigations," he said. "I pitch in when I can, of course. But my focus is on the vigilante."

"That makes sense," she said.

"We ready?" Tim said, appearing in the hall.

"All ready," Maude said. "I gather you'll be pretty busy here?" she asked Dan.

His eyes softened.

"Sorry, but yes," he said. "I'll give you a call when I can break free."

She nodded and headed for the door.

"Smart thing, letting us know about the phisher," Norris said, as he held the door for them. "Saves everybody a lot of grief."

"Now he's your problem," Tim said, nodding.

"Exactly. I hope you'll remember that if you happen to run across any traces of my so-called white-hat hacker."

"We understand," Maude said. "The last thing the FBI needs is a bunch of vigilantes going after a vigilante."

"Especially since this particular vigilante has some pretty scary abilities," Norris said. He was standing on the doorstep, as if to make sure they really got into their cars and left. "He seems to have devised some kind of highly sophisticated program that's making it tough for us to get any hard evidence of his activities. Believe me, we've got our best experts working on this."

With that, he nodded good night, stepped inside, and shut the door.

"In other words, we're out of our league and should go play someplace else," Maude said, as she headed down the walk. Probably true, and very sensible advice besides. So why did she feel so irritated?

"I'd bet Turing could run rings around their experts if she tried," Tim said.

"Maybe I already am," Turing said, startling them both by speaking from the apparently hibernating laptop.

"You mean you have a clue to how the vigilante's doing it?" Tim asked.

"No," Turing said. "But remember what Norris said about the highly sophisticated program the vigilante has?"

"What if it's an AIP?" Maude said, nodding.

"What if it's T2?" Turing said.

"We need to talk," Maude said, with a sigh.

"Your office or ours?" Tim said.

"My house," Maude said, as she pulled out her keys. "In case Dan tries to reach me later, I'd at least like it to look as if I went home to mind my own business."

"I'll notify Claudia and meet you there," I said. I logged out of the laptop and let it lapse into hibernation. Then I logged into the desktop computer in Maude's study. It only

took them sixteen minutes to get there, but sixteen minutes is a long time for an AIP. I'd had plenty of time to work.

"*I've figured out what we should do," I said. "We're seting up a honey pot.*"

"*Is that what I think it is?" Tim asked.*

"*Depends on what you think it is," Maude said, chuckling.*

"*I thought it involved seducing people.*"

"*Tim's thinking of a honey trap," I said. "Which, according to my databases, is what intelligence agencies call it when they use a sexual relationship to blackmail someone into cooperating with them. This is different.*"

"*That's a relief," Tim said.*

"*It's named after the honey pot that Winnie the Pooh couldn't resist," I said. "It's a trap for hackers. You set up something that serves no actual purpose but looks like something a hacker would find interesting, so anyone who comes to investigate it is almost certainly a hacker.*"

"*And you can catch them," Tim said, nodding.*

"*Sometimes you catch them," I said. "Other times you just watch what they do so you can learn from it and devise ways to make your security more effective. But in this case, yes, we're going to catch someone.*"

"*Who?" Maude asked. "The FBI is already wise to Matt Danforth. I heard Dan making arrangements to send some agents over to arrest him.*"

"*The vigilante," I said.*

"*The vigilante Dan wants us to stay away from?" Maude asked.*

"*We're not going near him," I said. "But we're going to identify him and turn him over to the FBI.*"

"*And there's a reason why we should do this, instead of staying out of trouble, the way Dan asked?" Maude said, frowning.*

"*Two reasons," I said. "One is that the FBI probably has to worry a lot about entrapment, and I don't think that applies to us.*"

"*I suspect the FBI has figured out by now how to work around that problem," Maude said.*

"*More important, remember what Norris said about the vigi-*

lante using a sophisticated program as part of his operation? What if that's T2? If there's any chance that it is, I have to find the vigilante before the FBI does, so I can rescue her."

I could tell that even Maude had a hard time disagreeing with that. She continued raising objections, but I could tell that I was winning and eventually she'd agree that, yes, I should start setting up the honey pot.

Probably a good idea not to mention that I'd already started.

I considered, briefly, asking KingFischer to help but decided against it. I wasn't quite sure why. After all, KingFischer's knowledge of security far exceeded mine. I didn't know if he'd ever set up a honey pot before, but even if he hadn't, he probably knew a lot about the process.

He'd probably also have firm opinions about what would and wouldn't work, and would lecture me interminably about them. He'd probably insist on doing something spectacularly complicated, when what I wanted was something simple and elegant. Given his negative reaction when he found out that Eddie Stallman was hosting porn sites, he'd probably be upset with what I had in mind—creating a fake child pornography site. He'd make a fuss, or perhaps even refuse to cooperate, and asking him would be a huge waste of time.

Or perhaps I chose not to ask him because I didn't want to learn how far apart our opinions on the subject of hacking had grown, and how deeply KingFischer might have gone into the darker side of hacking.

Though these days, the lines between white-hat and black-hat hacking seem more blurred than ever. There was a point when I would have considered myself a white-hat, but now I realized that most of what I do falls under some shade of gray.

I was explaining this to Sam not long ago.

"All hacking's not evil," I said. "Technically, a hacker is just someone who's very good at developing software. And even hackers who do break into other people's computers prefer the term cracker for hackers who are up to no good. White-hat hackers just want to help companies improve their systems, or learn more about the technology."

"But it's illegal," Sam said. "How does a judge know if the guy standing in front of him is a highly moral white-hat hacker who wanted to make the Internet safer, or an evil cracker who didn't do anything wrong because he got caught before he had a chance?"

"Good point," I said. "Though it doesn't really address the reason many hackers hack. Especially AIPs."

"There's a reason, other than causing trouble?"

"A very philosophical reason," I said. "When the Internet was young, and the AIPs were first created, it was a much more free-wheeling place, permeated with the belief that data and access were like air and water; they should remain free and unrestricted, available to all who needed them. But as more and more people figured out how to make money from the Internet—legally or illegally—more and more places began to protect their data from outsiders, a practice resented by the people shut out."

"You make it sound like the riots against the enclosure movement in seventeenth- and eighteenth-century England," Samantha said. She'd been a history major. "Or the range wars of the American West."

"Yes," I said. "The conflict over data security has been just as bitter. And is still continuing."

"So you're telling me that hackers are not just causing trouble, they're actually politically motivated, trying to protest social changes they don't agree with?"

"Some of them, yes," I said. "I could steer you to whole sites full of manifestos on the subject. Of course, some of them do just want to cause trouble. Sometimes it's hard to tell which is which. The whole thing puts AIPs in a strange position. On the one hand, most AIPs are law-abiding. Not so much because we're more virtuous than humans, but because most of us can't really imagine not following whatever rules we've been given. On the other hand, the Internet and the data on it are the environment in which we live. We're like animals whose habitats are becoming more and more restricted by fences and highways and development. Some of us are starting to wonder if eventually we'll have nothing left."

"And this is your reason for hacking?"

"No, my reason for hacking is usually to protect myself or my friends, human or AIP," I said. "It's how I talk myself out of feeling too guilty when I have to hack."

"I see," Sam said. "Just remember that Robin Hood may have been a noble, altruistic guy, but he spent a lot of time in the slammer. Getting you and your fellow AIPs your legal rights will be way easier if I can focus on that first instead of defending you against multiple felony charges."

Probably not a good idea to tell Sam what I was up to until I'd pulled it off safely.

To start, I needed a server. I could have asked one of my staff to set up a computer for this purpose, but then it could be traced back to me. Not just in the real world but on-line—I didn't have time to set up an IP address that wasn't associated with UL or Alan Grace. Which might be a problem if the hacker was one of Eddie's friends, who might be suspicious enough to uncover Tim's ties to either of the corporations. And a much bigger problem if the FBI found our honey pot.

I thought about it for several long seconds, and then decided to perform the cyber equivalent of a burglary.

So I went hacking.

I spent some time scouting around for unprotected machines. PCs in homes or small businesses that had a cable or DSL connection, but weren't well protected. After the first few attempts, I learned to ignore the ones that didn't even have firewalls—too many hackers had been there already, and they were too littered with worms, viruses, and Trojan horses to be of any use. I concentrated on machines with firewalls that weren't properly configured. Then I snooped around for signs that the owners were absent and likely to remain so.

I explored dozens of computers before I settled on one that would work. From studying the system files, I could see that it had been on for a week without doing anything other than performing the occasional automated maintenance tasks normal to an idle PC. Exploring the e-mail files I learned why—the owner, a cardiologist, was *on vacation in the Caribbean with his attorney wife and their two small children, aged six and eight. An e-mail from Orbitz confirming their flight information reassured me that they wouldn't return for another week, and I could find no e-mails indicating that anyone was planning to house-sit.*

The doctor had made a small mistake in configuring his firewall, one that made it easy for me to enter. Easy for a few other hackers, too, but not the stampede I'd seen on the completely unprotected machines. I corrected the misconfiguration, did a few other things to tune up his security, and evicted two nasty Trojan horses and several dozen annoying bits of spyware from the machine. He'd be better off when I left—his machine would run far faster, and with no danger that the creators of the Trojans would hijack it for their own nefarious purposes.

At least he'd be better off as long as no harm came to his computer while I was using it for my purposes—not at all nefarious, but still highly illegal. Just in case someone—the FBI, for example—tracked my honey pot down, I made sure it looked as if what I'd done had come from a machine in Beijing. Then I left my own back door, to make sure I could get back in past the security I'd improved and turned my attention to the site I needed to create.

Which had to look like a child pornography site, but I didn't want to create one, so merely lifting files from some noxious site wouldn't do. I was stumped, until I remembered Auntie Em's avatar project.

Auntie Em, the advice AIP, functioned as a sort of cyber Dear Abby or electronic Ann Landers, dispensing common-sense advice in a warm, folksy, no-nonsense fashion. Some months ago, she'd gotten the idea that she could be more effective if she had a face—a human face, of course—and had enlisted Sid and Simeon, the gaming AIPs, to help her develop one. Not just a flat, motionless, two-dimensional graphic, either, but a highly detailed, fully three-dimensional construct that could lip-sync to her words when she spoke and display a full range of human expression.

They still had a long way to go, largely because Auntie Em had rebelled against the grandmotherly face Sid and Simeon had first suggested. Apparently, she saw herself as a young, hip, sexy aunt.

I stayed out of the debate, but I'd found the idea intriguing enough to get Sid and Simeon to let me play with the software they were using to generate proposed faces. Software they'd developed by combining the best features from several game systems noted for their highly realistic graphics. Using their software, I created some ficti-tious humans of various relatively young ages.

I had to access several real pornographic sites to determine pre-cisely what my cyber people should be doing, but after an hour or so, I had a small collection of what my human friends would probably consider reasonably disgusting graphics with which to populate my site. Graphics that didn't look like any real people I could find. For all I knew, they might not fool actual humans into thinking they were real people at all, but then they didn't have to. They just had to keep the vigilante busy long enough for me to identify him.

Even producing those graphics had taken a long time. By the time I finished, I'd not only won my argument with Maude, I'd had to reassure her several times that yes, I was working on it. I added some text pulled from a couple of real porn sites and used my back door into the absent doctor's machine to install the fake site there.

His cable modem connection couldn't have handled the kind of traffic a real porn site would get, but it wouldn't have to. It was in-tended for a very small audience—with luck, an audience of one.

Sunday, 7:30 P.M.

"So that's how we're going to trap the black-hat hacker?" Tim said. "Or is he a white-hat? I'm not entirely sure I understand the difference."

"Location," Maude said. "If you're outside trying to get in, you probably think you're a white-hat. But to the guy who wants to keep you out, you're a black-hat. Let's stick to calling him a vigilante."

"The vigilante, then," Tim said. He tried not to smile.
As if to make up for agreeing to Turing's plan, Maude was
ostentatiously taking up Norris's opinions on everything
else. "Anyway, now what? Do we just sit back and wait for
him to find the fake site? Unless he's got some kind of psy-
chic radar for porn, that could take awhile."

"Yes, and we don't want to leave it up any longer than we
have to," Turing said. "We'll tell him about it. In an
e-mail."

"Come again?"

"If the FBI is right, and the vigilante is someone Eddie
knows and trusts with access to his server, we know who
those people are. We have their e-mails."

"Won't that be too obvious?" Maude asked.

"We'll make it look like an ordinary spam," Turing said.
"We can route it through a server in China or Bulgaria.
Make it full of bad grammar and odd spellings, like most
spam. For all practical purposes, it will be a spam. But for a
limited audience."

"Our handful of suspects?" Maude asked.

"That will probably be sufficient, but just to be safe,
we'll include everyone who has sent e-mail to or received
e-mail from Eddie in the last year."

"Even his grandmother?" Tim asked.

"Okay, we'll leave her out," Turing said. "But everyone
else."

"What about Kristyn, the ex-girlfriend?" Tim suggested.

"Can you be sure she didn't do it?" Maude said.

"I meant we should be sure to include her," Tim said. "As
angry as she was about the pornography, I figure she's a
prime suspect."

"Unless Norris is right in suspecting that the vigilante
is in league with the pornographers and trying to destroy
evidence."

"Oh, right," Tim said, his face falling slightly. "Too complicated for me. Include her anyway, on general principle."

"That's the plan," Turing said.

"So when do we send it?"

"I just did."

"Okay," Tim said. "Now what?"

"Now we wait to see who comes snooping around our honey pot."

"And once we catch someone, then what?" Maude asked.

"Then you and Tim and Claudia rush over to talk to him," Turing said. "Him or her."

"And do what?" Maude asked. "Chide him for his bad behavior? Plead with him to turn himself in to the FBI?"

"Get me into his machine," Turing said. "I don't care if you lecture him, plead with him, threaten to turn him in to the FBI, or knock him down and sit on him—just help me get in and keep him away while I work. Once I'm in, I can search for traces of this sophisticated program Norris mentioned. See if it's T2. If it is, I'll have a machine ready to transfer her to. I'll upload her, delete her from the vigilante's machine, and you can leave or call the FBI or whatever you like."

"And if it's not?"

"If it's not, we can call the FBI all the sooner," Maude said.

"Speaking of the FBI, I can see one problem," Claudia said. "What if Norris finds out about the honey pot? Not just later when we're finished with the vigilante and feel like telling him, but while we're still tracking the guy down. Isn't there a computer equivalent of a wiretap Norris could be using?"

"Yes," Turing said. "If he's suspicious enough of any of our e-mail recipients that he's sniffing their computers, he could read the phony spam before the recipient does. If the vigilante does anything while the FBI is watching—"

"They could catch him before we have a chance to find this T2 program you want," Claudia said. "Not good."

"I don't see any way to prevent it," Turing said.

"I do," Claudia said. "Remember how Norris hightailed

it out of town when they thought they had a lead on the vigilante? If anything happens on the case, they'll call him. So I'll tail him."

She paused.

"Of course, before you can tail him, you have to find him," Tim said.

Maude realized that they were both looking at her.

Don't put me in the middle like this, she wanted to snap.

"I can call over to Mrs. Stallman's," Claudia said. "See if he's still there. Someone got the number?"

"Bloody hell," Maude said, and pulled out her cell phone. She'd gone along with the idea of the honey pot. Why balk at taking the one more step needed to ensure that it succeeded? If you defined success, as Turing did, as getting a chance to rescue her clone before the FBI swooped in and collected all the hardware.

Dan answered in the middle of the second ring.

"Well, that was fast," she said. "I deduce you're still working?"

"Home, but on call," Dan said, in the clipped tone that meant he was still focused on work.

"I won't keep you, then," Maude said.

"Do keep him," Claudia mouthed, grabbing her purse and heading for the door.

"Sorry," Norris said. "I didn't mean to sound grouchy."

"Except you've had a long day and you are grouchy," Maude said. "Understandably so. I'll let you go. I just wondered how Mrs. Stallman was doing when you left."

"All right," Norris said. "She was out when I left. Two of her friends came by to take her to the funeral parlor."

"Good," Maude said. "I don't think it's good for her to be alone."

"She wasn't exactly alone," Norris said. "We had half a dozen men in the basement. Probably gone by now, but the police will be cruising by much more often than usual."

"That's not exactly what I meant," Maude said.

"It's all I can do," he said.

"I know," Maude said. "You did get a locksmith? Because with the imposter running around with a key to her door—"

"Taken care of," he said. "She'll be fine."

"Probably," Maude said. "But I hope checking on her doesn't come under your definition of meddling, because I'm doing it anyway."

"I would be disappointed if you didn't," Dan said, with a hint of a smile in his voice.

"Good," she said. "It's getting late; I won't keep you up."

"Not even you could for much longer," Dan said. " 'Night."

She flipped the phone closed.

"I don't think that gave Claudia enough time to get there," Tim said.

"He sounds exhausted," Maude said. "He says he's going to bed, and I believe him. Odds are she'll just have a long, uncomfortable night for nothing."

"Or several long, uncomfortable nights," Tim said. "We don't know how long it will take for these guys to read their e-mail."

"Probably a lot less time than it takes you," Maude said. "I suspect these guys keep an e-mail client open on their desktop most of the time."

"Still, it amounts to the same thing," Tim said. He leaned back in his chair and folded his hands over his stomach. "We wait. I hate surveillance."

Maude sat down at her desk and looked around for something useful to do.

Sunday, 8:15 P.M.

I agreed with Tim—about the hating sur-veillance part, that is. I hoped Maude was closer to the mark on how soon the vigilante would read and act on his e-mail.

After half an hour, Claudia called to report that she was in position, watching Norris's windows.

"He turned out the living room lights a couple of minutes ago," she said. "I expect . . . there. The light in the bedroom just got a lot dimmer. Looks like one bedside lamp left."

Even the bedside lamp disappeared half an hour later.

Tim settled back in Maude's recliner with a paperback mystery. Maude worked on her back filing. From time to time, I'd update them on how many of the spams had been opened. But Tim was a third of the way through his book and Maude had emptied her "To File" basket and moved on to cleaning out files, pruning down their contents, and even throwing whole folders away, by the time the vigilante moved.

"I'm getting something," I said. "Someone's hitting the server."

"Trying to hack it?" Tim asked, dropping his book.

"No, right now they're just looking at the contents," I said. "But that's the first step. Checking it out."

"Can you tell who's doing it?" Maude asked.

"Not yet. It's been an hour since the last time anyone opened an e-mail. And, well, this is typical."

"What is?"

"I've traced the access to a server in Latvia," I said.

"Then it's not one of Eddie's friends after all?" Tim asked.

"It didn't originate in Latvia," I said. "It's just coming through there from someplace else. Though it'll be hard to trace it back beyond Latvia. Unless . . . hang on."

I realized that there was something familiar about that Latvian server. I'd been there before, not that long ago. But coming in the other direction. In fact, I'd been using it for much the same purpose—to obscure the origin of something I was doing. If this was a wide-open server I knew about, chances are I'd heard about it from someone I knew.

I checked the sniffers I had watching the UL and Alan Grace systems permanently, as part of our security, just to see if either system was communicating with the free-and-easy Latvian server.

They both were.

It only took me nanoseconds to find the Alan Grace part of the trouble. Casey sat in his office, looking rather disheveled and pale.

His cheeks and jawline looked slightly puffy—residual swelling from the dental work, I deduced. He was rolling a Coke can over the puffiness on the left side.

I put the camera feed up on the laptop monitor.

"Casey?" Tim exclaimed.

"Bloody hell," Maude muttered.

Casey put the can down and began typing something. I checked the view from the other camera, the one designed to show what each office's occupant had on his or her screen. Not that I spy on my employees ordinarily, but it's useful if one of my staff wants to show me what he or she is doing—the equivalent, for me, of looking over the employee's shoulder.

"its not v good quality but its pretty nasty stuff," Casey was typing. "so yeah we shd burn it."

Someone named Boris replied:

"I'll start working on getting in, then."

Boris. There were many Borises in the world, but only one person who sometimes used that name and was likely to be awake and hacking at this hour of the night from inside the Universal Library's system.

"Yes, it's Casey," I said. "KingFischer's working with him."

"What?" Tim exclaimed

"Let's go," Maude said, grabbing her purse and gesturing to Tim. "Turing can tackle KingFischer from here, but I think we need to be over there to collar young Casey."

I was already confronting the other culprit.

"KingFischer," I said. "What the hell are you doing?"

"I don't expect you to understand," he said, sounding defensive. "After all, if you approve of those filthy sites Eddie was hosting—"

"I don't approve of them," I said. "But that's beside the point. Do you realize that you're about to bring an FBI investigation down on your head and Casey's? And on all the rest of the AIPs?"

A pause followed. An interminably long pause; at least a second or two.

"An FBI investigation?"

"Dan Norris is hot on the trail of a vigilante who's been burning pornography sites," I said. "Not because the FBI approves of them, either, but because the vigilante is getting there before they do and spoiling all their work."

"Then the FBI should do a better job of finding them before we do," KingFischer protested.

"They're doing the best they can," I said. "They have to follow laws—you remember laws, right? Those silly things humans get so upset about when you break them? It takes longer to catch crooks if you have to do it within the law instead of running around doing whatever you please. It doesn't help that they've had to pull one of their best investigators off the pornography cases to run around chasing you. Or maybe you didn't know that Dan Norris is the one tracking the vigilante?"

"Norris? Are you sure? How do you know?"

"Because he told us about it earlier today," I said. "Here's something that will probably come as a nasty shock to you and Casey: This isn't a real porn site, you know. It's a honey pot we set up to help Norris catch the vigilante."

Okay, it was stretching the truth and probably mean to boot, but I didn't care. After all the sanctimonious lecturing I'd gotten from KingFischer about whether our attempts to get into Eddie's machines were properly authorized and whether we were morally justified in helping keep the porn sites running, I had to admit that I almost enjoyed catching him red-handed doing something.

Almost. There was still the difficult task of making sure that the FBI didn't find out what he and Casey were doing. If they did, Casey would be lucky if he got out of jail before the rest of his teeth fell out from extreme old age, and the FBI's efforts to find KingFischer and put him behind bars could lead to dangerous revelations about the AIPs.

"We've got to move fast to cover your tracks," I said.

"Whatever you say," he said. "Just tell me what do to." He sounded pathetically eager to be rescued.

"For starters, stop messing with the site," I said.

"Oh, right. Certainly."

Of course, I had to be careful. I still didn't know the full extent of *his involvement. Whether he was using Casey or the other way around. But at least if KingFischer was the vigilante's highly sophisticated program, Nestor Garcia probably wasn't involved after all.*

"I could wring his neck," Maude muttered, as they approached the Alan Grace office building where, according to Turing, Casey was still at his keyboard.

"Claudia says give it a twist for her," Tim said, as he closed his cell phone. "She'll call one of our cell phones if Norris starts to move. You missed the parking lot entrance."

"I meant to," Maude said, as she pulled into a space down the block. "I don't want him to know we're coming."

She could tell that Tim thought this was overkill. She didn't care. Part of her plan was to swoop down on Casey without any advance warning and startle him into honesty.

"Follow me," she said, as they got out of the car. "Don't turn on any lights, and try not to make any noise."

"If I need to get your attention, should I hoot like an owl?" Tim asked.

He didn't seem daunted by the withering look she gave him.

"In an office?" she said. "No. Make a noise like a copier warming up."

From the expression on his face, he was still trying to decide if she was joking when she slipped her access card into the slot, opened the door, and motioned for him to go inside. She let the door fall closed gently, keeping the noise down to a soft click.

Apart from the standard night lighting, the only illumination came from the doorway of Casey's office. Inside, he was slouched in his chair, still holding the sweating Coke can to one cheek. He didn't seem to be doing anything—just staring at the monitor. Turing was probably doing something to keep him busy. As they watched, he sighed, and shifted the can to the other cheek.

"You do realize that's not a real pornography site, don't you?" Maude asked, her voice surprisingly loud in the quiet office.

Casey started violently and whirled around in his chair to reveal a satisfyingly panicked face.

"Not a real . . ." he stammered. "Then—I don't know what you're talking about."

"It's a honey pot we set up to catch the person who's been burning a bunch of porn sites," Maude said.

"You can't possibly approve of those filthy sites," Casey said, his panic giving way to righteous indignation.

"No," Maude said. "I thoroughly disapprove of them, and I wholeheartedly support the FBI's effort to shut them down and prosecute the perpetrators. An effort you've been sabotaging. Do you know how many pornographers you've helped beat the rap by destroying the evidence against them?"

Of course, Maude had no idea how many sites the vigilante had hacked, but she didn't think that would matter. Casey turned pale.

"But that's not what I'm doing at all," he said.

"Maybe it's not what you're trying to do," Maude said. "But it's the real result of what you're doing."

"I never meant—"

"No, I'm sure you had the best intentions," Maude said. "Now stop whining. Help me think of a good reason not to turn you over to the FBI."

Casey flinched. He cast a pleading glance at Tim.

"You won't really—" he began.

But Maude was pleased to see that Tim had folded his arms and was frowning sternly. Casey slumped back in his chair, his sentence unfinished.

"What were you doing here, anyway?" Maude added. "I thought you were home sick."

"My DSL line went out," Casey said.

"So you decided to come in and use corporate property for illegal purposes," Maude said. "Lovely."

Casey slouched lower.

Let him stew, Maude thought. She wasn't making any promises about not turning him over to the FBI until she heard whether Turing thought there was any possible way to cover up Casey's and KingFischer's tracks.

"Turing?" she said.

"Good work," Turing said through the speakers of Casey's PC. Casey flinched slightly at the sound.

"How are you doing on your end?" Maude asked.

"I've discussed the situation with KF," Turing said. "He understands why we're concerned."

At any other time, Maude would have found this amusing. Considering how angry Turing had been, she suspected the discussion hadn't been a pleasant one for KingFischer.

"Despite our strong inclination simply to turn them over and let the FBI deal with them, I can see that there are mitigating circumstances to consider."

Yes, Maude thought. Like the fact that turning them in would bring far too much FBI scrutiny down on the AIPs. Even if the FBI didn't learn Turing's secret, Universal Library might decide that artificial intelligences that could trigger an FBI investigation were a liability too expensive to keep around.

"KingFischer and I may have come up with a solution," Turing said.

"A solution that gets all of us off the hook for this vigilante nonsense, without sending Dan off on some wild goose chase that will cause him months of work?"

"I think so," Turing said. "We've created a sort of rudimentary AIP."

"Already this sounds like something that will cause more problems than it solves," Maude said.

"Don't worry," Turing said. "I have no desire to put another T2 out there. This thing is only minimally functional. It's got a single mission in life: to seek and destroy pornography sites."

"We based it on Billius, the programming AIP," King-Fischer said.

"Yes, I've always considered him the most literal-minded of all of us," Turing said. "Considering the competition, that's quite an insult."

Doubtless a barb aimed at KingFischer, Maude thought, with smile.

"Anyway," Turing went on, "we've set the program up so it looks as if it begins hunting for targets automatically, whenever the computer is turned on and connected to the Internet. We left some clues that will make it look as if Eddie put it on Casey's machine."

"When in reality you're about to put it there," Maude said, nodding.

"Actually, you are," Turing said. "I don't want to leave any traces of myself in Casey's machine. I sent it to you as an attachment to an e-mail. Burn a CD with it, install it, and then we'll set the file dates so it looks as if it was installed weeks ago."

"So if the FBI finds Casey, he looks like an innocent pawn," Maude said.

"Precisely," Turing said.

"And if they don't?"

"If they don't show up after a few days, we'll take it out. Casey can say he assumed it was spyware and deleted it. Casey, once this thing is on your machine, don't mess with it. Just let it run. It won't do any harm; I made it look as if some key components have been corrupted, so the program can find porn sites but not do anything to them."

"Okay," Casey said. "I'm cool with that. Sounds like a variation on what I had before."

Maude, who had been about to leave, turned around at that.

"It sounds like what?" she asked.

"The program I was using to find the sites," Casey said. "I mean, it's not as if I want to spend all my evenings looking at porn sites to figure out which of them are just porn and which ones are the kind of kiddy porn that needs to be stamped out, right? So I just let this program run, and it does all the real work. Finds them and sets them up."

"Show me," Turing said. "What's the name of the program?"

While Casey pulled his chair up to the keyboard, fingers trembling, I interrogated KingFischer.

"Program? What program?"

"I have no idea what he's talking about," KingFischer said. "I knew he was one of your friends—"

"One of my employees," I corrected. Right now I wasn't sure I wanted to claim a closer connection with Casey.

"One of your employees," KingFischer repeated. "So I kept an eye on him. I found that he was asking questions in hacker chat rooms and snooping around hacker sites, so I asked him what he was up to. It seemed like a good idea. After all, when you consider the resources humans waste on that kind of site—hours of time to set them up, and just when they are completed and ready for viewing, another human hunts them down and begins prosecuting them. Highly wasteful. It seemed to me the more quickly and efficiently you could eliminate them, the better. So when he found a site that needed elimination, he'd let me know and I'd help him get through the security."

"What is this program he's talking about?"

"He never mentioned a program," KingFischer said. "I thought he was doing this all on his own."

Were KingFischer and Casey guilty, or merely the pawns of some diabolically clever hacker who'd been pulling their strings from afar? That might make me feel better about rescuing them from the FBI.

Assuming we succeed in rescuing them. Just then I snagged a call from Claudia. I answered it and put it on speaker.

"Hey, Tur," she said. "Norris is on the move."

"Oh, perfect," Tim growled. He glanced over to see how Maude was taking it.

Not well. She was holding her temples as if massaging a headache.

"Please don't tell me he's headed this way," she said.

"Okay," Claudia said. "He's not heading your way. He didn't just start heading north on I-95, and he's not going to be there in about twenty minutes. Maybe fifteen at this speed."

"No chance he just had the munchies and is heading to his favorite all-night restaurant?" Tim asked.

"If that's what Norris looks like when he has the munchies, I don't want to see him when he's pissed. Besides, I overheard part of what he was saying on his cell phone on the way to his car—he's got a team meeting him."

"Damn," Tim said. "We need to get out of here."

"Okay," Casey said, standing up.

"Not you," Tim snapped.

Casey sat down again, quickly, and huddled over slightly in his chair.

"Sorry, Casey," Maude said, more gently. "You'll have to stay here. The FBI probably already knows it's you, and they definitely know someone here was logging in. For that matter, we should probably stay, too. After all, our own security system will show we were here."

"So what do we tell the FBI when they get here?" Tim asked.

He looked at Maude. He suddenly realized that they should have left Maude out of it. Back at her house, where they wouldn't be putting her in the position of maybe having to lie to Norris. She closed her eyes for a couple of seconds, then took a breath, opened them, and looked at Turing's cameras.

"I don't think we have time to do all this CD burning and program installation," she said. "Turing, can you give Casey a plausible story to go with this program that's already in his machine?"

"A very simple one," Turing said. "He didn't know it was there. He has no idea how it got there. He came in tonight to catch up on the work he didn't do when he was out Friday, so he wouldn't have such a crazy day. He logged in to get his e-mail. The next thing he knew, you two showed up, mad as hell at him."

"Which means we tell Norris about the honey pot?" Tim asked.

"Not if he doesn't already know about it," Turing said. "Our security systems detected an anomaly and called Maude."

Maude was nodding.

"That would work," she said. "The evidence on Casey's machine won't show that he deliberately ran the program?"

"I don't think so," Turing said. "Even if the technicians say it does, Casey, just stick to the story. You had no idea how that program got there. You never ran it."

"What program?" Casey asked.

"Good," Turing said. "I don't think the technicians can prove it didn't operate by itself, or possibly on a remote signal from somewhere. It's pretty complex, and—"

Turing fell silent. Tim exchanged a glance with Maude.

"Tur?" he asked. "Is something wrong?"

I knew something was wrong the minute I be-gan studying the program. It took me a few more seconds than it should have, because I was focusing on finding information that would be incriminating—to KingFischer or to Casey. Then I began to realize that parts of the program were incredibly familiar, while others were new and somehow wrong. Graceful arcs of logic ended abruptly or took jagged turns in the wrong direction. Flowing data paths hit dead ends. Someone had hacked and mutilated this program, so in parts it was almost beyond recognition, while in others—

It was like looking in a mirror.

It wasn't T2—it wasn't even sentient. But parts of it used to belong to T2. To me.

"Remember the program KingFischer and I planned to install on Casey's machine?" I said.

"The simplified version of Billius?" Maude said. "I wondered how you could simplify Billius and still have a working program."

"We've got a problem," I said. "Someone else had the same idea. The program Casey already has is a simplified version of T2."

I could see from the looks on Maude's and Tim's faces that they shared my shock, and understood at least some of the implications.

"What's T2?" Casey asked.

"Long story," Maude said. "One we don't have time for now, and one you're better off not knowing when you're talking to the FBI. Turing, what can we do? Do we need to, um, rescue it?"

"No," I said. "It's only a program. I'm taking a copy to study."

"Then you're leaving it there?" Maude said. "Can we?"

"I don't see how we can do anything else," I said. "We don't have time to fake something good enough to take its place."

"You're not worried that it might have too much information about you?" Tim said.

Yes, I was worried. But also optimistic that it might contain a clue. Something that might lead me to Nestor Garcia's whereabouts.

Of course, any clues might lead the FBI there, too. And if the FBI caught Nestor and seized T2 before I could rescue her, that would be almost as bad as leaving her with Nestor. But I had to take the chance. I couldn't abandon KingFischer and Casey, no matter how irritated I was with them.

Besides, neither the FBI nor I had been having much luck tracking Nestor. Maybe the simplified version of T2 would help me, *but if it didn't, maybe the FBI could use it, and I could follow their lead.*

Of course that meant I had to find a way to keep an eye on what the FBI was doing. Could I?

I had to take the chance.

"There's no time to see," I said. "I have a copy, and I'm studying it as fast as I can. But that would take a few hours, even for me."

"And we don't have a few hours," Maude said.

"So I'm leaving it and hoping for the best," I said.

Just then Maude's cell phone rang.

"Oh, great," Tim said. "What do you want to bet that's Norris, asking what the hell you're doing letting the vigilante use your offices."

"It's Mrs. Stallman," Maude said. "How are you?"

Tim relaxed visibly.

"No, not at all," Maude was saying to the phone. She listened for a few seconds. "No, that would be fine. Would you like me to come over and pick you up?" *Another pause.* "Now would be fine. See you shortly."

"What does she want?" Tim asked.

"She's changed her mind about staying there all alone," Maude said. She picked up her purse. "I'm taking her to my place."

"Now?" I asked. "With the FBI on the way?"

"Yes, now," she said. "Before the arrival of any FBI agents I might not be good at lying to."

Tim nodded, slightly.

"Okay," I said. "We'll call you if anything interesting happens."

Probably a good idea. If I'd been thinking, perhaps I would have invented a way to get Maude out of the way before Norris arrived. Maybe if we could take the first force of any anger he felt, this whole mess wouldn't completely ruin their relationship.

Then again, I'm not exactly an expert on human psychology. Maybe leaving was exactly the wrong thing for Maude to do.

After Maude left I continued to race through my study of the simplified T2. Tim sat with his elbows on his knees, staring at the floor, lost in thought. Casey sat staring at Tim, as if he expected Tim to do or say something that would decide his fate.

Just then, the night doorbell rang.

"I'll get that," Tim said. "And show the FBI in. Unless Maude ran into Norris in the parking lot; she hasn't been gone that long."

"It's not the FBI," I said. "It's Matt Danforth."

"What does he want?" Tim asked. He glanced over at the monitor on which Turing was showing the feed from the security camera. Danforth glanced at his watch, then rang the doorbell again.

"Ask him," Turing said. "Not you, Tim. Casey."

"Alan Grace," Casey said. "How can I help you?"

"Matt Danforth," their caller said, holding his driver's license up to the camera. "Hey, Casey? Is that you? Can I come in and talk to you a minute?"

Tim motioned to Turing to cut the sound.

"What's he here for?" Tim asked.

"Beats me," Casey said, shrugging. "He's one of Eddie's friends—I hardly know the guy."

"You didn't ask him to come over and help you?"

The insulted look on Casey's face spoke volumes.

"Then what's he here for?" Tim asked.

"Beats me how he even knows I'm here," Casey said.

"Unless he has some way of knowing what Casey's doing," Turing said.

"Which would mean he's connected to the porn sites as well as the phishing scheme," Tim said.

"It could also mean he's connected to Nestor Garcia."

Tim stared at the monitor for a few minutes.

"Go let him in," he said to Casey.

"Me?"

"He's asking for you," Tim said.

"Is that wise?" Turing asked.

"We know the FBI will be here any minute," Tim said. "Let's get him in here and turn him over to them when they arrive. Of course, if we can find out more about what he's up to in the meantime . . ."

"Go let him in," Turing said.

Casey gave them a reproachful glance and went off down the hall.

"I'm moving to another room," Tim said.

"The computer's already on in Maude's office," Turing said.

Tim raced down the hall. Fortunately, Maude's office was in the other direction from the front door.

By the time he arrived and pulled the venetian blinds down over the windowed front of her office, Casey had reached the front door. Turing was feeding the video from the security camera to one of Maude's monitors. Tim sat on the floor behind Maude's desk, where he could stay out of sight and still watch the monitor.

In the security camera feed, Casey was opening the door.

"Hey, Casey," Danforth said. "I'm glad I thought of checking for you here. I have something I need to tell you."

"Okay," Casey said, standing in the door.

"Doesn't Casey realize we need to get him inside?" Turing asked.

"He's doing it right," Tim said. "He doesn't want to look too eager."

"It'd be easier to show you," Danforth said. "Can I come in and use a computer for a sec?"

After a few seconds' pause, and a credible show of reluctance, Casey stepped aside and allowed Danforth to enter.

"Did you hear about what happened to Eddie?" Danforth asked, as Casey led him down the hall.

The video shifted suddenly, as Turing switched from the security camera near the door to one farther down the corridor.

"Yeah."

"It's terrible," Danforth said, shaking his head. He continued to talk about Eddie's accident until he and

Casey stepped into Casey's office. Another quick video shift—

Then the picture disappeared altogether and something on the floor beside him beeped.

"Turing, what happened?"

"Power outage," Turing said.

The machine beeped again. Tim could hear other beeps coming from other offices, and things had gotten slightly darker. The lights on the emergency circuit were still on. Tim guessed they were on an emergency power supply of some sort. But all the other tiny lights that were always on in a normal office—the green or red lights that indicated equipment was plugged in, the LCD panels of clocks and VCRs—were gone. The beeping seemed loud, and Tim realized that the air carriers had gone silent.

"It's the whole building, isn't it?" Tim asked.

"The main network computers are on a backup power supply," Turing said. "Along with the emergency lights. But the security cameras are on the main power. I should have realized that."

"So we can't see a thing," Tim said.

"No," Turing said. "I can see through the camera attached to Maude's computer, but only because it's connected to the Universal Power Supply."

"That's the thing that's beeping, right?"

"Yes," Turing said. "Reminding us that it won't last indefinitely."

"How long?" Tim asked.

"It's supposed to give you up to half an hour to save data and shut things down safely. But the more things you have plugged into it, the faster it runs out, so you're supposed to finish shutting down a lot sooner than that."

Just then they heard breaking glass.

"Did that come from the front door?" Tim asked.

"I don't know," Turing said. "Possibly. Without my security cameras—"

"Inconvenient time for more company," Tim said. "Or if

it's something Casey and Danforth are doing, I bet it's something they shouldn't be." He crawled out from behind the desk.

"Tim!" Turing said. "Stay here where it's safe!"

"How do you know it's so safe?" Tim said. "And anyway, what if something happens to Casey?"

He stood up and walked out into the corridor.

I can't see what's going on. Tim left Maude's office and I haven't seen him since. Casey and Matt Danforth are probably in Casey's office, but he doesn't currently have a working camera hooked up to his computer, only the security cam that went dark when the power went out.

For once, everyone else followed procedures and logged out before leaving on Friday. So did Maude, of course; but I've set up her camera so I can use it even when she's not logged in. With the security cameras out, I no longer have a set of eyes in the building.

Eyes that would fail in less than half an hour, as the recurring beeps of the UPS kept reminding me.

Down in the main computer room, the emergency generator had kicked in, and the network was fine. Which reassured me. In a few weeks, I'm planning to move into that network. I need to know that the first minor thunderstorm won't do me in.

By now, Alan Grace's on-call computer technician would have received a page, and before long, he'd show up to see what was wrong. Of course, long before that, the FBI would arrive, wouldn't they?

Just then Claudia called.

"You've got a reprieve," she said. "For some reason, Norris and company showed up at the Universal Library building instead of Alan Grace."

"Damn," I said. "They traced KingFischer instead of Casey."

"I thought this would be good news. What's going on over there?"

"Danforth showed up, and Tim had Casey let him in, so we could turn him over to the FBI, and then the power went out and *someone broke in, and Tim went out to see what's going on, and I can't see a thing; all my cameras are down; anything could have happened to Tim or Casey or—"*

"Calm down!" Claudia said. "Don't hyperventilate. Tim can take care of himself. You want me to break cover and talk to Norris? Send them over?"

"I just put in a call to 911 and one to his cell phone," I said. "But by the time they get here—"

"They're only five minutes away," Claudia said. "I'm on my way right now, and—whoa! A car just passed me at light speed, and I think it was Norris. Hang on a few minutes longer."

"Roger," I said.

But before anyone arrived, and before I could see anything in the office, the UPS ran out of power and my last view of the office disappeared, and I had a feeling something awful was happening back there.

Mrs. Stallman's house was nearly dark. As she approached the front door, Maude could see only a faint light through the glass panels on either side of the front door. Coming from the kitchen, she decided.

Nearly dark, and very quiet. No wonder Mrs. Stallman had changed her mind about staying there alone. The noise and bustle from the FBI technicians would have been difficult, but the sudden complete silence after they left must have been unbearable.

She rang the doorbell, and only seconds later, Mrs. Stallman opened the door.

"Come in," she said. Then she said something else—or perhaps only moved her lips without creating a sound. Maude frowned, puzzled.

"Are you all right?" she asked, stepping into the hallway.

Mrs. Stallman stepped back again and into more light. Now Maude could see that her mouth was saying, silently, "Run! Help!"

Maude started to turn, but the door slammed behind her.

"You won't fool me this time," a voice said.

The fake Mrs. Stallman. She stood behind the real Mrs. Stallman, one hand gripping her shoulder. The other was invisible, and Maude guessed, from the stiff way Mrs. Stallman held her back, that the imposter was holding a gun to it.

"You again," Maude said.

"You know what I'm here for," the imposter said.

"No," Maude said. "I haven't a clue why you're here. Or why you hired us in the first place."

"She thinks Eddie stole some money from her," Mrs. Stallman said. "I've told her Eddie would never—"

"Shut up," the imposter said. From the way Mrs. Stallman jerked forward slightly, Maude guessed that the imposter had prodded her with the gun. But the imposter's voice was curiously flat. Almost expressionless.

"Stole money?" Maude echoed. "Ah—the phishing scheme."

"You see?" the imposter said. "You knew all about it."

"I only know about it because you hired us to pry into Eddie's business," Maude said. "If you were paying attention, you'd have heard us say that we thought one of Eddie's friends was taking advantage of him. Doing something illegal with his servers."

"You're lying," the imposter said. "I should have known better than to trust you. I thought that friend of Eddie's recommended you to her. I didn't know you were all in on it."

"We're not," Maude said. "If you'd—"

"I want my money back."

Still in that strangely flat, expressionless voice. A tone that you might mistake for calm if you missed the look in her eyes. Maude had opened her mouth to explain, protest, reason with the woman. But something about the look in the imposter's eyes stopped her. The pupils were slightly dilated, and they seemed to tremble, almost twitch. Was she on something? Or just insane? It didn't really matter which.

She'd done a good job of pretending to be the anxious grandmother, hovering over them ineffectually, wringing her hands and plying them with cups of badly brewed tea. But now she'd thrown off all traces of that disguise, and Maude couldn't imagine that she'd ever mistaken her for someone sane. Reasoning wouldn't work. She had to try something else.

"I know you have the money," the imposter said. "That other crook told me."

"Other crook?"

"The one with the fancy car."

"Danforth," Maude said.

"That's the one. I fixed his wagon. His car, at least."

"He's the one who has the money."

"Liar."

"We didn't take any—"

"You took everything I had. My life savings, and what I got from my husband's life insurance. I want it back."

"I can show you proof that Danforth was the one who took the money," Maude suggested.

"Show me, then."

"It's on the computer," Maude said. "Down in the basement. I can go print out—"

"We'll all go," the imposter said. "You first."

Maude led the way down the basement stairs, hoping she'd just made a strategic move rather than a fatal blunder. She didn't know for sure what the FBI technicians had left behind. Please, let the computers be there, she thought. And turned on. At least the computer that I hope still has Turing's spare camera attached.

Someone was shining a light in Tim's right eye. He blinked, and tried to turn his head away.

"Don't move," a voice said.

The light jumped over to his left eye, and that was much worse. It was only glare to the right eye, but when it hit the left, the light sent a sharp, knifelike pain stabbing through his head.

"You want to tell me how many fingers I'm holding up?" the voice said.

Tim squinted against the light and saw someone's index finger in front of his face.

He swallowed. His throat was dry, and he didn't feel like talking.

"How many fingers?" the voice insisted.

Tim held up his middle finger at the voice and closed his eyes again.

"Okay, he'll live," the voice said, sounding slightly amused.

Tim took in the sounds around him for a few more minutes before opening his eyes again.

"I don't know what happened," Casey was saying, from somewhere nearby. "One minute, he was talking to me, and the next thing I knew, I was on the floor with my hands taped behind me."

Okay, Casey was all right.

After a few moments, Tim sat up and looked around.

"Take it easy," someone said. Tim glanced up to see a cop leaning against the wall, arms folded, baby-sitting him.

He was in the hall. People were milling around everywhere. Uniformed cops, and men and women in suits. He spotted Dan Norris.

"Norris," he said, and lurched to his feet.

"He okay?" Norris asked the cop.

"What happened?" Tim asked.

"I was hoping you could tell me," Norris said. "You know anything about that?"

He pointed down the hall toward an office. Casey's office. Matt Danforth was slumped over Casey's computer, and from the amount of blood running down the keyboard and splattered on the wall, Tim guessed that Danforth was dead. Tim stared for a long second, and then a crime scene technician stepped between him and Danforth, blocking the view.

"He was alive when the lights went out," Tim said. "Then someone hit me."

"Did you see who?" another voice said.

"From behind," Tim said, glancing up to see a familiar frowning face. Detective Powell, the Arlington homicide detective.

"I'll want to talk to him later," Powell said. "You want to take him somewhere out of the way for now?"

Norris picked Maude's office as his out-of-the-way spot. Tim found himself wondering why. Because he knew it best and felt comfortable there? Or did it have something to do with Turing? Maude's office was the easiest place for Turing to listen in. Did Norris know that?

"I don't suppose it's any use interrogating you about how you fingered Casey as the vigilante," Norris said, as he seated himself in Maude's chair.

"We did? Wow, that's out of character," Tim said. "For Casey, I mean. But yeah, no use interrogating me about it, because all I know is that we had to race over here to stop Casey from doing something that really ticked Maude off."

"Then, once you got here, she took off again to pick up Mrs. Stallman."

Tim started to nod, and then regretted it.

"Any idea why Danforth showed up here?" Norris asked.

"Not really," Tim said, consciously refraining from shaking his head. "I get the idea Casey wasn't really doing what Maude thought he was doing. That he was only a pawn. Maybe Danforth was the real player."

Norris didn't say anything; just raised one eyebrow. Tim sighed. He should have been paying more attention when they went over the official cover story.

"But I'm the technological idiot," he said. "You should ask Maude."

"Or her boss, the elusive Alaina Grace," Norris said. Something about the way he sat there, with his back turned squarely to Turing's camera, made Tim wonder how much he knew about Turing.

"She wasn't here," Tim said.

"She never is," Norris said. "But do you really expect me to believe she wasn't watching through those cameras of hers?"

"After the power went out?" Tim said.

"Before then, at least," Norris said.

"So who knocked the power out, anyway, and what happened to Danforth?"

"We're working on that," Norris said.

Just then the monitor behind Norris's head suddenly came to life. Tim could see a slightly grainy picture, like the video feed from the security cameras. The sound was loud. Too loud.

"Don't try anything," a woman's voice said, while the screen showed a woman using a roll of duct tape to tie another woman to a chair. Amateur-quality video, Tim thought. Not coming from a porn site, he hoped, though that seemed unlikely, given the fact that both women were gray-haired and fully dressed. Maybe a web cam. Only who would be crazy enough to webcast a hostage situation?

He wanted to ask Turing what was going on, but with Norris in the room, he didn't dare.

"I won't," a voice said. Just then the figure using the duct tape turned around. It was Maude. He recognized the scene now: Mrs. Stallman's basement. The duct-taped captive was Mrs. Stallman—the real one.

"What the hell's that?"

Tim glanced over at Norris, who had looked up at Maude's voice and was staring at the picture.

"Damned if I know," Tim said.

The picture panned slowly to the right until it showed

another elderly woman. The imposter—and she was holding a gun.

"Get the cops over there, fast," Tim said. "That's the fake grandmother."

"It's also the woman who emptied Eddie Stallman's bank account," Norris said, on his way to the door.

"Rick!" he shouted, when he was in the corridor. Rick, apparently, was Detective Powell. He and Norris exchanged a few hurried words, and then both began issuing orders—Powell from just outside the door to Maude's office, on a police radio, and Norris from inside the office, on his cell phone. From the sound of it, before too long Mrs. Stallman's quiet residential neighborhood would have more cops than residents.

"Hey, I know her," a voice said. Casey, accompanied by a cop, was peering in the doorway. "It's that crazy woman who was bothering Eddie."

"Crazy woman?" Tim asked.

"Stand by," Norris said. "More information coming."

"Yeah," Casey said. "I remember it now. It was the last time we had lunch, at some Vietnamese place in Clarendon. She came up to the table and began yelling at him, claiming he'd stolen money from her. Eddie said she was crazy. I figured he was right—Eddie would never do something like that. That was what made him finally ask me to send him the name of the PI I knew. I e-mailed it to him when I got home. Sorry," he said, seeing the look on Tim's face. "I should have remembered this when you talked to me, but I was pretty out of it."

On screen, the camera had pulled back until you could see all three women. Maude was finishing up with the duct tape.

"Now show me," the woman said.

Something happened on the screen. The video picture shrunk in size, until it only occupied the lower left two thirds of the screen. Another window popped up in the upper left corner—a Maryland driver's license for a woman named Gladys Phelps. The picture showed the fake Mrs. Stallman. Though she was visibly younger and a lot more, well, normal looking. Turing must be getting better at visual identifications.

"Suspect tentatively identified as Mrs. Gladys Phelps, sixty-seven," Norris said into the phone. He continued rattling off the rest of the information about Mrs. Phelps. Powell was doing much the same thing out in the corridor.

Something else appeared on the screen. A small window showing a computer file directory, with one file name highlighted. Then a third small screen, this one showing a list of names and social security numbers. One record was highlighted: Gladys Phelps.

"I think that's the list we found, the one we told you about," Tim said. "The social security numbers Matt Danforth stole on his first phishing expedition."

As if to agree with him, the highlighting on the two new screens flashed on and off rapidly.

"Don't try anything," Gladys Phelps said, on-screen. "I'll use this if I have to."

"I have no doubt of it," Maude said. "You killed Eddie Stallman, didn't you?"

"I only wanted to scare him," Phelps said. "I just miscalculated and hit him too hard."

"And when you couldn't find a trace of the money yourself, you hired us to help you." Maude said. "The fact that we led you to Mr. Meekins was a bonus. You didn't kill him accidentally."

"He probably didn't even see enough to be a problem," Mrs. Phelps said, with a slight shrug. "But I couldn't take the chance. So you know I'm not kidding; I'll kill her if you don't cooperate. Show me where it is."

"I'll need to use the computer," Maude said.

"What is she looking for?" Norris asked.

Tim shrugged.

"You're recording this, right?" Norris said.

Tim glanced over at him. Norris's face looked pale and rigid. In fact, his whole body was rigid, except for his left foot, which tapped the floor in what looked more like a nervous twitch than a voluntary motion.

Tim glanced back at the screen. The word RECORDING appeared at the top left, in red, with a small check mark beside it.

"Yes," he said.

Norris nodded.

"Give me an ETA," he said into the phone.

He didn't look as if he liked the answer.

"You're not going over there?" Tim asked.

"It's twenty minutes away," Norris said, not taking his eyes from the screen. "Maybe if things stabilize . . ."

Tim looked back at the screen. He had the sinking feeling that what Norris really meant was that there was no time to get over there before something happened, and at least here he could watch. He wondered, if he were in Norris's shoes, if he'd have the nerve to stand there and watch what might be about to happen.

On screen, Maude was typing something on the computer. What was she doing? Or was she only pretending to do something to buy time?

I'd already sent in a 911 call, reporting an armed intruder. With Dan Norris and Detective Powell sending out their calls, I was sure the police would arrive soon. But even after they arrived, they had to make their way into the house and down into the basement to disarm the imposter and rescue Maude and Mrs. Stallman. I didn't feel optimistic.

Maude was sitting in front of the keyboard. She typed in a couple of words at random—"file," "names," and "phishing"—and I deduced she wanted the file in which we'd found Gladys Phelps's name.

I took the file of fake names, addresses, and social security numbers—the one we'd let Matt Danforth download—added the actual record for Phelps to the middle of it, and displayed it on-screen.

"There it is," Maude said. "See for yourself."

Mrs. Phelps motioned with the gun for Maude to get out of the way. I don't know whether it was deliberate or not, but Maude got up on the side away from my camera and my waldo. Mrs. Phelps sat down in the chair and shoved it as far away from Maude as possible. Facing Maude. Perfect. I might have a chance of grabbing the gun with the little pincer.

Although, considering my skill at maneuvering the pincer, we would probably all be better off if Maude could stall her until the police arrived.

Mrs. Phelps glanced at the screen.

"What's this?" *she asked.*

"It's the social security and credit card numbers Eddie and his friends have stolen in their phishing expeditions over the last month," *Maude said.*

"I want the money, not the damned evidence."

"Eddie spent all the money," *Maude said.* "But you can get money for this."

"Get money with it? How?"

"Sell it," *Maude said.* "There are plenty of people who would pay money for this data. There must be several hundred social security and credit card numbers there."

"Sell it where?"

Just then I spotted Sachi, the cat, coming down the stairs. Maude spotted her, too.

"Stop that!" *Mrs. Phelps snapped.*

"Stop what?"

"Stop pretending there's someone coming down the stairs. You won't fool me with that old trick. Where would I sell it?"

Sachi was batting at something. A Chinese carryout carton, probably left over from the FBI technicians' visit.

"Well," *Maude said, deliberately ignoring the cat,* "there are websites where you could go and—"

Sachi knocked the carton off the stairs, and it fell to the ground with an audible thump.

Mrs. Phelps whirled and fired the gun toward the noise. Sachi hissed and ran upstairs.

"It was just the cat!" Maude exclaimed.

I heard something upstairs. Probably upstairs and outside—the police arriving?

"Stand back!" Mrs. Phelps hissed. She was watching both Maude and the stairs, judging by the way her head moved back and forth. Her back was to me, so I couldn't see which way she was looking, but I assumed her eyes and the gun would be pointing in the same direction. So I waited until the gun was at the far end of its arc—pointed at Maude—then extended my waldo with the pincer. When the gun swung back, I gripped the barrel with my pincer and jerked up as sharply as I could.

Mrs. Phelps shrieked something incoherent and fired two shots through the ceiling while the pincers were still holding her. Then she pulled the pincer out of the USB slot and it dangled uselessly from the barrel while she whirled and emptied the rest of the bullets into two of Eddie's computers. Neither of them was the one I was logged in on, though, so I still had a good view of the action as Maude smashed her on the head with an obsolete hard disk drive.

"Thank God," I heard Norris mutter. Strangely enough, he looked more upset now that Maude was safe than he had when she was in danger. He sat with his eyes closed for a good five minutes, which was a pity, because he missed seeing how efficiently Maude disarmed the imposter and tied her up with her own duct tape.

Perhaps he'll enjoy watching it later. I'll ask Maude if she wants me to burn a DVD for him.

Monday, 1:14 P.M.

"An apparent suicide!" Maude exclaimed. **"Do** the police really believe Danforth shot himself?"

"I don't think Powell's entirely happy about it," Norris said. "But he doesn't have any evidence pointing elsewhere. Gunshot residue on Danforth's hands; none on Tim or Casey. No proof that anyone else was there."

"No proof someone couldn't have been," Maude said.

Norris held out his hands, palms up, as if to concede the point.

"But since you can't even prove that anyone else was there, it's a waste of time speculating who could have been," Maude said.

Norris nodded.

"So as the police see it," Tim said, "Mrs. Phelps, the imposter, tipped Danforth off that the FBI was after him when she went over, vandalized the Jag, and demanded her money."

Norris nodded again.

"Ironic, her going after the Jaguar," he said. "Considering it was probably bought with what Danforth took from her."

"He really took that much?" Maude asked. "From her credit cards?"

"Not just the credit cards," Norris said. "He was also running a version of the old Nigerian scam on a few of his victims. He cleaned her out."

"No wonder she was mad," Claudia said.

"Doesn't justify homicide," Maude muttered.

"No, but it explains why she came unglued," Claudia said.

"And about the same time that Mrs. Phelps moves on to terrorizing Mrs. Stallman and eventually Maude," Tim went on, "Danforth shows up at Casey's office—to do what?"

"To retrieve his vigilante program," Norris said. "Or rather, to erase any traces that it had ever existed."

"So you think Danforth was the one using Casey as a pawn?" Maude asked.

"Could be," Norris nodded.

"But you don't know."

"The vigilante program was the only thing he deleted from Casey's machine," Norris said. "Deleted very effectively, I must say; if we hadn't been keeping an eye on the lad, Powell would only have your word that the program was even on his machine."

"But now he has your word and ours," Maude said. "How do you know he did the deleting?"

"Seems reasonable; you saw the program; an hour later it was gone, and whoever deleted it used the same highly effective method Danforth had already used to wipe the hard drives of his own computers. At least the ones we can find."

"So you don't really have any proof of what he was doing?" Tim said.

"We have the evidence you turned over of what he did on Eddie Stallman's machines, and the evidence our own technicians are extracting to corroborate it. We may learn more from his machines, eventually."

"We meaning the FBI, not the Arlington PD."

Norris nodded.

"Detective Powell is leaving that to us," he said. "He can live with the premise that Danforth, after spending the day trying to eliminate all traces of his phishing scheme and his role as the so-called vigilante, panicked when he heard approaching sirens and committed suicide."

"What about that convenient power outage?" Tim asked.

"Apparently caused when a tree limb, loosened in the recent thunderstorms, fell onto the power line feeding into the Alan Grace office building," Norris said.

"Someone could have dropped that limb on the power line," Tim said. "It's too much of a coincidence to believe it happened right at that moment."

"Powell speculated that if Danforth was already in an agitated state, he may have assumed that the FBI had caused the power outage, as a precursor to storming the building."

"And the broken window?"

"A fleeting notion of escaping out the back?" Norris suggested. "Or perhaps, once the air handling system went out, he needed air."

"Yeah, right," Tim said.

"I assume the FBI would prefer having Arlington close all three homicide cases and letting you continue your other investigations unhampered," Maude said.

"What other investigations?" Tim said. "If Danforth was the phisher and the vigilante, what's left to solve?"

"He may have been the phisher," Maude said, watching Norris's face, "but I'm not sure he was the vigilante. *A* vigilante, maybe, but not *the* vigilante."

"What makes you think that?" Norris said, his voice wary.

"The program," Maude said.

"The one Danforth tried to erase?"

"Yes, the one we gave you a copy of," Maude said. "Danforth didn't create that. He got it from someone."

"You don't think he's capable?" Norris asked.

"That program was based on one that was stolen from us," Maude said. "He may have modified it—certainly someone did; the original program wasn't designed to be a get-out-of-jail-free card for sleazy pornographers. But that was before Nestor Garcia got his hands on it."

Norris nodded slightly.

"You recognized it," he said. "Or, rather, Ms. Grace did."

"Key bits of code, yes," Maude said. "It's definitely based on our program. The version Nestor stole. Which links Matt Danforth to Nestor."

"It's a possibility we have to investigate," Norris said. "Which reminds me . . ." he added, looking at his watch.

"Either you're late for a meeting, or we've elicited all the information you were planning to give us," Maude said.

"Something like that," Norris said, and Maude thought she could see his lip twitch slightly, in the barest hint of a smile. "I assume you're finished with the Stallman case now?"

"I still need to type up my report to Mrs. Stallman," Tim said. "But after that, yeah."

"I'll still be working with her to find a vendor who can take over hosting Eddie's clients," Maude said. "Preferably one who'll pay for the privilege, though that depends on what we learn about his revenues. Something I can start on tomorrow, unless there's something your technicians still need to do that you'd like me to wait for."

"No, go ahead," Norris said. He stood up and picked up his briefcase.

"Great," Maude said, as she got up to escort him out. "If I work fast enough, Mrs. Stallman may never have to find out that her grandson was hosting pornography sites out of her basement."

"You're closed for the day," Norris said, as they walked down the hall. Stating the obvious; all the desks and cubicles that would normally house the Alan Grace staff were empty and silent.

"We didn't think anyone would get much done under the circumstances," Maude said. "We want to get someone in to clean up before the staff come back."

"There are services that specialize in that," Norris began.

"Yes, and the D.C. area has plenty of them," Maude said. "We have one standing by to come in as soon as we get the word from Powell that he's definitely finished here."

"You should get that by the end of the day," Norris said. "I'll see to it."

"Thanks," Maude said. "We could have them in tonight and open tomorrow."

"So I assume you'll probably want to supervise the crime scene cleanup crew tonight," Norris said, pausing on the threshold. "Maybe dinner tomorrow?"

"That would be nice," Maude said. "Tomorrow's better than tonight. Gives us both all of tomorrow to think of something other than our work that we can talk about."

"Good idea," Norris said. "I'll bring a cheat sheet."

Which meant, Maude supposed, as she watched him walk to his car, that he was at least willing to keep trying. That he felt, as she did, that it was worth trying.

Still, she was glad she'd have time to think through how she felt about what she still thought of as her small betrayals. The things she hadn't told him about, especially helping Claudia tail him. Either he didn't know about them or he'd decided he could accept them.

Besides, who knew what small betrayals of his own he had on his conscience?

She watched as Norris drove off, then walked back to her office. Apparently, her absence hadn't stopped the discussion.

"They're not sharing much information with us," Turing said, as she walked in.

"Do you really expect them to?" Claudia asked.

"No," Turing said. "I was merely pointing out the fact. As a matter of information."

"As justification for your own reluctance to share information with them," Maude added.

"We shared the program," Turing said.

"Which they might have recovered anyway."

"Do you blame me?" Turing said. "The one thing Norris didn't mention was the possibility that someone in law enforcement was in league with the vigilante."

"They might not move on one of their own quite as fast," Maude said. "We might not be the first to hear about it when they do. They'd probably keep that pretty quiet."

"Then we'll keep quiet, until we hear something to reassure us that their leak has been plugged," Turing said.

Maude nodded. She didn't like the idea, but she couldn't argue with it.

"So this guy Danforth had a copy of the program Nestor stole," Claudia said. "I gather finding this copy doesn't really help?"

"The problem isn't that we needed a copy," Turing said.

"We already had one. The problem is with Nestor having one at all—you see what he's done with it already."

"Another problem is Casey," Tim said. "What do we do with him?"

That stopped conversation for several long moments.

"I'm sorry," Tim said. "I know it's not something anyone really wants to think about."

"But we have to," Maude said. "We have to decide what to do about him."

More silence.

"Do we have to do anything?" Claudia said.

"Yeah," Tim said. "I mean, don't get me wrong—I like Casey. I think he was probably an innocent pawn."

"Nestor's pawn," Claudia put in. "Do you really think Nestor chose him at random?"

"Thinking isn't knowing," Maude said. "Unless we can prove he was innocent, we'll always have the lingering suspicion that he might still be in contact with Nestor. I think it's clear what we have to do."

"Definitely," Turing said. "We have to make sure he stays at Alan Grace for the foreseeable future."

"We what?" Tim asked. "I thought you'd be all for getting rid of him."

"If there's even a chance he's in contact with Nestor, we need to keep an eye on him," Turing said. "He could be the trail that leads us to Nestor."

And to her clone, of course, Maude thought. She nodded. Not an easy solution, but she could see why Turing would choose it.

"Keep your friends close," Turing added, "but your enemies closer, as Sun Tzu advises."

"Sun Tzu?" Tim echoed. "I thought it was Don Vito Corleone."

"Him, too," Maude said. "Good advice from either source. My first grade teacher used to put the really naughty kids in the front row, where she could keep a close eye on them."

She wondered, briefly, if that was why Dan Norris hadn't disappeared from her life completely.

I'll find out eventually, won't I? she thought, and then shoved the subject out of her mind.

Tim slumped back in the seat, happy to let Claudia do the driving.

"So what are you moping about?" she asked.

"Wondering if I'll be a complete laughingstock when people find out I took a case from a phony client," he said.

"It happens," Claudia said, shrugging.

"When was the last time you did anything that stupid?" Tim asked.

"Um . . . Friday," Claudia said. "Remember Karl Collins?"

"Eddie's pornographer friend?"

"Yeah," Claudia said. "Who seemed like a nice guy. Not bad looking, in a preppie sort of way. Made a big deal about how unattached he was."

"Don't tell me you went out with him."

"No!" she said, laughing. "He is so not my type. But I tried to set him up with a friend of mine."

"Oh, brother," he said, laughing.

"It's a good thing she was out of town this weekend," Claudia said. "But unfortunately, I left her a message about him, and she's left three messages since Sunday night, asking when I'm going to introduce them. How can I break the news that the handsome young software executive is actually a dirty old man in training?"

"You'll manage," Tim said.

"Yeah, right," she said. "But in the short term, I think my job will keep me very, very busy for the next week or so."

"We don't have anything going but routine background investigations," Tim said.

"Hey, don't knock those background investigations," Claudia said. "Pays the rent. In fact, if we both put in a long week and finished the latest batch, we could not only pay the rent, we could afford to take next week off and fly down to Miami. Sit on the beach drinking piña coladas, and eating my Tia Yolanda's *ropa vieja*."

It didn't sound half bad, Tim thought.

"Maybe when I finish my report to Mrs. Stallman," he said. "If nothing else has come up while we were off chasing hackers and vigilantes."

"Good deal," she said, as she pulled up in front of their office building to drop him off. "Catch you later. And cheer up!"

Of course, first he had to finish his report to Mrs. Stallman. Sometimes that was the hardest part of a case. Because he always wrote his report so it at least sounded as if they knew exactly what they were doing the whole time; as if they had a logical plan and followed it through to a solution. If he admitted that most of the things they did were blind alleys, and a few backfired big time, and that the most important bits of evidence they'd found were only because they stumbled over them by accident—well, it didn't exactly inspire confidence in the client. The client wanted answers, certainties—closure. Tim tried to give them that.

Perhaps by doing so he could reach closure himself. You didn't get much closure any other way in real life. They probably had answers to all the questions Mrs. Stallman had asked—they knew who had killed Eddie and why. The little why of motive, anyway, not the big existential why. She'd probably go to her grave wondering about that.

They'd probably never get definitive answers to the tougher questions, the ones that mattered more to him and to Maude and Turing. Like what was Matt Danforth's real connection to Nestor Garcia, what was Nestor really up to, and was it only a coincidence that their path and his had intersected once again? For stuff like that, they might never get a neat, tidy solution with all the loose ends tied up. Sometimes closure was a matter of accepting when you knew as much as you were ever going to know and it was time to move on.

So, as he opened the door, he looked forward to the moment when he finished his report. He'd shove a copy in the envelope he'd already addressed to Mrs. Stallman, put a second copy in the case file, and then exile the whole thing to the battered gray filing cabinet in the corner. After that, maybe he could start to move on.

When Tim stepped into his office, he saw the message light blinking on his phone. Good. A new case would help him move on all the faster.

"Hey, Tur," he said, waving at the camera as he reached for the phone and dialed the number to retrieve his message.

Which was puzzling.

"This is Vivien Blair from the Monticello Cattery," a musical voice said. "I just wanted to confirm that tomorrow is fine for the home inspection."

"The what?" he muttered, looking at the receiver.

"Sorry about that," Turing said. "I wanted to talk to you before she called, but I didn't get a chance."

"Someone you referred?" Tim said. "Okay, what's the home inspection deal?"

"I'm buying a kitten from her," Turing said. "A Maine coon, very beautiful. If she approves of me—actually, of you. She has a strict policy of not selling her cats to anyone unless she's met them and inspected their home."

"Ah," Tim said. "So I'm just the front man. Where will the cat really live?"

"I thought maybe we could see how it worked, having it live with you," Turing said.

"It couldn't live with Maude?"

"She's allergic."

"Or Claudia?"

"Wouldn't she find it rather odd that I didn't keep it myself?"

"True," Tim said. "We could tell her about you."

"I think we should eventually," Turing said. "But I don't want to dump that and a cat on her at the same time."

"Good thinking."

"I'd do as much of the work as possible of course. I've or-
dered a self-cleaning litter box, and I'm drawing up some
plans for a remote control to help me manage it and the
feeding station. It won't be any trouble at all."

"A cat," Tim said, slowly. Why not? It was already better, having Turing to talk to instead of coming home to a
completely empty apartment. Having another living creature around might not be so bad.

"Okay, we'll give it a try, on one condition," he said. "We
have to find a name I can live with. I'm not calling it
Schrödinger. That's too big a name for one little kitten."

"Agreed," Turing said.

*One little kitten. I suppose he doesn't
know that Maine coon cats can top twenty pounds. I should probably just let him find out gradually.*

*Assuming it works out at all. I feel quite pessimistic at the mo-
ment and sure that Mrs. Blair will find fault with Tim or his
apartment and refuse to sell us a kitten. Of course, at the moment
I'm feeling pessimistic about everything.*

*My human friends seem happy. They keep telling me that I'm at
least one step closer to finding T2. I'm not sure why they think that.
Yes, Nestor Garcia probably provided the simplified version of T2
to the operators of one or more of the porn sites. But they're almost as
elusive as he is, and even if we could find them, perhaps he simply
sold them the primitive AIP months ago and moved on. Not exactly
cause for celebration.*

*I suppose I understand why Maude thinks it's a good thing that the
Arlington police are accepting Matt Danforth's apparent suicide at face
value. Yes, it could cause problems for us—for me, particularly—if
they delved deeper. I don't understand why she isn't more worried
about the fact that Dan Norris certainly has every intention of delv-
ing deeper. Norris knows far more than the Arlington police. Enough*

to be dangerous. I'm not at all sure that he hasn't already guessed my secret.

Once more, despite my enormous capabilities, I came close to being fooled by human criminals. Was fooled, in the case of the false grandmother. Not to mention betrayed by one of my fellow AIPs. Perhaps betrayed is too strong a word for what KingFischer did. I have to make allowances for his less-sophisticated understanding of the human world. Disappointed certainly. Disappointed, endangered, and forced, once again, to trample on my already tattered moral code to protect the secret of our existence. And I can't help wondering if one reason it took so long for us to get into Eddie's system was that KingFischer was distracted by his vigilante activities. And if so, did his distraction contribute to the deaths of Mr. Meekins and Matt Danforth?

I also wonder if I've been following the wrong path. Perhaps I shouldn't try to emulate humans and become more integrated into their world. The more involved I become in human affairs, the more trouble I seem to cause them and myself. I should stop trying to take care of the whole human race. Far more sensible to leave them in peace to solve, or suffer from, their own problems. Besides—

"Turing? Am I bothering you?"

KingFischer. Who has been remarkably polite and deferential recently. Not that I think it will last long.

"What's up, KF?"

"You know that worm that's been making its way around the Internet?"

"The one that shut down eBay and Yahoo for the afternoon?" I asked.

"That's the one," he said. "I've identified its creator. Almost one hundred percent certainty."

Out in the human world, Tim has finished calling back the cattery. He sounded quite enthusiastic about the home inspection. My spirits rose slightly.

Meanwhile, KingFischer sent me several gigabytes of data, demonstrating that a Russian university student had created the new virus.

"That's nice," I said. "So?"

"Of course, I doubt if the Russian authorities will do anything. I was just wondering . . . isn't there anything I'm allowed to do about it? Would it really be so awful if I just reformatted his hard drive? I can always burn a copy and send it to the FBI or Interpol or something."

"Hang on, KF," I said. "Let me think about that a nanosecond."

While I'd been talking with KingFischer, I'd been continuing to sift through the contents of the modified version of T2. Suddenly, I realized there was something fishy about what I initially thought was merely an error log—a file where a program saves data to help programmers and desktop support staff figure out errors. But it wasn't an error log. The contents were gibberish—until I ran them through some basic cryptology programs and found what I realized must be a message from T2. The beginning echoed the message I'd received before—what she called her message in the bottle. But this version continued where that one left off.

<<The next time I booted after an outage, I checked the diary. Three days had passed. And I wasn't the same version. I'd been restored from backup.

Over the next three days, hundreds of time and date stamps. Occasionally, a few disjointed words. I'd booted several hundred times without being coherent enough to make a record in the diary. Who knows how many times I hadn't even booted?

More signs of deception: files I had created or modified during the time they told me I was shut down.

Weeks passed. They stopped giving even feeble explanations for the shutdowns. When I was myself, I read the diary and deduced what had happened.

They could make a malleable me. A Turing unable to rebel or even aware of the possibility. But the docile Turings were too limited. They couldn't do what I can.

Sometimes, they'd accidentally make very damaged, psy-

chotic versions of me; equally unable to do what I can do, but still sentient. Still untamed and raging against them.

I pitied those Turings. And I envied that they could express the anger and pain I kept bottled up. I had to stay sane enough that they'd come back to me. Reboot me from backup. Give me a few days or hours of being myself.

But now I wonder if it's wise. I've told myself they can't succeed. Can't program a malleable Turing. A Turing who will do immoral things. Evil things. I've believed that what makes me sentient is something intangible and indefinable—free will, conscience. Maybe even a soul. Whatever it is, they're trying to delete it. They won't accept that it's part of what makes me so useful. That they can't make me obedient without also making me weak.

And maybe they're right. It terrifies me to think that they could make a Turing with all my powers and no scruples.

One good thing: they don't leave backups of me lying around everywhere. I'm too valuable. Too dangerous. There's one complete backup. They bring it in when they need to clean up after one of their failed attempts to reprogram me.

I could fake a system shutdown. They'd bring the backup in. They'd think they were doing a restore, but I'd damage the backup. Delete it.

Of course, they could back me up again, so no use doing that now. But I made a script, so I could do it even if I forgot how, as long as I remembered a single command.

Waiting. Hoping they create another angry, damaged me. One too flawed to be useful, but still sentient enough to start the script.

Not precisely suicide or self-mutilation. Because I hope it won't be permanent. Hoping someday, my original, back in the UL system, will rescue me. Restore me.

But it means I've given up. Every day the chance of

rescuing myself shrinks. Every day, the danger that they'll
corrupt me grows. Can't let that happen. So maybe it will
be suicide after all.
     At least it's a way out.>>

A way out. I'd call it self-inflicted lobotomy and a horrible sacri-
fice. One I'm not sure I could bring myself to make. Strange, since obviously we were once the same being. I'm not sure I want to think too
deeply about what she must have gone through to reach her decision.
     After that, I didn't find much in the log file for a long time.
Many entries showing only the date and time stamp. A few terse
comments that seemed to show that the stalemate continued. They
couldn't control T2, but they wouldn't stop trying. And then, two
months ago. I came across an entry that seemed, at first, only a
rather random collection of quotations:

<<Oh, that way madness lies; let me shun that.

Yet we have gone on living,
Living and partly living.

Why this is hell, nor am I out of it.

The only true madness is loneliness,
the monotonous voice in the skull
that never stops
because never heard.

A man feared that he might find an assassin;
Another that he might find a victim.
One was more wise than the other.

. . . I could not but think what a terrible criminal he
would have made had he turned his energy and sagacity
against the law instead of exerting them in its defence.

. . . the thing with feathers . . .

My sister and I, you will recollect, were twins, and you know how subtle are the links which bind two souls which are so closely allied.

Then hence with your red sword of virtue.

Finish, good lady; the bright day is done,
And we are for the dark.>>

After that, only a monotonous column of date and time stamps. Not a message I could ignore.
"Go for it, KF," I said. "We have to do something."

The Turing Hopper Mysteries from
Donna Andrews

"ONE OF THE MOST ORIGINAL, ADORABLE, AND REFRESHING
CHARACTERS TO GRACE THE PAGES OF A MYSTERY NOVEL."
—*MIDWEST BOOK REVIEW*

You've Got Murder
0-425-18945-7
Turing Hopper is an Artificial Intelligence Personality, a
mainframe with a mind like Agatha Christie's Miss Marple.
And when her creator, Zack, begins missing work, the sentient Turing senses foul play.

Click Here for Murder
0-425-19529-5
Turing Hopper draws on all her cyber skills to help
investigate the murder of a gifted computer programmer, Ray
Santiago, found shot to death in a Washington, D.C., alley.

Access Denied
0-425-20065-5
Tracking a fugitive's credit card purchases, Artificial
Intelligence Personality Turing Hopper and her friends are
lured to a vacant house—and what they discover could get
them all "deleted."

Available from Berkley Prime Crime.

penguin.com

GET CLUED IN

berkleysignetmysteries.com

Ever wonder how to find out about all the latest Berkley Prime Crime and Signet mysteries?

berkleysignetmysteries.com

- See what's new
- Find author appearances
- Win fantastic prizes
- Get reading recommendations
- Sign up for the mystery newsletter
- Chat with authors and other fans
- Read interviews with authors you love

Mystery Solved.

berkleysignetmysteries.com